MW01165073

Regards,

Larry Feirman

Malpractice

Copyright © 2003 by Larry J. Feinman

ISBN 0-7414-1609-3

Published by:

INFINITY
PUBLISHING.COM

519 West Lancaster Avenue
Haverford, PA 19041-1413
Info@buybooksontheweb.com
www.buybooksontheweb.com
Toll-free (877) BUY BOOK
Local Phone (610) 520-2500
Fax (610) 519-0261

Printed in the United States of America

Printed on Recycled Paper

Published October 2003

To my wife Sheryl, and my children Matthew, Alex and Michaela, without whom I surely would never have gotten beyond the first page of this book. Your patience and love has allowed me to devote far too much time to this endeavor and far too little time to you.

This book is dedicated to the men and women toiling in the trenches of our nation's hospitals; hopefully the medical profession can be saved before outside influences destroy it.

*First they came for the Jews and I did not speak
out because I was not a Jew.*

*Then they came for the Communists and I did
not speak out because I was not a Communist.*

*Then they came for the trade unionists and I
did not speak out because I was not a trade
unionist.*

*Then they came for me and there was no one to
speak out for me.*

-- Pastor Martin Niemöller

PROLOGUE – September 1312

The young girl lay sweating and delirious in her bed, her mother mopping her brow with cool rags torn from her own skirt. The father busied himself in the great room, trying to avoid looking into his daughter's sunken eyes. He knew the Black Death was in her, and he well knew the road that they were traveling. He had seen it before: the swollen glands in the neck, the fevers, the chills, the need to lie on the floor for days at a time. But no, that was only the beginning. No, the fates could make it worse, much worse.

He had seen his friend die of this dreaded disease, and the most chilling part was the bleeding. Yes, that was the worst to witness, the worst suffering he had ever seen. His friend William had been sitting by the night table and talking to him, when suddenly he coughed and the man saw a streak of blood stream from William's right nostril. Another cough, then a gurgle, and William spit up a cup of blood. He started to breathe faster and faster, and then the blood came from the corner of his eye as if he were weeping his own blood. The man knew that he could not stand to see his friend perish in this fashion, started to cry, and ran from the room; but as he crossed the threshold, he heard a thud and turned in time to see William crash to the floor, dead. Yes, the bleeding was definitely the worst.

Now, it was his daughter's turn. The man had never told his wife about the horrors of William's death. But now, she would have to witness such a terrible end for herself. Slowly, agonizingly, his daughter tried to catch her breath, but she couldn't. Mercifully, she slipped out of consciousness and fell silent, and his wife took the opportunity to leave her bedside. His wife came into the great room and took a bowl of the stew that was slowly cooking over the fire. There were tears in her eyes; the man wanted to console her, but he knew that there was nothing that he could say to ease the pain. It was better if he said nothing.

His wife went back to their daughter's bedside, and the man sat in a chair at the foot of the bed. Soon, the man and wife were both asleep. In a few hours, they awoke to the hacking cough of their daughter. The man jumped to her bedside in a panic, but when he looked into his daughter's eyes he thought he saw life. He woke his wife, and yes, their daughter was going to live, he told her. They quickly got her a glass of water fresh from the well, and the man ran into the great room to fetch her some bread. He shooed the mice from the table and cut a piece of the loaf sitting on the counter. She ate the bread and drank the water greedily. Yes, she was going to live.

The man saddled his horse and rode into town. There he got the doctor, an old man who had tended the sick for more years than most people had breathed, and they returned to the man's home. The doctor examined the girl and proclaimed her disease as the pox, not the Black Death. He decreed that the treatment of the pox should be leeches, and he made them ready. Soon, the girl was shrieking as the slimy animals crawled across her arms and began the search for their blood meals. In short order, seventeen of these worms were tightly attached to the girl's body, and in one hour, seventeen fat, sluggish leeches were returned to their jar and the doctor was on his way.

That night, the girl developed a fever and started to hallucinate. She called to people who were not there and punched herself in the belly to try to exorcise the demons that were causing such pain. But, alas, there were no demons, only bleeding into the abdomen; and as the bleeding continued, her blood pressure fell. As it did, the light dimmed in her eyes, and her father saw his child slip away into the eternal darkness.

The man buried his only daughter, but he could not get the actions of the doctor out of his mind. He went to a lawyer and asked if there was any way the lawyer could help him. The lawyer told him that he could sue the doctor for negligence and try to make the doctor suffer for his misdiagnosis, for surely it had been a misdiagnosis. His daughter had been awake and laughing and eating to regain her strength before the doctor arrived, and she died only hours after he left. The man's anguish was immeasurable.

After a time, there was a trial. The doctor told the magistrate that he had indeed seen this disease before, and he knew the girl did not stand much chance of living, in spite of her false recovery long enough to eat a final meal, and that he had applied the only treatment he knew for this ailment, the only treatment that he thought might save her, the only one any competent doctor of his day would have used. And more than this, he said, he had given the mother and father hope because these small gestures were all he could give them. But another doctor, from a village several leagues away with a reputation for saying whatever his listener wanted to hear, testified that this was not so. He testified that surely the blood of the young girl had revolted against the leeches and turned on her, had become a boiling enemy within her flesh and taken her life. The doctor who treated her, he said, had indeed killed her.

The doctor was found guilty of medical negligence and given a sentence of biblical proportion. He was sentenced to death for causing the death of the man's daughter. The doctor died by hanging the next day, and the emptiness in the father and the mother of the young girl who had died of the plague grew deeper.

CHAPTER 1 – CURRENT DAY

The beeper went off at 2 am, the absolute worst time to be awakened. It was too early in the morning to have gotten anything close to enough rest, and too late to take care of business and then go back to bed again before the sun came up. And Steve Boxley knew that he wouldn't be sleeping until tonight, many hours from now. He knew that the beeper only sounded when the resident was in trouble, and he had one of the third-year guys with him this month. By the third year, waking the attending was an admission of failure, a pathetic cry for help. Thus the beeper and Steve's certain knowledge that he was in for a long haul before he found his bed again.

He called the switchboard immediately. "Good morning, Dr. Boxley," the operator said. "Dr. Land needs you in the trauma room. I'll connect you now."

"Dr. Boxley on the line," Sharon said to Mark Land, and Steve could imagine Mark grabbing the phone with a shaky hand to match the uncertainty in his voice. "Dr. Boxley, I have a 50 year-old man with a fractured pelvis, ruptured spleen, and a collapsed lung, all from a motorcycle accident. I can't keep his blood pressure up, and his oxygen saturation is terrible. I need help." Steve told him to intubate the patient and call the OR; he was on his way in.

The ride to the hospital in the middle of the night was always relaxing, even when he knew that he was going in for a disaster. The roads were empty, and in central Florida, no matter how hot it was during the day, there was a damp coolness to the night that you could smell. The radio played oldies, and his mind wandered to the upcoming operation. A 50 year-old guy on a motorcycle. What was this world coming to, he wondered? Why wasn't this guy driving a safe family car? He was not a kid anymore, after all. The collapsed lung could be treated with a chest tube, albeit somewhat brutally — a ¾ inch hose forced into the chest cavity to re-expand the lung — and the low oxygen could be treated with a breathing tube. The ruptured spleen was the easiest of the problems to repair — just remove it. On the other hand, the fractured pelvis was a big problem. All of the small blood vessels around the bones of the pelvis would be torn and bleeding, and no matter how experienced a surgeon was, he could never stop that particular type of bleeding. The best he could hope for was to stabilize all of the other problems, and then hope that Mother Nature would stop the free flow of the patient's blood from the pelvis before he died. He smiled a bit at the thought of Mother Nature in the mix but never getting sued when things didn't go well.

His mind went back to the road as he turned into the hospital parking lot. "So, if you're injured as a result of a doctor's negligence, or even if you just think he may have been negligent, call us and we'll review your case at no charge to you. We're 'For the Little Guy.' Morris, Cuney and Howe," the ad on the radio finished up. Steve figured out why his mind had strayed to suing Mother Nature. He couldn't listen to his radio or watch TV without being accosted by a cute little ad from that bastard at Morris, Cuney and Howe. "Someday, that guy's dick is going to fall off, and no doctor in Florida will sew it on," Steve thought.

Steve crashed through the doors in the Trauma Room, and a nurse threw him a gown to put over his clothes. "John is his name. That's all we know," Mark Land said. "His BP is 90 over 60, heart rate 110, oxygen about half-normal at 85%. We intubated him and his oh-two came up to 95%, but now he can't talk to us."

"Hi, John. I'm Dr. Boxley. I'm a trauma surgeon, and I'll be caring for you. Do you hurt anywhere?" John nodded. "Here?" Steve said as he pushed on John's chest. Another nod. Still another with a push on the belly and a bigger nod with pressure over the pelvis. Steve said to Mark, "Did you do a retrograde cystogram to check for a bladder rupture?"

"Yes, it's OK," Mark replied. "Get a Foley in him, someone." One of the nurses placed a Foley urinary catheter into the bladder, and about 200 c.c.s of bloody urine came back.

"Are you allergic to anything, John?" A shake of the head told him no. Steve asked the charge nurse to tell X-ray that they'd be coming over for an IVP to check John's kidneys, then she should tell the OR they'd be on the way up. He also told her to tell the orthopedic service that they'd need to come into the OR to stabilize John's pelvis once he finished the operation for the ruptured spleen.

Steve told the resident to stay with the patient, and he'd meet them in the OR. He stripped off the bloody gown and went upstairs to lie down. At 46, he wasn't as enthused about the late night cases as he was when he finished his residency. He needed more sleep with each passing year, and he now saw these trauma patients as nothing but a liability to his own health. He closed his eyes and was asleep before his head hit the pillow.

***

The makeup artist wiped the extra makeup off of Jake Morris' face and backed away. While she was fixing him up for the cameras, he started to think about the road that got him into this TV studio. Jake was a scrawny man, the object of taunting, and he had been in more than a few fistfights growing up on account of his diminutive stature and scrawny arms and legs. He'd showed those bullies. He studied hard, went to business school, and then to night school at Penn State for his law degree. He originally had wanted to be a criminal lawyer, to devote his career to helping people wrongly accused of crimes. That brought a faint smile to his lips; how could I ever even sit in a room with those dirtbags, let along work for them, he thought.

He thought about his first medical malpractice case. He had moved to Florida to be near his in-laws, and he opened an office in a storefront. A painter had put "Jake Morris, Criminal Lawyer" on the window, and he hired a high school dropout to sit in the front room filing her nails, answer the phone, and greet the occasional client that walked in off the street. Marlene was an adorable 6 year-old girl who had gone into the hospital for a tonsillectomy. Her parents were told that the operation would take about 20 minutes, and the surgeon would be out to talk to them soon afterward. But that didn't happen. The anesthesiologist was not able to place a tube in her windpipe for the surgery, and all hell broke loose. When it was over, the beautiful angel was brain dead. Her parents walked into Jake's criminal law office and asked if he could help them. He didn't know anything about medical malpractice, but business was so slow, he hated to turn down any work. He got the medical records and promptly filed suit against the anesthesiologist. Then he remembered what one of his professors had told his class: In malpractice cases, sue everyone — they all have insurance.

So Jake added the name of the surgeon to the court papers. He couldn't think of any logical reason to include the surgeon, but he figured that, at worst, the surgeon's lawyer would threaten Jake with a countersuit and Jake would quickly drop the surgeon. At best, however, the surgeon would say a few unkind words about the anesthesiologist at the trial, thereby helping make Jake's case. But he had it figured all wrong, and he had that same feeling in his chest now that he got every time he allowed himself to think about that case. The anesthesiologist's insurance company called Jake two days after he filed the lawsuit to offer the 1 million-dollar policy in full, if only Jake would drop the case and not go to trial. He nearly wet his pants: one million dollars for filing a complaint. He had just started to draw up the papers to drop the surgeon and settle the case when the surgeon's lawyer called to ask if he'd settle with the surgeon for two-hundred-and-fifty thousand. Jake figured he'd break the guy's balls a bit just for fun, and said he'd settle for a half million. When the surgeon's lawyer said OK without even a second's hesitation, he couldn't speak. In less than a week, he had written a three-page filing and had offers totaling one-and-a-half million dollars. He allowed himself to think of his commission: he got 35% of any settlement, so his take was $525,000. That was the moment that Jake decided that he didn't really want to do criminal law. Medical malpractice was the only way to go.

The settlement made the news, and all of a sudden, Jake was an expert medical malpractice lawyer. But he knew he really wasn't an expert, that he needed help. Samuel Cuney was a lawyer who did specialize in medical malpractice, but he had such a bad personality; no one would hire him. Jake made him a deal he couldn't refuse. Jake would use his notoriety to be the rainmaker, which is to say that Jake would bring in the cases, and Sam would work in the background using his legal skills to win the cases. It was brilliant. Which brought Jake back to the present. He was getting made up for another TV commercial. Every person living in Central Florida who had a TV set knew Jake's face, and everyone with a radio recognized his voice. He had made a lot of enemies over the years, but it didn't bother him in the least. His company's advertising budget alone was 12 million dollars a year, and every one of those dollars was worth it.

"Three, two, one, go," said the producer.

"Hello, I'm Jake Morris. Have you or a loved one been injured in a hospital? The AMA has said that pain control is a fundamental right of every patient in pain, but the hospitals just don't have the nurses to give out the pain medicine on time. If your medicine is late, you've suffered; and if you've suffered, you have a right to be compensated. Call me, Jake Morris, at Morris, Cuney and Howe, 'For the Little Guy'."

"Great job," the producer said, and Jake stripped off the mike. He now did every one of these commercials in one take. It took longer to get made up and cleaned up than it did for him to rattle off the spiel. The makeup artist cleaned his face off, and Jake headed for the limo to return to the office. He took his cell phone from his pocket as he walked and called his wife. "Just wait until the hospitals see these ads. They'll shit," he said. "There's no way they can argue about the AMA guidelines, and no way they can hire enough staff. We have them by the balls." He hung up and allowed himself to smile. As somebody says in a Mel Brooks movie, he thought, "It's great to be king."

Jake walked out of the studio and headed for the street. His limousine was waiting for him, and James, his always proper British driver and man-servant was polishing the car. James looked up when he approached. "Good afternoon, sir."

"Good afternoon, James," Jake replied. "Let's take a ride along Beach Boulevard, then head to the office."

"Very good, sir." James held the door open for Jake, who slipped into the dark leather seat and poured himself a small glass of single malt scotch. James put the car into gear and slowly drove towards the Gulf of Mexico.

Jake pushed a button on the console and the privacy screen slid up from behind James' seat. Jake was now suitably alone, and he picked up a secure telephone. He dialed a number from memory, and Stan Large answered on the first ring.

"Stan Large here," he answered, right after the private line rang in his back office.

"Stan, how did the Novella thing end up?"

"Fine, sir. The problem has been terminated. No loose ends anymore."

"Very good, Stan. Thanks."

Jake sat back in the warm leather seat of the limo and let his mind wander to this instance of Stan's enormous usefulness as he sipped the scotch.

Melinda Novella had been the only thing standing between Morris, Cuney and Howe and a three-million-dollar settlement. The firm's payoff on a three million dollar settlement, after inflated expenses, would be 1.2 million dollars. The case was a personal injury suit against a hospital. Their client was the wife of a wealthy, retired businessman, who went into Samaritan Hospital for a routine operation on his enlarged prostate gland. The operation was supposed to take about an hour, but bleeding had caused it to last two hours. The wife was concerned, and when she couldn't get answers from the volunteer manning the information desk in the surgical waiting room, she set out to find out what was going on. She somehow managed to navigate the corridors of the operating room, and unbelievably, was directed to the room in which her husband was undergoing surgery. She burst in as the surgeons worked feverishly to stop the bleeding. The shock of seeing her husband in surgery, and the nausea of seeing his blood on the drapes and the floor, caused her to pass out. As she fell, she struck her head on the floor and suffered a subdural hematoma, a blood clot on the brain. She required emergency neurosurgery to relieve the hematoma, and recovered rather uneventfully. But, as had become the custom in Central Florida, she sought consultation regarding her injuries with an attorney: she came to Morris, Cuney and Howe. Jake Morris chose to handle this case himself because he wanted to make it a landmark case; he wanted to try to make a big splash and expose the weaknesses in hospital security. The fact that his client was allowed to wander into an operating room without being accosted was certainly a breakdown in security if ever there was one.

The case made the headlines as it wended its way through the preliminary hearings, depositions and discovery. However, Melinda Novella, the head of security at the hospital, had been subjected to an unsworn deposition. That was a type of deposition in Florida in which a witness could be questioned without being placed under oath, which allowed a plaintiff's attorney to find out what the witness would be saying under oath. As much as this process discriminated against the defense, it helped the plaintiff. Jake learned that his client had been stopped by Ms. Novella three times, and she had literally forced her way into the operating room, pushing Ms. Novella aside on her way by. However, there were no witnesses to that altercation, and it would be his client's word against Novella's. But at the unsworn deposition, Morris learned that Novella was a retired security agent for the sheriff's department and had been given high level clearance. Her word would carry quite a bit of weight. If she testified under oath against his client, he knew he'd lose the case. Thus Melinda Novella was the only thing standing between him and a three-million-dollar settlement.

That morning, Melinda was heading out of her apartment to her job at Samaritan Hospital. She started her car and drove off. As she approached the intersection at the corner, she applied the brakes to slow down. Nothing. She pushed harder on the brake pedal. Still nothing. She tried pumping the brakes. No help. A tractor trailer was crossing the intersection as her car flew into the intersection at 60 miles per hour. The Toyota Celica hit the side of the semi and burst into flames. Melinda was incinerated, and her testimony died with her.

Jake raised his glass in the air as he rode in the limo toward the Gulf. "Here's to you, Melinda," he said softly.

Jake had known all along that without Melinda's testimony, the hospital would settle for it's entire policy limit in the mediation phase, three million dollars. Anything to avoid the publicity of a trial.

The beach flew by as James drove down route A-10, known to the locals as Beach Boulevard. Sadly for Jake, they made good time and were at the office in 20 minutes.

***

"Wake up, Dr. Boxley, it's time for surgery," said Shana, the new OR tech. Steve hadn't gotten to know her yet, but she seemed pleasant enough. He'd soon get to see how she worked under stress. "Let me splash some water on my face, and I'll be in." Steve went into the men's locker room and started washing his face. Mark had just finished changing, the two men nodded in greeting, and Steve told Mark to start without him. "Who's your junior resident tonight?" Steve asked.

"The new guy."

"In that case, you do the procedure and let him assist. I'll watch you."

Boxley walked into the OR, snapped on the radio, oldies again, and took a step stool over to the anesthesia side of the drapes. He stood on the stool and watched Mark's tentative hands open the belly. He made a midline incision from the end of the breastbone to the pubes. For some reason, maybe watching Quincy on TV all those years ago, Steve always thought of an autopsy when he saw that incision. The skin fell apart, and then the fat, muscle, and finally the last coverings of the abdomen. Blood came pouring out of the hole, and Mark jumped back. "Suction," he yelled at the first year resident. "Get the retractor in there," he told the nurse. Soon, the operative field was free of blood, and he had the spleen in a pan on the back table. "Look here" he told his assistant. "This is why they bleed to death from pelvic fractures. See this huge hematoma coming out of the pelvis? We can't do a thing to stop this bleeding, and if we try to be heroes and open the hematoma, all hell breaks loose. So, we just leave it alone and say a quiet prayer that it stops. It will have a chance to stop once the orthopods fix the fractures."

Steve always marveled at the constant teaching going on. This is the way it always was, and how it always would be. His senior residents had taught him, he had taught the junior residents, and they taught the medical students. A great system, he thought. "Very nice, Mark. Close however you want, put him on antibiotics, and be sure the ortho resident does as good a job as you did. I'm going home now, but I'll stop to talk to his family on my way out. Call me if you want." Mark laughed a little. He knew he'd never live it down if he called Dr. Boxley twice in one day.

The sun was coming up over the river as Steve drove home, and there were a few more cars on the roads and the drive-time traffic report was on. The reporter was talking about a delay on I-75 due to a motorcycle accident from 4 hours ago. There was still an investigation going on, and gasoline was still on the road. Four hours. Had he been there that long? He looked at his watch; it was 6 a.m. "Christ, 6 a.m. and I'm going home. What a life." *Satisfaction* came on the radio, and he sang with it. He cut the engine in front of the house and headed up the steps to the shower. Another day with too little sleep. Well, it was his half day, so it could be worse.

As he entered his empty house, he thought of Ellen for the millionth time, of how her last few days with him must have been. Picturing what was merely one more in a series of his transgressions from her perspective made him feel better somehow, feel better by seeing how much his work life had been a burden on her. He could both take responsibility and know that he had done nothing more than what he had to do, so her discomfort was both his fault and not. He was both absolved by the exercise and felt remorseful, but lately he seemed to have to perform the exercise every time he came home.

The invitation had plainly stated that the affair started at 7:00 p.m., black tie optional. Ellen had been looking forward to this night for weeks. The kids were safely at her mother's house, and would be there all weekend. She knew that afterwards she and Steve would come home to a childless house and that he had arranged to be covered by his friend, Dr. Nan Freedman, for the whole weekend. Ellen had the rest of the weekend planned in her mind, as she always did, a trait that he found both endearing and maddening. First the affair, then a nice intimate night in bed without the phone or children, then maybe breakfast in bed Sunday morning. Her mind would have wandered to the thought of her sexy husband and no beeper, Steve thought, and he smiled as he searched a drawer for clean socks. She would also have thought that maybe this weekend they could recover whatever had been missing from their marriage, and Steve stopped smiling.

Steve had been laboring in the operating room for hours, trying in vain to stop the bleeding from the right lobe of his patient's liver. He neglected to have the circulating nurse call his house, to tell Ellen that he would be late. So, by 6:00 p.m., Ellen would have been getting concerned. She had showered and probably had selected a skimpy black dress to wear, knowing that it would compliment Steve's tuxedo perfectly. She had spent an hour doing her hair and make-up, and as always she would have looked great. The dark ringlets of her hair cascading over her shoulders, framing her beautiful face — the image made Steve ache a bit. Even Ellen, self-critical and suffering from an inferiority complex, would have known that she looked great. Her pictured her: she closed her eyes and thought about the night. Their neighbors, the Steens, had invited Ellen and Steve to the wedding of their son, Scott. Ellen and Steve had built their home two properties away, and they made fast friends with the Steens. Scott was about six years-old when the Boxleys had moved in, and as the Boxley kids had grown up, Scott had baby-sat for them. All of a sudden, Scott grew up. He went to college at the University of Pennsylvania, and was now working his way up the corporate ladder at a technology company in Tampa. And, tonight, he would be married.

Steve pictured Ellen going to the family room where she inevitably waited for Steve. In his imagination she pulled out their wedding album and slowly looked through the pages. How happy they had been. Steve was a surgical resident when they met, and even though he was busy, his days and nights were predictable. When he was on-call, he was off-limits to Ellen. But, when he was off-call, he would be home, sometimes for a whole weekend at a time. How different that was to now; he was in private practice, and every call, every new patient, every problem had to be discussed with Steve, and more importantly, he now had no free time. In Steve's imagination, she then opened the family album and looked at the pictures of the kids. There were a few of the whole family, but most of the pictures were of the kids, taken by Ellen, or they were of Ellen and the kids and taken by a stranger. Here were the pictures of the family vacation in the Bahamas, the one that Steve had missed because of an unexpected emergency as they were packing up the car. Steve had given a report of the patients to Nan Freedman, but he had neglected to tell the answering service that she was now taking his calls. So, the beeper went off, and a frantic resident had blurted out a plea for help. Steve had sent Ellen and the kids to the airport and told them he would take care of the emergency and meet them before the plane took off. Ellen grimaced in Steve's mind, and Steve grimaced now too. Not only did he miss the plane, but he never made it to the resort.

Steve imagined Ellen looking at her watch. It was 8:15. Tears rolled down her face; she really wanted Steve to be with her, and it was obvious that the only way she would be able to go to the wedding was alone. She got her bag and left. Before walking out she wrote Steve a note, telling him to meet her at the wedding and that she loved him. He never showed up, and when Ellen got home, he still had not gotten there. She called the hospital and the secretary at the operating room desk told her that Steve was still in the same case, and that he would probably be there all night. She went to bed alone, and she woke up alone.

The next morning, she went to her mother's house and picked up the children. They returned home, and Ellen packed up her and the kids and moved out. They went back to her mother's house and moved in.

Steve looked around the empty house, at his sport jacket over the chair where he had thrown it when he came in, and he felt quite lonely. It was times like this, when he came home from a tough night and pictured Ellen's final time in these rooms, that he wished Ellen and the kids still lived there. His marriage was not a bad one, but his life revolved around the hospital and his patients, not his wife and children. Ellen had packed up her belongings and the kids' belongings and moved in with her parents, and he didn't realize they were gone for two days. He had called her cell phone to ask where she was, and that's when she told him she had left two days before.

"Well, that's the life you chose," Steve thought, "your brother's a GP, and he's home every night. No beeper, no hassle. You wanted the excitement, and you got it."

He was showered and dressed and in the office 45 minutes later.

CHAPTER 2

Gunshots rang out in the night, fired from an unseen car speeding along the access road at 55 miles per hour. Raymond Grayson fell to his knees and was only able to gurgle, "I'm hit," before his temple hit the ground and he lost consciousness. Fortuitously, one of the patrons at the bar that Raymond was standing in front of heard the gunshots and pulled out his cell phone.

"9-1-1, what is your emergency?"

"Shots have been fired."

"Where are you located?"

"We're at the corner of Oklahoma Road and 4th Street."

"Has anyone been hurt?"

"I don't know. I'm in a bar, and I am afraid to go outside."

"Stay put. Help is on the way."

Moments later, two squad cars screeched up to the corner and two policemen jumped out of their cars, hands on their guns. They saw Raymond lying in a puddle of his blood, and one of the policemen used the radio on his sleeve to call for an ambulance. That officer stayed with Raymond while the other went into the bar.

"Turn the lights on, and turn off the music, now," the cop demanded of the bartender. He did as he was told, and in a moment, about twenty people were blinking to adjust to the lights. "Someone was shot outside this bar. One of you called for assistance. Who knows what happened here?"

One of the patrons, a muscular, tattooed skinhead stepped forward. "I'm Cueball," he said. "I called the cops. No one saw a thing. We were all in here, and I was nearest to the door. I heard three shots, and called you on my cell phone. No one has had the balls to leave since then."

Just then, the cop's partner walked in and said a few words to him. "Alright, the victim was Raymond Grayson. He's on his way to Middle Florida Hospital as we speak. He's been shot in the head, and is gravely injured. Any of you know him?"

Most of the patrons shook their head from side to side, but then one of them said, "Yes, I know him. I was speaking to him a few minutes ago, and then he got a phone call and said he had to leave. A minute later, Cueball yelled that someone had been shot."

"Any idea what the phone call was about?"

"None, except that he seemed kinda pissed, then he yelled, 'I'm on my way,' into the phone, then left."

"Who does he hang around with?"

"No one in particular, but I do know that he runs with a gang, the Bluebloods."

After some more questioning, the cops left the bar and headed to the hospital to see what they could find out there about the victim. As they walked out into the night, they found the crime scene technicians already hard at work on the scene, photographing the sidewalk and blood-splatter patterns, taking samples of the blood and other bodily fluids that Raymond had left behind. Other cops were beginning to question patrons as they came out of the bar; and still others were searching the area for shell casings or bullets to help identify the type of gun that had been used in this crime.

At the hospital, the two officers found that Raymond was already in surgery. The neurosurgeon was Dr. Bob Carney. They settled down into two comfortable sofas and waited for the operation to be over.

In the operating room, Raymond was being prepared for surgery. One of the nurses shaved his head with a standard

Norelco electric razor, and his hair was placed into a plastic bag to be given to Raymond's family. Sometimes the family wanted to make a wig for their loved one to use until the hair grew back. Next, soap was scrubbed into the scalp, and a disposable Bic razor was used to complete the shave. Finally, the head was rewashed and then placed into a frame that looked like it had been made by Torquemada for use in the Inquisition. It was a semicircle with six screws protruding from below the frame. Dr. Carney situated Raymond's head in the position that he wanted it in for the surgery. Then, the six screws were turned, biting into Raymond's scalp. This would keep the head in a fixed position throughout the surgery. Another wash of the head, then iodine paint was used to disinfect the skin. Finally, surgical towels and drapes were placed, and Dr. Carney could begin.

"The bullet entered the head just in front of the right ear," Carney said to the medical student who was watching the procedure. "We have seen pulsatile bleeding from the wound, so it seems likely that an artery was hit. What artery would be in the path of the bullet?"

The student shrugged and said, "This is just a guess, Dr. Carney, but I would say that it might be the anterior cerebral artery."

"No, that would be an incorrect guess. The artery is the middle meningeal. We will need to find it and stop the bleeding before we do anything else."

Carney made a half-circle incision in Raymond's scalp, and then deepened it into the muscle layers below. The student had witnessed a few surgeries before this one, but he gasped at the amount of bleeding. He was slightly in awe of just how unruffled Dr. Carney remained. He seemed to expect the bleeding and was not fazed. White clips were applied to the scalp, almost like some type of grotesque hair treatment, and the bleeding from the scalp ceased. Next, Carney used a jigsaw to cut the bone; he removed a circle of bone about three inches wide. Bleeding from the cut bone was impressive, but it stopped when Carney used bone wax on it. Now, he could see the damage caused by the bullet. The cut edge of the middle meningeal artery was visible, and Carney quickly tied the artery to stop the bleeding. But the damage to the brain was extensive.

"Normal brain tissue looks kind of like a cauliflower, with ridges and bumps on it," he said to the student. "This area of the brain looks like the cauliflower has been boiled and charred. The charred area is from the bullet, and the spongy area is from the concussive force of the bullet. All of the tissue you see is dead." With that, he began to meticulously remove all of the dead tissue from Raymond's head, stopping the debridement when he reached brain matter that he thought was viable. After about three hours, he had completed his job. He stood up and stretched. "I'm going to take a break for a minute or two. Let the student gently irrigate the brain," he told those assisting, "and I'll be right back."

Carney headed for the bathroom, and after emptying his bladder, he washed his face, rescrubbed his hands and returned to the operating room. He placed a drainage catheter into Raymond's head, and then he carefully closed up the hole he had made. The circle of bone was cleaned up and sutured back where it belonged, the muscles were closed, and finally, the skin was sealed. The screws holding Raymond's head to the table were released and bandages were placed over the wound. Raymond was not allowed to wake up; Carney wanted a day or two to be able to control his breathing, and therefore the pressure in his brain, while Raymond began to heal.

As the nurses got Raymond off of the table and into the recovery room, Carney went to the waiting room. There he found the two officers and Raymond's family. He asked the officers to wait a few minutes and went to see Raymond's relatives. A man who looked to be about fifty years old introduced himself as Raymond's father, then turned and introduced a woman as Raymond's mother, and finally a young girl was identified as his sister. Carney asked them to sit down and began to speak. "Raymond has suffered a terrible gunshot injury to the head. I retrieved the bullet, and the police will take custody of it for testing, but I suspect that it was a high caliber bullet. You see, with small caliber weapons, the bones of the head usually stop the bullet from entering the brain. The patient can still have some brain injury from the force of the bullet striking the bone, but usually, the bullet can't penetrate the skull and directly injure the brain. In Raymond's case, the bullet passed through the skull and continued into the brain, killing brain tissue as it went along. I needed to remove about ten percent of the right side of the brain. I suspect that he will have memory problems, difficulties using the left side of his body, and maybe even blindness in his right eye. That is, of course, if he lives."

The boy's mother and his sister were now weeping quietly as the father stared vacantly at the doctor, his lower lip trembling.

"Now, Raymond is being taken from the operating room table to the neurosurgical intensive care unit. You'll be able to see him once he's settled, but I need to tell you that we will make no effort to wake him up after surgery. In fact, we'll be keeping him asleep intentionally. If he were to wake up, he would get agitated and start thrashing around, which would raise the pressure in the brain and cause bleeding, or worse, swelling in the brain. By keeping him asleep for a few days, we can control the pressure and allow him to start healing.

"Unfortunately, however, by keeping him asleep, we can't examine him to see how much damage there is. We won't be able to determine that until we let the sedation wear off in a few days."

"How bad could it be?" asked his mother between sobs.

"It could be terrible. When we wake him up, he may have the mental ability of a two-year old, or he could be essentially brain dead. We won't know until we turn off the sedatives."

With that, Carney excused himself, and asked the Grayson family to remain in the waiting room. He told them that he needed to speak with the police and that after he was through, the police would need to speak with them. The father nodded in agreement, and Carney walked over to the policemen.

"Good morning, gentlemen," Carney said as he looked at his watch. "Christ, it's four o'clock in the morning. Well, how can I help you?"

The older officer spoke. "Hi, Doc. We'd appreciate any information you could give us. First, do you have the bullet?"

Carney held out a plastic bag and handed it to the officer. "Here you go," he said. The cop placed a red sticker that said 'EVIDENCE' on the bag and pocketed it. Carney went on, "The bullet entered the right temporal bone and continued into the temporal area of the brain."

The cop interrupted, "Hold it Doc. Let me tape this, ok?"

Carney nodded and the cop turned on a hand-held recorder. He continued, "As I said, the bullet entered the right temporal bone and continued into the temporal area of the brain. It severed – that's cut – the middle meningeal artery, which needed to be tied off. That artery supplied blood to some of the brain, and therefore, the tissue may die later if the brain doesn't have adequate alternative blood flow to that area. We then identified a considerable amount of unquestionably dead brain tissue and proceeded to remove it. I'm concerned that the concussive injury may have caused damage to the right optic nerve, and maybe even to the left as well; those are the nerves to the eyes. If both are lost, he's completely blind."

"Doctor, would you explain what you mean by concussive injury? I thought that the only injury was direct, from the bullet."

"No, the concussive injury can even be worse than the bullet injury. You see, the bullet passes quickly through an area, and it kills what it hits. However, the brute force of the bullet, the energy that it possesses, is dissipated in waves around the bullet's path. Think of it like dropping a stone in a pond. The center of the injury is where the stone hits the water. The rings around the center are due to the energy being dissipated around the bullet. These rings of damage are devastating, and cause much, much more injury than the bullet itself."

"Thanks for the explanation. When will you know how bad he was injured?"

"We'll be keeping him asleep for another two or three days, and then we'll turn off the sedation. After that, we'll be able to assess him and tell you how bad the injury is."

"Thanks, Doc." The cops excused themselves and went to speak with the Graysons. Carney walked to the doctor's lounge. He wanted to get a bit of sleep before starting another day of neurosurgery.

***

"Do you swear to tell the truth, the whole truth, and nothing but the truth?"

"Yes."

"Dr. Semben, you are an expert in urology, are you not?"

"Yes, I am"

"I have asked you here as an expert to testify on behalf of my client, regarding the care rendered to her by her own urologist, Dr. Franks. Is that correct?"

"Yes, that is correct."

"Would you briefly review your credentials, please?"

"I went to college at the University of Georgia, medical school in the Bahamas, and did my urology residency at Pickett Hospital in Georgia."

"After that...?"

"I went into private practice in urology in rural Georgia, where I continue to practice."

"How long have you been in practice?"

"Four years."

"Did you review the records of my client?"

"Yes."

"And have you formulated an opinion as to the malpractice committed by Dr. Franks?"

"Objection, your honor," the defense attorney yelled. "Mr. Cuney knows that malpractice has not been established, and that in fact we are actively trying to show that Dr. Franks' care of this patient was actually exemplary."

"Objection sustained. Mr. Cuney, please restate your question."

"Yes sir. Dr. Semben, have you formulated an opinion regarding the level of care given to my client while she was Dr. Franks' patient?"

"Yes, I have. Dr. Franks removed her kidney unnecessarily."

"How did you come to that opinion? You know that she was bleeding, and Dr. Franks' operative report states that he had no choice but to remove the kidney. He couldn't repair the hemorrhaging blood vessel, and she was dying as he worked."

Dr. Semben smiled. The questioning was going just as Cuney had told him it would. "I don't care what Dr. Franks put in his report. Every kidney can be saved by an experienced urologist."

"Bullshit," whispered Dr. Franks to his attorney, a bit too loudly. "He's lying through his teeth, and they both know it."

"I know, but you need to be quiet. The judge and the jury heard you."

Cuney continued, "So it's your opinion that Dr. Franks was negligent in his care of my client?"

"Absolutely."

Cuney looked at his opponent and said, "Your witness."

"Thank you. Dr. Semben, I'm Matthew Johnson, Dr. Franks' attorney. Am I correct that you practice in rural Georgia?"

"That's correct."

"How many miles away from Central Florida is that?"

"Objection. What difference does that make?" bellowed Cuney.

"It makes quite a bit of difference. First, a medical expert is supposed to testify about the community standard of care. How can he know the community standard of care in a community that's a thousand miles away? Second, he lives in Georgia, for Christ's sake; couldn't you find someone to lie for you that lives closer?"

"Mr. Johnson, that's enough," said the judge. "But, Mr. Cuney, Mr. Johnson has a point. I'll let Dr. Semben testify, but I'll also allow the line of questioning."

"Thank you judge. Dr. Semben, how far do you live from Central Florida?"

"It was a six hundred mile trip for me to come here."

"And how much are you getting paid to say what Mr. Cuney wants you to say?"

"Objection!"

"Sustained. Be careful, Mr. Johnson."

"Sorry, your honor. Doctor, how much are you getting paid for this case?"

"I get $300 per hour and $2000 per day."

"So, for this entire case, what's your fee?"

"I spent three hours reviewing the records, one hour writing up my report, one hour on the phone with Mr. Cuney, and two days for the trip here to testify."

"Your bill, sir?"

"$5,500."

"Now, have you ever testified in a medical malpractice case before?"

"Yes."

"How many times?"

"I don't recall."

"Come now, sir. At $5,500 a pop, I'm sure you must be able to remember."

"Maybe 20 cases."

"In how many years?"

"Four."

"So, you've testified since you've been in practice. Is that correct?"

"Yes."

"Dr. Semben, the Internet is a wonderful tool. I researched court records, and the truth is that you've testified in 35 cases, and you have given depositions in 40 more in those four years. Isn't that so?"

"If you say so."

"How much money did you make last year by giving medical opinions? Before you answer, remember that I can check that too."

"Why don't you just tell me, and I'll agree."

"Based on your income statement, it seems that you earned $120,000 last year alone by testifying."

"Ok, I agree."

"How many of these opinions were for the defendant, Doctor?"

"None."

"What percentage of your opinions are for the firm of Morris, Cuney and Howe?

"Over ninety percent, I would guess."

"So, you are a plaintiff hack. Is that correct?"

Cuney shouted," Your honor," but before the judge had a chance to respond, Johnson continued, "Question withdrawn. Do you see trauma patients in your practice in Georgia?"

"No, I don't."

"Doctor, have you ever had the need to remove a kidney?"

"Yes, but it had cancer in it."

"You mean to tell me that in four years of practice, you've only had one occasion to remove one kidney?"

"That's correct. I told you that I'm in rural Georgia. We aren't very busy there."

"Dr. Franks is a busy, respected urologist. How can you, having only removed one kidney in your career, and not having done any trauma surgery whatsoever, testify against him regarding the procedure in question?"

"Mr. Johnson, whether you like it or not, I'm an expert and qualified to testify in court. That's how."

"I have no further questions, your honor," said Matthew Johnson as he returned to his seat.

"In that case," said the judge, "we'll recess for lunch. Be back in one hour."

While Dr. Franks didn't feel much like eating and just picked at his salad, Matt Johnson ate heartily. "How can that son of a bitch lie like that in court and get away with it?" he asked.

Johnson shrugged, "That's the system, like it or not. He is an urologist and therefore he can testify against you. There's no law that says he can't come into your state and lie through his teeth. This is a civil trial, not a criminal trial, so he's not subject to perjury for lying. But, if it makes you feel better, the jury knows he's full of shit. Remember, however, that the jury is made up of six people who are too stupid to get out of jury duty." That made Franks smile, his last one for the day.

"Has the jury reached a verdict?"

"Yes, your honor, we have."

"What say you?"

"In the matter of Shaff versus Franks, we find on behalf of the plaintiff."

"And what damages do you assess?"

"We find on behalf on the plaintiff in the amount of $600,000."

"Thank you. We are adjourned."

Cuney hugged his client, accepted congratulations from his law clerk, and enjoyed his moment in the sun as the reporters crowded around him in the hallway of the courtroom. He did a quick calculation: 35% of $600,000 is over $200,000, a few thousand for that whore Semben, and the rest is gravy. He'd have to tell the rest of the trial lawyers about Semben at the next meeting. That guy would say anything for a buck. Jake can have the limelight with the TV commercials, Cuney thought. He'd take the courtroom antics any day.

Dr. Franks hadn't cried since his father died 5 years before, but today he cried like a baby. He saved that bitch's life, dealt with her family, literally slept in the ICU at her bedside, and now these people award her $600,000 on the lying testimony of a hick who hasn't practiced real medicine in his entire career. Without a word, he left the courtroom, got in his car in the parking garage and headed home, but he would never get there. He really couldn't see too well while he was driving, couldn't see through the tears that he was so unaccustomed to peering through; and maybe he didn't really want to go on living anyway, a subliminal wish tucked away in his subconscious that this verdict had awakened just enough to keep him from driving all the way home. His convertible Mercedes hit the train bridge abutment at 70 miles per hour, and there really wasn't much the paramedics could do for him but cover his face with a blanket.

CHAPTER 3

The investigation of Raymond Grayson's shooting was progressing nicely. The investigators found all three shell casings, and the two bullets that had missed Raymond had hit the stucco wall behind him. They were severely deformed from the impact, but they were retrieved and studied. The bullet that entered Raymond's brain was photographed and carefully examined as well. It was determined that the bullet was a 45 caliber ACP load.

After the detectives interviewed the patrons of the bar, they found that Cueball was correct: Raymond belonged to the Bluebloods. The investigators began to surmise that this was a not a random drive-by shooting, but instead, an attempted execution. The SWAT team of the Florida Highway Patrol stormed a meeting of the Bluebloods in an abandoned warehouse in downtown Tampa. The members were immediately separated and taken to different interrogation rooms, and after sweating the prisoners for a few hours, the detectives got what they wanted. The Bluebloods were in the middle of a gang war with the West Side Skinheads over distribution of crack cocaine in Central Florida. The Bluebloods had started a fire in a building that the Skinheads used to store their drugs. The Bluebloods thought the building was empty, but unbeknownst to them, one of the Skinhead brothers was killed in the fire. This death prompted retaliation, more death, and the execution of one of the lieutenants of the Bluebloods, Raymond Grayson, had been authorized.

A similar raid on a meeting of the West Side Skinheads produced a cache of arms and about 20 kilograms of crack cocaine, as well as a methamphetamine lab. Twenty members of the gang were arrested, and after their interrogation, the police suspected that Jimmy Delano was

27

the shooter. They tested all of the weapons recovered, and ballistics determined that a Sig P245 was the gun used in the shooting. Shortly after Jimmy's arrest, he confessed to the shooting. He was charged with numerous weapons offenses and attempted murder.

Raymond Grayson was having a slow and complicated recovery from the gunshot wound. He developed bleeding from the brain, and required another operation to control it. Later, he developed pneumonia and needed prolonged respiratory therapy. But, by far, the worst part of his recovery was related to the brain injury itself. The bullet had damaged the right side of Raymond's brain, and the destruction that it caused rendered the left side of Raymond's body almost unusable. He needed physical therapy three times daily to try to restore some function. He also had been blinded in the right eye, and he was having problems using his right side to help himself with tasks the whole body would normally be needed to accomplish. His memory was affected; he had trouble remembering much of anything, or even recognizing his family. Finally, he was having a terrible time speaking, and the doctors doubted if he would ever be able to speak normally. But, all in all, he was lucky. He wasn't dead. And he was recovering, however loosely defined the term might be in his instance, no matter how arduous the process.

Raymond's medical bills were staggering. The doctors' bills from the surgeon, various medical specialists and rehabilitation physicians totaled roughly $50,000, and the hospital and rehabilitation center bills were over $150,000. Not surprisingly, Raymond did not have health insurance. He fell through the cracks, as the politicians like to say: he was over 21 years old, and not a student, so he didn't qualify to be covered on this parents' plan, and he was unemployed so he didn't have his own insurance. The bills started rolling in, and because he lived with his parents, they got them. As the amount due mounted, the Graysons turned to the legal system to try to have someone else foot the bill. Roberta

Grayson called Morris, Cuney and Howe, and within a few hours, she and her husband Harold were seated across the table from Brian Jeffries, one of the staff lawyers.

"Please tell me as much as you can about your son and the nature of his injuries," Jeffries inquired.

Mr. Grayson began, "Raymond is a good kid. Unfortunately, he made the wrong friends, and as much as his mother and I tried to stop him, he got involved in a gang. We begged him to get out, but the excitement and the money were too much, and he wouldn't leave. He was arrested a few times for minor charges, but a few weeks ago, he got in over his head. From what the police tell us, his gang, the Bluebloods, was in a turf war with the West Side Skinheads over the crack distribution in Central Florida, and Raymond's gang burned down a building where the Skinheads made and stored their drugs. One of the Skinheads was killed in the fire. Raymond was targeted for execution, and they damn near succeeded." Harold Grayson nearly choked up at this point and had to stand and walk to a window, where he stood peering out into the Florida sunshine.

Mrs. Grayson continued, "Raymond was shot in the head, and there was extensive damage. He is now out of the hospital and in rehab, but it will be months before he can come home. Once he is released, he'll need around-the-clock help, probably for the rest of his life." She began to sob, and her husband stood behind her and put his hand on her shoulder. After a few moments she regained her composure, blew her nose, and went on. "His medical bills are already over $200,000, and they go up every day. We've been told that his home care will cost us about $300 per day. Mr. Jeffries, my husband is a laborer and only earns $150 per day, and we have no savings. Even if we declare bankruptcy, and have the medical bills erased, we could never afford the care after he comes home." She began to cry again.

After a moment, Jeffries spoke. "If we are to shift the financial burden away from you and to a defendant, we need to identify someone or something that we can blame. The first target would be the shooter. Do we know who that was?"

"Yes, his name is Jimmy Delano; he's a member of the Skinheads."

"Ok, the next possible plaintiff is the gun manufacturer. Have the police identified the gun?"

"Yes, it was made by Sig Arms. It's a Sig P245," Mr. Grayson replied.

"If we go against the gun manufacturer, it will be very difficult to win, but we can keep that option in mind for now. Who owned the building that the Bluebloods burned down?"

"It was an abandoned warehouse. I have no idea who owns it, but here is the address." Mr. Grayson wrote an address on a piece of paper and Jeffries circled it in red pen.

"Finally, the last option is to sue the neurosurgeon. Right now, based on what you told me, I don't know how we could do that, but financially speaking he'd be a great target; and if Raymond is as bad off as you say, we'd get a lot of sympathy in court. In addition, the surgeon would probably be the only potential defendant we could get to."

The Graysons signed papers authorizing Morris, Cuney and Howe to obtain Raymond's medical records, agreeing that Morris, Cuney and Howe would get 35% of any settlement and approving Morris, Cuney and Howe as the only law firm working on this case. The distraught parents walked out of the office, Mr. Grayson's arm around his wife's shoulder, her head buried in his chest.

***

The alarm rang in the resident's quarters at five o'clock, and Mark Land jumped out of bed quickly. He had a zillion things to do before the first scheduled case of the day. Dr. Boxley had 3 cases scheduled, and the first was going to be a tough one. Mr. Kane had a large rectal tumor, just a few centimeters up from the anus. These tumors were difficult enough to get out, but to make matters worse, Mr. Kane was the size of a small house. Dr. Boxley had been letting Mark do most of the cases by himself, and he wanted him to handle this one, too. He had spent a few hours in the library during the night reading about just this type of surgery. He was ready for Boxley's questions and thought he might be able to go skin to skin without asking for help. But he knew that there was no way Boxley would be at all generous if Mark didn't have rounds done first. So, he hopped out of bed, jumped into the shower, and put on scrubs. Most of the rounds went well, and he discharged the laparoscopic gall bladder patient from the day before. Next stop, ICU. He walked in and went to the bedside of the motorcycle trauma patient, John. He seemed to be doing well, and his breathing was quite regular. The ventilator was pushing air easily into his lungs. Mark woke him, and John smiled. Mark told him to breathe deeply, in and out. He disconnected the ventilator and quickly pulled out the tube. John coughed once, and then spoke in a very quiet voice. "Holy shit, what happened." Mark sat down in the easy chair next to him and went over the events of the past couple of days. John said he remembered driving down I-75. A car had sped past him, one of the teenagers in it flicked a cigarette at him, and as he brushed it off, he lost control of the bike. That was the last thing he remembered. Mark finished at his bedside, made his chart notes, and headed to the OR.

Steve Boxley was chatting with the nurses when Mark arrived. "How is everyone doing?" he asked Mark.

"Fine. I discharged 305-B and 202-A, transferred the aorta to the floor, and extubated the motorcycle guy. He's awake and doing well."

"Great," said Steve. "We'll make rounds together between cases. Get into OR 3 and get the rectal tumor patient ready for surgery. Have the nurse page me when you start."

The two men went their separate ways, Mark to the OR and Steve to the lounge. He ran into Bob Carney in the bathroom, and the two of them struck up a conversation about the topic closest to each of their hearts, the current malpractice crisis. "I'm thinking of leaving town. I can't take the constant ads on TV and radio by that asshole Jake Morris, and I don't like looking over my shoulder all the time, wondering when I'm going to be sued. As far as I'm concerned, that prick Morris' head could explode and I wouldn't help him. His partner Cuney could use masking tape to hold his cranium together, for all I care."

"You're pissed," said Steve, "and I understand, but that doesn't help the situation. I hate to see this area implode for lack of medical care. I'd prefer to see if we can get a solution."

"Sure, there's a solution, Steve. As Shakespeare said, 'First, let's kill the lawyers.' That would be a solution I can get behind." Boxley chuckled and headed for OR 3.

The cardiac monitor showed a heart rate of 95 beats per minute and blood pressure at 120 over 70, both normal. The oxygen level was 99%. The patient was quite large, and the nurses, with Land's help, had struggled to get Mr. Kane into the correct position for the operation. He looked like a beached whale, with his legs up in stirrups like a woman getting ready to have a baby. Well, he'd have a delivery alright, but instead of an 8 pound girl, he'd have an 8 pound tumor. Land had opened the abdomen and placed a large self-retaining retractor into the belly. He had packed the intestines away from the lower abdomen and was dissecting the lower colon and rectum when Steve walked in. "Hi, Dr. Boxley. This is Alan, my second-year resident."

"Hi Alan," Steve replied. "What structure is in jeopardy with the dissection that Dr. Land is doing now?"

"I would say that that would be the ureter, Dr. Boxley," replied the resident.

"Correct, Alan. You can stay for the rest of the case. Mark, do you need my help yet?" Land said no, and Steve sat on a chair in the corner and was quickly lost in thought. He was overwhelmed by the turn of events in Central Florida, doctors leaving the area, and his own concern with a malpractice insurance policy he couldn't afford. "Oh well," he thought, "things will work out."

"What did you say, Dr. Boxley?" one of the nurses asked.

"Huh, I didn't know I was talking out loud," Steve replied. "Nothing."

Steve went into the next room and scrubbed his hands to the Beatles tune *Help*.

The case took 3 hours, but Mark did a beautiful job. The anesthesiologist decided to leave Mr. Kane asleep on the breathing machine for a while, so Mark didn't need to be so attentive after the procedure. He told the second-year resident to write the postoperative orders and note, and to stay with the patient. This gave the two men a chance to do rounds together. Steve let Mark lead him around the hospital. He listened to Mark review each patient's progress and condition. When they got to ICU and John's bedside, Steve spoke with him for awhile. Boxley felt that he was well enough to leave the ICU and instructed the nurses to let him go. Rounds done, they went for coffee in the surgeon's lounge, waiting to be called for the next case.

CHAPTER 4

Every week, the partners of Morris, Cuney and Howe had a meeting with the staff attorneys. The junior lawyers would review any cases they had signed up since the last meeting, and the senior lawyers would discuss the merits of the case and the potential profit to the firm. Money drove this meeting, always; a potential plaintiff could have been seriously wronged, but if the damages were not enough, the firm would refuse to take the case. Furthermore, even if the plaintiff wasn't wronged, but his injuries were great, which thereby increased the potential pay out, the firm might be willing to take a chance on the case.

Brian Jeffries took his seat at the conference table. The other junior associates sat around him at the far end of the table. Jake Morris sat at the head of the table, flanked by Sam Cuney and Jay Howe. One by one, the junior associates reviewed cases, and the entire group discussed them. The main discussion topics were causation and damages. Cuney was responsible for quickly determining the method of attack, and Jake Morris had the final say.

Finally, it was Jeffries' turn to speak. He quickly presented Raymond Grayson's case to the group and identified possible targets. "I have investigated the potential defendants in this case. Of course, the main target would ideally be Jimmy Delano, the guy who shot Raymond. However, he has nothing. He lives in a flop house with his prostitute girlfriend. He has no assets, no bank accounts and no job. I would rule him out as a target as there is nothing we can go after if we win.

"The next targets I've identified are the gangs, both the Bluebloods and the West Side Skinheads. But, while they have names for their organizations, they are not legal names; there are no corporations or assets to go after. All of the people in these gangs are derelicts; none has any assets of significance. Therefore, I figure we can't go after them either.

"Next, I looked at the property where the shooting took place and the warehouse that the Bluebloods burned down. I thought that we might be able to make a case against the bar for inadequate security. After all, Raymond was shot on their property. Unfortunately for us, the bar has no liability insurance and the owner has no assets. So, we could sue the proprietor, but we couldn't recover anything. The warehouse was abandoned 5 years ago, and the owner is nowhere to be found. The county has a back tax lien on the property for $150,000, so even if we found the owner and sued him, the first $150,000 in assets that we found would go to the county. So, I've ruled the property owners out as well.

"An interesting target would be the gun manufacturer. The gun was made by Sig Arms, and we could sue them, alleging that Raymond would not have been shot if they didn't make a product whose only use is to kill or maim. I know that this would be a difficult case to win, but I thought I should mention it.

"The last remaining target is the neurosurgeon. His name is Dr. Bob Carney. While I don't have any evidence for it, we could probably come up with a theory of medical malpractice. He would be a great target, because we know that he has malpractice insurance."

Brian took a deep breath and sat down. He waited while the partners mulled over his speech, and finally Jake Morris spoke. "I would defer to Mr. Cuney about medical malpractice, but I would immediately rule out the gun manufacturer as a target. This firm is not interested in setting public policy, and I don't want to get embroiled in social issues. Sam, what do you think about this as a medical malpractice case?"

Cuney responded, "Jake, I like this case. The damages to the victim are tremendous, and if we could get the full value of the neurosurgeon's policy, our cut would be almost $350,000. I'm sure that we could come up with a theory of malpractice; that should be the least of our problems."

Cuney stood up and started pacing around the room. The assembled people watched him. They knew that he was lost in thought. Finally, he brightened up, and almost shouted, "I've got it. I've been toying with a new claim for medical malpractice. It's the opposite of wrongful death. With the claim of wrongful death, we assert that the defendant caused the death of our client's loved one, and that he or she *shouldn't* have died. This claim will be wrongful life. In this instance we can assert that the plaintiff *should* have died because the injuries were so devastating that any thinking, competent doctor would have let him die. But in this case, we will argue that an incompetent doctor, thinking only of a paycheck, saved the plaintiff and now this doctor should have to pay for the ongoing expenses and for the pain and suffering of the family. Actually, I've been saving this theory to use in a bad-baby case, but I think that this would be a perfect opportunity to try it out."

Everyone turned to Jake Morris. He thought about it for awhile, and then a smile broke out on his face. "Sam," he asked Cuney, "do you think that we could threaten to tack on putative damages here. Could we convince the doctor that we could get the jury to punish him for allowing this man to live? If we could, they would be much more inclined to settle the case, and not go to trial."

"I hope so, Jake. That was my initial thought when I came up with this wrongful life theory."

"Great. I vote that we take the case."

Brian Jeffries was beaming. This was his case, and he was going to milk this new strategy for all it was worth.

***

"Shit happens. That about sums up all of the bad things that can happen that are out of a doctor's hands. Wounds get infected. Arteries that were tied off start bleeding. People who never heard of heart disease because they show no signs can suddenly have heart attacks after an operation. Injections given in the correct place can hit a nerve, causing terrible pain and paralysis. One especially disastrous complication of surgery is called a pulmonary embolism.

"Patients undergoing major surgery need a breathing tube in the windpipe so the anesthesiologist can control the breathing. In order to place the tube and push air into the lungs, the patient must be given a medication to paralyze the breathing muscles. This medicine does its job, but it paralyzes all of the muscles, including the muscles in the legs. The muscle paralysis promotes clotting in the veins of the legs, and if clots form, it is known as deep venous thrombosis, or DVT for short. These clots can then flow with the blood out of the legs and eventually end up in the heart and then in the lungs. They lodge in the lungs and stop the blood flow, thereby causing the normal oxygenation of blood to stop. This is called pulmonary embolism, and many times it's fatal. If the patient has a severe pulmonary embolism and survives, he can have permanent lung damage. For this reason, we need to be both proactive, trying to prevent DVT in the first place, and reactive, aggressively treating it when it occurs."

"Thank you Alan," Steve said. "That was a very interesting and concise explanation of this terrible problem. Now, who can tell me which patients are at higher risk for this problem?"

One of the third-year medical students raised her hand. Steve acknowledged her, and she responded, "Smokers, sedentary patients, and especially obese patients. Also, patients undergoing pelvic, orthopedic or gynecologic surgery are especially at risk."

"Good," Steve replied. "Now Dr. Land, tell these people what we've done to protect our first patient today from DVT and pulmonary embolism."

"I asked the nurses to put TED hose on him. TED stands for thromboembolic disease. You students will remember that those were the white stockings he was wearing into the OR. It would have been nice to add heparin, a blood thinner, but the operation was pretty bloody and he's so fat that I was afraid to give the drug to him. Hopefully, the TEDs will be enough."

"Would anyone like to comment on that answer?" Steve asked. A first year resident's hand went up. "Yes?"

"I disagree with not giving him heparin. Mr. Kane is at extremely high risk. He's terribly obese, a smoker, and he's sedentary. He's a poster child for someone who gets DVT and pulmonary embolism. I think that it's worth the risk of bleeding to place him on heparin, because we can fix bleeding but we really can't fix pulmonary embolism."

"Any further comments?"

The hospital risk manager raised her hand. "Sandy, why don't you first explain to everyone who you are and what you do."

"Thank you Dr. Boxley. I am Sandra DeStefano, the hospital risk manager, which is a new position, and I'm sad to say it's a necessary one. In my earlier career, I was a nurse. Now I monitor the activity in the hospital and try to minimize malpractice risk for the hospital and the doctors. Therefore, my answer is more from a legal perspective than from a medical one. And, all of you students and residents, unfortunately, need to start thinking of decisions from both the standpoint of the best medical decision and the best legal decision. Don't kid yourself and think that they're the same. I assure you, they are not.

"Before I comment on the question at hand, let me give you a quick example. A 12 year-old boy playing ball gets hit in the head with a softball, falls down, is unconscious for maybe two seconds at most, then gets up and wants to return to the game. The coach refuses and makes his dad take him to the emergency room. The ER doctor examines him and everything is fine. Does this boy need a CAT scan? First, let's hear from one of the medical students."

A young woman with sharp features and an intense demeanor answers. "No. We were taught that a momentary loss of consciousness coupled with a normal examination is associated with only a 1% or less chance of serious brain injury. There is no need whatsoever for a CAT scan. The father should be given instructions to watch the boy for the next 12 hours, and if he's fine after that, there's nothing to worry about."

"Good. Now the first-year resident?"

The resident who answered the heparin question responded. "I agree with the student. The risk of the radiation from the CAT scan to 100 people to find the one person, the 1%, with a real injury is not at all worth it."

"OK, now what about the expense? Dr. Land?"

"A CAT scan costs the patient or his insurance company $600. Multiple that by 100 scans to find one abnormal scan, and the cost becomes $60,000 for one abnormal scan. That is a terrible waste of resources."

Sandy smiled. "You are all correct. However, we would fire an ER doctor who didn't order the scan." A murmur went through the crowd. She continued, "For the one missed brain injury, society would not be willing to pay $60,000. So, society would say, 'don't scan all 100 of these people.' However, we live in a litigious society, and the family of the one patient who had the injury would sue us, even if there were no damages. In a perfect world, the father would be given instructions as you said, and if the kid were to start acting funny, he'd be brought back to the hospital and treated properly. However, the lawyers would contend that something, somehow, should have been done sooner, and a sympathetic jury would throw a million dollars at the client. Now, the question is, 'Should we waste $60,000 of other patients' money, of the health insurance companies' money, or lose $1,000,000 of ours?' Of course, that's an easy question to answer: we scan everyone. If they get brain tumors 20 years from now from the radiation, that's their problem.

"So, back to Mr. Kane, and the risk of DVT. This is what we call a no-win situation. If Dr. Boxley decides to treat him with heparin, and he bleeds, we have to answer for that. If he decides not to treat him with heparin, and he gets the clots, we will answer for that, too. Now, there's something you don't learn in medical school."

Steve ended the conversation. "We had a similar case - a trauma patient – recently, and just as with the case under discussion, we felt the risk of bleeding was too great. In this patient, Mr. Kane, we chose to use the TED hose but not heparin because we felt that if he started to bleed, and required more surgery to control the bleeding, he'd die from his bad heart. We can only hope that we made the right choice."

Time would tell, and Mr. Kane would do fine. Unfortunately for John Davis, who was resting quietly in his semi-private room just outside the ICU as this meeting adjourned, he wouldn't be so lucky.

***

Susan Parks got out of her sporty Mazda RX-7, covered the open convertible with a drape, and went into Hot Stuffs, the new Southwest-theme bar just outside of Tampa. She was dressed for the place: bare midriff top, short dress, and open shoes. Her long blonde hair framed her lovely face, and quite a few men's heads turned as she walked by. This was her day, her 25th birthday, and her friends were meeting her here for drinks and dinner. Her eyes adjusted to the dark, and the hostess asked if she could help. Susan told her who she was and the hostess led her to a private room. Everyone was there, all 4 of them and Susan made 5, her crowd. They had graduated together from the Business Institute of Florida just 6 months ago and had stayed in contact afterwards. They all made the effort to get together for special occasions: birthdays, showers, divorce parties and the like. Susan was the only one who had never been married, but she hoped to be changing that soon. She gave each of her friends a kiss and settled into the chair at the head of the table. There was a margarita waiting for her, which she downed while the girls sang the school's fight song for her. She got a refill and the party started in earnest.

She opened her gifts, and two of her friends had gotten her a porn DVD. She thought that it might be fun to watch it Saturday night with David. Another got her a cute blouse, and the last gift was a string bikini. She thought that David would enjoy these gifts as much as she did, probably more. Dinner came, then more drinks, and by 10 o'clock that night, she had been there for five hours, six margaritas, and two enchiladas. She hugged her friends and was on her way.

Susan had landed a prime job out of college, in the accounting department of a major law firm, Morris, Cuney and Howe. She would be a bookkeeper, responsible for accounts payable and accounts receivable, and reported to the CFO herself. She had done well for herself, she thought as she made her way home: a great boyfriend, good friends and a wonderful job.

The next day, Susan stretched at her desk. The columns of numbers were mind-numbing. She had passed three of the needed five tests for her CPA designation, which was good, but she felt like she would only be a glorified bookkeeper until all five were behind her. No problem, she thought. A few more classes on the weekend, and she'd have the CPA within a year. Maybe someday, she'd be the CFO. "Hmmm, chief financial officer. That sounds nice," she thought. "Of course, Mrs. Murray would need to resign the post, first." Morris, Cuney and Howe was a big firm, the names on the marquee belonging to the only partners, but there were 15 associates in the firm.

Associates, she thought and giggled. Slaves would be a more descriptive term. The associates got their asses worked off, sifting through hundreds of possible cases until they saw one with real potential. If the case didn't have potential, the firm wrote a few nasty letters, shaking the tree to see what fell, as David described it, to see if a lawyer or insurance company on the other side wanted to give them a few bucks to go away. If the associate thought there was potential, he would run it by Mr. Howe, and if Howe liked it, it would be presented at the weekly meeting. The associate would get to do the running around, and get very little of the credit. If the opposing lawyer and the insurance company took the case to trial, then Mr. Cuney would try the case with the slave-associate sitting second chair, mostly for ornamental purposes only.

David had sat second chair for Dr. Franks' trial, and he had come home crying that night. He had said all along that Dr. Franks hadn't done anything wrong, that Cuney had paid a doctor to lie on the stand. He bawled like a baby when he heard that Franks had died, because he said he thought the whole firm was responsible. Well, he seemed to have gotten over it, anyway. The one she couldn't figure out was Jake Morris. She knew that he was in all the radio and TV ads, but even though she had been with the firm for 6 months, she hadn't seen him do anything that could be interpreted as practicing law. Oh well, she thought, that's not my worry. Back to the numbers.

At precisely 5 p.m., Susan grabbed her sweater and headed for the break room. She needed to clock out, and

Morris, Cuney and Howe didn't want the clients to see a time clock, so they hid it in there. She scanned her ID in the time clock and headed for David's office. Well, he called it that. She knew better. It was a cubicle. When the clients called, they knew to use David's line and a secretary would answer, "Mr. Archer's phone." Then the secretary would put the call to David's desk in his little hole in the wall. When David met with a client, the meeting would be scheduled so that he could use a beautifully outfitted office, one that was shared by all of the associates. Since each client only saw one associate, each client thought his associate had a beautiful, expensive office. If only they knew, she thought. If only they knew that all 15 associates shared one office and one secretary, they'd probably fire the firm and go somewhere else. But the secret was safe with her. Being in the accounting department, she knew that this setup saved the firm about $500,000 per year. Well, she thought, something has to give to be able to pay for that pig Morris' plastic surgery and makeup girl.

David was just about finished on the phone. Susan sat in a folding chair and waited. Before long, David hung up. "Hi hon," he said. "What do you want to do for dinner?"

"Sushi would be nice."

"Great, let's go."

David closed the file on his desk, put a few things in the metal file cabinet, took Susan's arm and headed out the door.

CHAPTER 5

A sheriff's deputy arrived at Dr. Carney's office and asked his secretary to sign for some papers. She did so, and then looked at the packet he had given her. She didn't fully understand the legalese that was written on it, but she did realize that Dr. Carney was being sued by Harold and Roberta Grayson, as representatives for Raymond Grayson, for medical malpractice. Dr. Carney was in his consultation room with a patient, and shortly, the door opened and the patient left. The secretary walked into Carney's office and put the papers down on his desk. "I'm sorry," she said, and turned and walked out.

Carney picked up the papers and began reading them. He was being sued by Morris, Cuney and Howe on behalf of Raymond Grayson's parents for wrongful life. *What the hell is that,* he thought. He dutifully called his malpractice insurance carrier and notified them of the lawsuit, and the representative he spoke to said she had never heard of this charge either. Then he closed the door and began punching the desk.

The next day, Carney was called by his malpractice insurance agent and told that Matthew Johnson would be his defense attorney. Carney called Johnson and a few hours later was seated in his office downtown. It was on the 17th floor of a high rise that catered mostly to law firms. The attorney was youngish, but not too young, thought Carney, feeling slightly guilty for his bias. But something told him that he would need someone with some miles under him if he was to survive this suit. Or maybe he only felt this way because of who the Graysons had retained to represent them, and this thought made him feel even worse, that these bastards could give rise to anything resembling fear in him.

"Mr. Johnson, what in the world is wrongful life?"

"Well, Dr. Carney, I've read the complaint, and basically, it seems that you are accused of saving Raymond Grayson's life when, in fact, you should have let him die. Therefore, if this theory prevails, all of the mounting medical bills and future care expenses would be your responsibility."

"Is there such a thing as a wrongful life precedent?"

"Dr. Carney, legal theory is dynamic. That means that any attorney can come up with a theory of the law, and it is up to the judge or the jury to accept or reject it. While I don't wish to upset you, I could see that this theory just might fly. You see, if a patient were doomed, it would be incumbent on the doctor to honestly tell the family that, and let them make the decision to withhold surgery and let nature take its course. By not giving the Graysons the opportunity to withhold treatment, the case could be made that you caused the ongoing expenses and suffering that would have terminated with Raymond's death. Therefore, if you were to lose, by civil court rules, you are responsible to pay those costs. Unfortunately, the medical bills, future medical and rehab expenses and the suffering of the parents would amount to far more than the one million dollar medical malpractice policy you have in force."

"Shit," Carney muttered. "What now?"

"Did you have the opportunity to speak with the Graysons before surgery?"

"Not really. When I got to the hospital, Raymond was in the emergency room and the CT scan was already done. The police had reached his parents by phone and they were en route to the hospital when I arrived. There was no way that I could have seen them before surgery. I was told that they arrived about 5 minutes after I started."

"Could you have left the operating room and gone out to the waiting room to talk with them?"

"No, I couldn't. Raymond was hemorrhaging from the middle meningeal artery, and I needed to stop the bleeding as fast as I could. Once I did that, his head was already open and the operation had already started."

"Well, that will provide us with some cover. You didn't see the parents and never had the opportunity to speak with them. So, we could claim that you made the best decision that you could based on the information you had but without the benefit of input from the parents because they were not available. Now, Doctor, did you think, based on what you saw in the emergency room and on the CT scan, that you could offer Raymond the possibility of a decent recovery. Or, honestly, did you believe that Raymond would be a vegetable after surgery?"

"Mr. Johnson, hope springs eternal. Every time I'm called to see a patient with terrible injuries to his brain, I realize that that person may end up a vegetable after surgery. But, every once in a while, I'm pleasantly surprised and the patient recovers with minimal or no long term deficiencies. Should I let every one of them die to avoid this type of suit?"

"No, I would think not, but if there was no hope in this case, it will be tough to defend your actions in trying to save Raymond."

"Mr. Johnson, that is appalling. I have dedicated my life and professional career to saving people with brain tumors and injuries, and to think that I might simply let someone die after a brain injury is offensive."

"Well, Dr. Carney, as appalling as it may seem, we have a big hurdle to clear if this case is to be resolved in your favor."

With that, Bob Carney walked out of Matthew Johnson's office and into the sweltering Florida afternoon.

***

John was sitting up in bed when his wife came to visit. "Hi, sweetheart. You look great," she said. She gave him a

---

small kiss on the cheek, and sat down in the chair beside the bed. John introduced her to his roommate, a 16 year-old kid who had an appendectomy the day before.

"Hi, Mrs. Davis," the roommate said. "John seems like a great guy, and he loves motorcycles. I want a cycle, and he says he'll help me pick one out once we're both out of here."

"John is not going to be riding any more, and call me Nadine, please. But, if you're stupid enough to ride after you see what it's done to John, I'm sure he can help you pick a bike. Just remember to wear your helmet. If John didn't have one, he'd probably be dead."

"Yes ma'am."

"So Nadine, what's going on?"

"Nothing, how're you feeling, John?"

"Fine. The only problem is some cramps here in my left leg. Would you massage it for me?"

"Sure." Nadine started to rub his leg. She suggested John tell the nurse about the cramps, and he said he'd try to remember. But he never did tell anyone but his wife.

When John was on the OR table, the blood in his legs was not flowing well due to his low blood pressure and pelvic fractures. Clots had formed in the left calf during the surgery, and now these were feeding off themselves, quietly getting bigger. The Orthopedic frame around the bed and the tangle of wires holding his pelvis steady didn't help, and the clots kept enlarging. It was only a matter of time…

John sat up in bed, and Nadine helped him get the dinner tray situated in front of him. It looked pretty disgusting to her: salty beef broth, apple juice and weak tea. But, for John, it was a feast. His first meal since the accident. He ate hungrily, and almost licked the bowl. Nadine straightened up the room, and they settled in to watch the television until visiting hours were over. Reruns of *M*A*S*H* were on, and they laughed until it hurt. John rang his bell for a pain shot.

He didn't want to worry Nadine about his leg, so he told her that the laughing had hurt his belly and that's why he needed a pain shot. He knew that the Demerol would take away the leg pain, and this way Nadine would be none the wiser.

The intercom cracked to life. "Yes, Mr. Davis?"

"Can I get a pain shot, please?"

"Sure, I'll tell your nurse."

It took a whole episode of *M*A*S*H* for the nurse with the pain shot to arrive, so they both knew it was a half hour until the relief came. The nurse rolled John a bit and injected 100 milligrams of Demerol into his right buttock. Ten minutes later, as he was starting to get groggy, a commercial came on the TV. John thought it was hilarious, something about waiting for pain medicine and suffering, and suing somebody, and something about 'the Little Guy'. Well, he just waited for pain medicine, and he was certainly suffering, so maybe he'd sue someone. He drifted off into a drug-induced sleep just as Nadine kissed him goodnight for the very last time, just as a blood clot the size of a dime broke loose from behind his left knee and started to travel into his vena cava and onward to his right lung. His last thought on this earth had something to do with suing Hawkeye Pierce, or was it Hotlips?

***

Susan always got a kick out of the name of the place. "Japan Palace" seemed more like a ride at Disney World than a restaurant. But David thought they made the best sushi in Central Florida. The place was a bit crowded, but they were seated by 7 o'clock. Susan had some Japanese beer, and David had a glass of warm sake. They made small talk while they waited to be served. The alcohol started to loosen David up, and he began to talk about Dr. Franks' death again. "We took in 35% of $600,000 for that case, all on the testimony of a liar. I can't go on like this. I feel responsible for his death."

Susan tried to console him. "No, David. It's not your fault. Mr. Cuney tried the case, and you just sat second chair. Unless you lied to me, you didn't say a word during the whole trial. How can that be your fault?"

"Susan, I'm an officer of the court. I swore an oath. I know that people lie in court all the time, and their lawyers always tell them that they don't want to know if they're telling the truth or lying. This is different. We needed to turn over a lot of rocks to find this guy Semben, and then Cuney needed to go over the testimony three times until the shithead got it right. That's not what I went to law school to do. I went to uphold the rights of the downtrodden. This is bullshit."

The waiter brought their food, and they didn't get a chance to finish the conversation. The walked home through the quiet streets of Central Florida, and Susan mentioned that maybe they should hurry, as she nuzzled into his shoulder just a little provocatively. David didn't need a second hint. They got into the house and Susan had his clothes off before they got to the bedroom. Just as David let his brain go on autopilot, he thought that Susan had great hands. Nobody had ever made him feel like this, and maybe he should marry her before she got away.

***

John had been playing beach volleyball with his friends and one of them spiked the ball at him. It had hit him squarely on the forehead and bounced away. John was knocked over, but he quickly jumped back up and ran after the ball. He chased it and then watched as it rolled to a stop next to a chaise lounge. The girl on the lounge chair was lying face down, with her bikini top open to get a full tan on her back. John ran up to her and smiled sheepishly. She was beautiful and he was tongue-tied. "Excuse me," he stammered. "I need to get my balls, er, my ball."

"Sure, help yourself."

John grabbed the ball and threw it to his friends. "I'll be there in a minute, guys," he shouted.

John looked at the beauty lying before him. "I'm sorry; I'm not very good at this. You are lovely, and I don't want to walk away. My name is John Davis," he gushed.

"Hi, my name is Nadine Faulkner. I think you're lovely, too," she said and she laughed.

Nadine tied her bikini top, and rolled over. She was more beautiful than he allowed himself to imagine when she was lying face down. He kept his eyes glued to the lines on her face from the nylon material of the chair, which kept him from staring at her rather impressive breasts. They made small talk, and Nadine asked him if he'd like to join her for dinner.

At dinner, she learned that John was on vacation with his friends from Virginia, where they were all enrolled in an apprenticeship program to become electricians. John was about to receive his certification and looking forward to making a real living. He and his friends would be in town for another three days. Nadine was a graduate of the Middle Florida Technical Institute, and was working as a graphics designer at a local firm. She had been born and raised in Central Florida and did not ever intend to leave.

The next three days were wonderful for both of them. They fell in love that very first night, and they made love on the beach the evening before John and his friends returned to Virginia. They spoke on the telephone almost nightly and visited each other as often as possible. Nadine rented a U-Haul truck and drove all night to Virginia a few days before he graduated from the apprentice program, and afterwards, she and John packed his belongings up and moved him to Central Florida. John got a job in one of the many construction companies in the area and Nadine continued to work as a graphics designer. They were married about six months later, on the beach where they first met. In their 30 years of marriage, Nadine had been unable to conceive, so they only had each other, and they had not been apart for more than two days at a time in over 30 years.

John drifted off to sleep just as the clot reached his vena cava. From there, it paused for a while, letting gallons of blood flow past. Then, John coughed in his sleep, and the clot started to move again. It passed the veins leading from the kidneys, and if John had been luckier, it might have lodged there, and maybe no one would ever have known about the clot. But instead, it kept going, now leaving the abdomen, and entering the chest. In the atrium, the upper chamber of the heart, it mixed with blood returning from all over the body, and the clot swirled around for a minute or two before entering the ventricle. From that point on, John was doomed. The clot quickly exited the ventricle and was forced into the right pulmonary artery, and then to the right lung. It followed the branches of the pulmonary artery until it lodged in a branch that supplied about one half of the right lung. An 18 year-old athlete, or perhaps John's young hospital roommate could tolerate that, but a fifty year-old electrician and biker couldn't. His blood oxygen level started to fall, first to 95%, then to 90%, then to 85%. His lips started to turn blue, but in the shadows, his roommate didn't notice. John's brain tried to tell him that something was terribly wrong, but the Demerol kept the message from reaching John's consciousness. When the oxygen level reached 70%, John started to cough, and the roommate looked over. John's head was at a strange angle, and he started yelling, "John, John, wake up." There was no response. He jumped out of bed, and just about puked from the pain in the appendectomy incision. He slapped John on the face, and still no response, but John's face was cold. How could that be?

"Help! We need help in here," he screamed. "Now. Help us, please!"

Three nurses ran into the room. One grabbed John's roommate and led him out of the room. The other two took a look at John's blue lips and clammy skin and started CPR. "Call a code," one shouted into the hallway, and moments later, "Code blue, room 445" could be heard over the hospital loudspeaker. Once a code is called, all available personnel respond. Mark Land recognized John Davis' room number and started to the room at a dead run. Two of the on-call medical students were having dinner in the cafeteria and ran for the room as well. Nadine Davis was just about out of the hospital and heard the page. She knew that either John or that nice boy who had had the appendectomy was dying. She started running for the room, too.

In the room, controlled mayhem broke out. John was hooked up to an EKG machine, and one of the medical residents had placed a breathing tube into John's windpipe. One of the surgical residents placed a subclavian catheter, a large IV, directly into a vein feeding the heart. A nurse was pressing rhythmically on John's chest, quietly keeping her rhythm by whispering, "one-one-thousand, two-one-thousand, three-one-thousand," and a respiratory therapist was squeezing the Ambu bag, forcing air into John's lungs every time the nurse said five-one-thousand. A senior medical resident was in charge, barking out orders for medications. "Atropine, one ampoule; epinephrine, one ampoule. Stop CPR, and let me look at the EKG strip. Restart CPR."

Steve Boxley got to the room at about the same time as Nadine Davis. Steve asked her to wait outside, and he walked into the room. He took one look at John and knew everything that had happened. The blue lips, the blue face, the oxygen level of 45% despite getting pure oxygen in the tube: John had suffered a fatal pulmonary embolism. There was nothing Steve could do that would save him. Steve told the crew to stop CPR and pronounced his patient dead at 8:31 p.m.

Steve left the room and found Nadine leaning up against the counter at the nurses' station. She was crying and was white as a sheet. "Tell me he's alive, Dr. Boxley. Please tell me he's OK," she begged. Steve just shook his head, and she knew. "Oh no," she wailed, and collapsed into Steve's arms. He helped her sit down and stayed with her for the next 15 minutes or so. He helped her call the family, and the charge nurse took over. Then Steve headed for home, exhausted.

The charge nurse explained to Nadine that in a situation such as this, the sudden death of a postoperative patient, the hospital needs to notify the coroner. The coroner may wish to do an autopsy, and if he did, the law said he could do it, even without Nadine's approval. The coroner did want to do an autopsy, and the Medical Examiner's office sent a hearse to collect John's body. Nadine walked into the humid night and went home alone.

Nadine went to bed, but sleep wouldn't come. It was too early to think about funeral arrangements, and too late at night to call her friends and cry. She flipped on the television and watched Jay Leno for awhile. The studio audience thought that he was hysterical, but Nadine didn't see much humor in the monologue. After the monologue was finished, Jay said he'd be right back after these commercials. First there was an ad for a new hamburger combo that the ad guys at McDonalds had dreamed up, and then there was the smiling, fatherly face of Jake Morris of Morris, Cuney and Howe, working 'For the Little Guy.' Well, there wasn't a guy littler than John at this moment, and Nadine figured that dead was about as injured as you could be. She wrote down the 800 number that Jake Morris said would reach him, shut off the TV with the remote, and turned out the light.

CHAPTER 6

Following the usual order of things, Morris, Cuney and Howe hired Dr. J. Marcus Semben as an expert witness to testify against Dr. Carney. Matthew Johnson arranged for both Dr. Semben's and Dr. Carney's depositions to be taken at Johnson's office. Semben went first, and the court reporter swore him in.

"Hello, Dr. Semben, I'm Sam Cuney. As you know, I represent Raymond Grayson and his family in the matter of a malpractice claim against Dr. Bob Carney, a neurosurgeon. We've engaged you as an expert to testify today, and as you know, this is a deposition. While a judge is not here, this is still a legal proceeding; and, as you see, you've been sworn in. Either Mr. Johnson or I may object, and if one of us does so, please do not answer until we instruct you to answer, after we've settled the objection. If needed, we can call the judge to settle the question. Do you understand?"

"Yes."

"With us here in the room are Dr. Carney, the defendant; Brian Jeffries, an associate attorney working with me from Morris, Cuney and Howe; Harold and Roberta Grayson, Raymond's parents; and Mr. Matthew Johnson, Dr. Carney's lawyer."

Semben nodded in turn to each of them, and Cuney continued. "Dr. Semben, have you come to any conclusions regarding the care that Dr. Carney gave to Mr. Grayson?"

"Yes. I reviewed the CT scan films and the reports of the CT scan. I also read Dr. Carney's dictated admission report, and I read the report of the ambulance drivers and of the emergency room doctor. The reports showed that Mr. Grayson was shot in the right temple and lost consciousness almost immediately. When he arrived at the hospital, he was bleeding profusely from the gunshot wound, and he never regained consciousness in the emergency room. The CT scan showed extensive damage to the right side of the brain. In my opinion, the damage was so great that Mr. Grayson had no chance whatsoever to survive the injury if he were not operated on; and if he were operated on, the best outcome would be one of total dependence for all of his basic needs for the rest of his life."

"Do you have any opinion as to whether or not Dr. Carney should have undertaken the procedure?"

"Yes, I do." Semben smiled ever so slightly. Cuney was great at leading him to say whatever he wanted him to. It was like a dance they'd done so many times that they didn't even have to rehearse. The basic steps were always the same, with just minor variations like the name of the victim and the grievance. "This operation was foolhardy. There was no way that Mr. Grayson could have been saved, and the operation only served to turn him into a vegetable and to enrich Dr. Carney's bank account. It did nothing at all to help Mr. Grayson or his family."

"On the topic of money, do you have any idea of the long-term costs of caring for Mr. Grayson?"

"Not with certainty, but offhand, using simple common sense, I'd say that Raymond could live for another 20 or 30 years, easily, so all you'd need to do is multiple his yearly care costs by 30 to come up with an estimate. Judging by what I've heard, home care costs around $300 per day." As planned, Semben pulled out a pad and pen and started to do some calculations. Three hundred dollars a day times 365 days a year equals $109,500 per year. Let's round that off to $110,000 per year, and this does not take inflation into account. Multiply that times 30 years, and the total cost is over 3 million dollars."

"Thank you, Dr. Semben." Cuney looked at Matthew. "Your witness, Mr. Johnson."

"Thank you. Dr. Semben, I'm Matthew Johnson, and I represent Dr. Carney. I remind you that you are not on trial. You are here as an expert witness. As such, you are not permitted to ask Mr. Cuney for advice on how to answer a question. Do you understand that?"

"Yes."

"Now, please state your full name and credentials, sir."

"My name is J. Marcus Semben, M.D. I am an urologist. I went to college at the University of Georgia and medical school offshore. Then, I did a residency at Pickett Hospital in Georgia."

"What do you mean by 'offshore'?"

"I attended medical school in the Bahamas."

"Did you attempt to get into medical school in the United States?"

Semben looked at Cuney for help, but he waved for Semben to go on. "Yes, I did, but I wasn't accepted."

"How many years did you apply in the US before you tried the Bahamas?"

"I applied for two years, then gave up and went to the Bahamas."

"Where did you learn to do brain surgery, sir?"

Cuney held up a hand to silence Semben. "I object to the question, Matthew. I won't allow him to answer the question."

Johnson looked at Cuney and smiled. "Let the record show that Mr. Cuney refuses to allow Dr. Semben to respond to a question regarding his expertise in brain surgery. Mr. Cuney, correct me if I'm wrong, but this case revolves around brain surgery, right?"

Cuney waved for Semben to remain silent once more and scowled, but the he seemed to change his mind. "Go on, answer him Marcus, or we'll be here all day."

"Very well. Doctor, do you have any formal training in brain surgery?" Johnson asked again.

"No."

"Have you ever done any brain surgery?"

"No, I haven't."

"Yet, you feel comfortable testifying against a brain surgeon in a matter of medical malpractice?"

"Yes, I do."

Cuney cut in. "Matthew, we stipulate that Dr. Semben is not a brain surgeon, nor has he ever done brain surgery. However, he is recognized by the Florida courts as an expert, and like it or not, you have to deal with that. Now, please, let's move on."

"Do you practice in Florida, Dr. Semben?"

"No."

"Have a Florida license?"

"No."

"Have you ever examined or even seen the plaintiff, Raymond Grayson?"

"No, never."

"So, how have you formulated whatever opinion you are about to give the court?"

"As I stated previously, I reviewed the chart from Middle Florida Hospital and the chart from the rehabilitation center, as well as the records from the ambulance and the emergency room."

"Specifically, what evidence did you use to come to the conclusion that Raymond would not recover from his injuries?"

"Simply the way he looked when he arrived at the hospital and the magnitude of damage to his brain on the CT scan."

"So, doctor, if this were your child, you would not have allowed Dr. Carney to operate; instead you would have simply let him die?"

Semben hesitated for a moment, and then said with conviction, "Absolutely."

Johnson glared at him and said, "I know you're lying, Doctor, but I can't prove it. I'm finished for now."

Semben was excused and they all took a break. When they returned, Dr. Carney was sworn in.

Matthew began. "Dr. Carney, could you please review your training and experience."

"Certainly. I have been in practice for 18 years. I am board-certified in neurosurgery. I did my residency at Stanford, and I attended medical school at the University of New York. Currently, I restrict my practice only to brain surgery and have done so for the past six years. Before that, I did both spinal and brain surgery. However, orthopedic surgeons are doing spinal surgery now, and there is a real need for brain surgeons in this area, as I'm the only one for fifty miles. I estimate that I've done over 2,500 operations over the course of my career."

"Do you participate in research?"

"Yes, I do."

"Do you have any specific area of interest in your research?"

"Yes, I have a special interest in trauma. The Middle Florida Hospital is a level-one trauma center. That means that we get all manner of trauma cases, and we accept transfers from level-two and level-three centers. So, as the only brain surgeon for fifty miles, I get all of the regional trauma."

"Do you get many gunshot wounds?"

"Sadly, yes. As the drug trade has increased in Central Florida, so has the incidence of gunshot injuries. As the incidence of gunshot wounds in general rises, so does the incidence of those to the head."

"Have you written any articles about this type of injury?"

"Yes I have. I invented the device that holds the patient's head steady for the surgery, making the operation safer and easier to perform. I wrote a major article about that. In addition, we have compiled statistics of survival after surgery for gunshot wounds to the head, which I have written up for several journals"

"Dr. Semben has testified that Mr. Grayson's injuries were so severe that you should never have chosen to operate on him. He says that you should have left him to die, and by doing this you would have saved the family thousands of dollars and a lot of heartache. Would you like to comment on that assertion?"

"Where should I start? First, Dr. Semben is not a neurosurgeon and is therefore unable to testify from experience. I would suggest that his type of doctor will give whatever testimony the plaintiff's attorney wants, for a price. I would certainly prefer to be judged by one of my peers, by a neurosurgeon. Secondly, he can say whatever he, or his employer, wants; but in reality, our statistics indicate that people with injuries such as Mr. Grayson's have a twenty percent chance of reasonable recovery and an eight percent chance of full recovery. Reasonable recovery in this case would consist of the ability to speak, walk, perform complex tasks such as writing, and maybe even to return to work on a limited basis. Those statistics may be somewhat bleak, but they beat the hell out of Dr. Semben's suggestion that we do nothing and allow him to die."

"Can you back up your statistics with medical articles?"

"Yes, I published an article in the *International Neurosurgical Journal* in January 1995 that discusses the statistics I just mentioned."

"Dr. Carney, I'm sure that at trial Mr. Cuney will put one of Raymond's parents on the stand and ask them if they would have consented to the operation if they were aware of the statistics beforehand. What would you answer if they said they didn't want you to proceed?"

"Mr. Johnson, you and I both know that if they were presented with those statistics, they would have jumped at the opportunity for their son to be saved. I have never had anyone refuse surgery once that kind of statistical outcome was conveyed to them. Further, I had no opportunity to speak with them, so I had to do what I thought was best. And, I must say, I still think that was the best choice."

"Thank you, Doctor. I have no further questions."

It was now Cuney's turn, and he began immediately. "Dr. Carney, as you know, I'm Sam Cuney and I represent the family of Raymond Grayson. How much money do you get paid for the type of surgery that you performed on Raymond Grayson?"

"I bill $2,700 for that operation. But, Mr. Cuney, I got paid nothing for the surgery on Raymond."

"Yes, I know. But, when you came to see him, did you know that he had no insurance?"

"No, I didn't."

"So, you had reason to believe that you would collect $2,700 for the surgery."

"I suppose."

"How much would you get paid to step aside and let Raymond die?"

"I wouldn't get paid anything if I didn't operate on him, of course."

"So, I can assume, then, that you have a financial incentive to operate rather than to do nothing."

"No, you can't assume that, sir. I don't base my decisions on whether or not I will make any money, and I'm disgusted to think that you would accuse me of doing so. I didn't know that Raymond didn't have insurance because I didn't check, and I never check on a patient's ability to pay. I would have operated on him regardless of his insurance status."

"Well, it is obvious that all of your good deeds went unappreciated. Raymond is barely existing. He's almost a vegetable and he should have been allowed to die."

Matthew Johnson pounded his fist into the table. "Sam, enough already. If you have a question, ask it. If not, move on."

Cuney responded, "I'm done with you, Doctor." He motioned to Harold Grayson, and Raymond's father got up and walked out of the room. He returned a moment later pushing a wheelchair. Raymond was sitting in the wheelchair, slumped over to his left side, a large line of drool coming from the corner of his mouth. He looked at his mother and coughed, and then a tear appeared in the corner of his eye. It seemed that someone had tried to clean him up for this trip because he had a few razor nicks from his morning shave and his clothes seemed rather clean. There was, however, the distinct smell of urine, and the urinary catheter bag could be seen lying on the chair beside Raymond.

After walking Raymond's chair to the table, Harold Grayson sat down. Cuney said, "Matthew, I want you to think long and hard about something. This young man should not be like this, locked into a body he'll never be free of, existing like this for years on end, never walking, never smelling the flowers, never loving or having children. Then I want you to think about how the jury will respond when they think about those same facts. Then I want you to think about making the Grayson family an offer that will help to ease their suffering. Then I want you to call me."

With that, Cuney rose, patted Harold Grayson on the shoulder and walked out. Brian Jeffries followed him, then Mr. and Mrs. Grayson left, pushing Raymond in front of them. Matthew looked at Carney and said, "Bob, we have a lot to discuss."

***

Three days later, Bob Carney walked into Matthew Johnson's office and sat down at the conference table. He was introduced to a gentleman he had not seen before, the adjuster from his malpractice insurance company. "It's my job to assess the risk that we face, and to determine if we are going to fight this thing or settle. My job involves money, plain and simple. I have nothing to do with determining whether you were right or wrong," he said. "Basically, what will it take to make this go away?"

Matthew began. "Bob, I know that you didn't do anything wrong in your care of Raymond Grayson. I know that you did your best, and that if you had it to do all over again, you would do the same thing. But, we need to acknowledge that Raymond will be in this vegetative state for the rest of his life and his expenses will be tremendous. If we go to court with this case, and we lose, the damages could be astronomical. I think we should settle."

"Matthew, that's ridiculous. First of all, I didn't screw up. All of the surgical care was perfect, and the outcome was expected. This bullshit they're suing me for, this 'wrongful

62

life,' what the hell is that? I keep asking this question, but I have yet to get an answer that makes any damned sense."

"That is a legal term thought up recently. The logic states that if we can sue someone for causing a death, called wrongful death, then we should be able to sue someone for saving the life of someone that should otherwise have been allowed to die, and this has been termed wrongful life. I know that you think it's bullshit, but the judge will allow it, I promise you."

Matthew looked at the adjuster and asked his opinion. "I think that we are looking at a tremendous liability here. If a jury feels sympathetic towards Raymond and his family – and I assure you that they will – they could decide in his favor and award him much more than you think. Dr. Semben, at his deposition, said that it could cost as much as 3 million dollars to care for Raymond over his life span. Dr. Semben is wrong, because he didn't figure for inflation and future medical bills. People with brain injuries like this are in the hospital frequently and run up considerable medical bills long after the operation that kept them alive. In addition, inflation runs at between three and seven percent per year. We had an actuary look at this case, and he figured that Raymond's expenses could run as high as 7 million dollars over his lifetime. Seven million dollars, Doctor. I know that the insurance company is not willing to pay that much, and I know that you can't afford it. So, we're willing to settle, as long as the amount is reasonable."

Carney looked at him, his mouth hanging open. "Wait a minute," he shouted. "Do you mean to tell me that you're going to pay them to go away, regardless of the fact that I saved Raymond's life and that I didn't do anything wrong?"

"Yes, Doctor Carney, that's exactly what I'm saying. The insurance company doesn't care whether or not you did a good job. The insurance company is a business. Businesses like to minimize expenses and maximize profits. We know that it will cost us a certain amount of money for your defense in this case, and we know what it will cost us if we do defend your actions and we lose. We can also estimate what we'd be willing to settle for given these circumstances. We've already decided that the risk would be tremendous if we were to lose, so we're willing to settle for 1 million dollars. If they demand more than that, we'll probably go to trial."

Carney looked up at him after staring into his lap as the other man spoke. "End of story?"

"End of story, Dr. Carney."

***

Bob Carney had never been in such a surreal meeting as the one he had to attend next. They all sat around an oblong table: Matthew Johnson, Sam Cuney, the adjuster from the insurance company, Harold and Roberta Grayson, Brian Jeffries, a mediator, and himself. The mediator spoke first; it seemed that he was speaking directly to Carney.

"This is mediation. This is not a court, but we have the authority to settle this case without going to court. Dr. Carney, I assure you that this proceeding will only settle in favor of the Graysons. If your insurance company offers nothing, then there is no settlement, and you will be headed to court. If the offer is accepted, this case goes away today. The way this works is simple. Mr. Cuney will have the opportunity to speak for a minute or two to explain the plaintiff's side of the case, and then Mr. Johnson will speak to explain the defense's position. You will then go into separate rooms, and I will act as an intermediary. If a settlement can be reached, great. If not, I report to the judge that we reached an impasse, and you proceed with a trial. Now, Mr. Cuney, please begin."

"Thank you. Dr. Carney, we are not questioning your abilities as a surgeon. We know that you did your best when you operated on Raymond. However, we believe that Raymond should never have been operated on; instead, he should have been allowed to die. You chose to operate on him, without permission, I might add, and he is now left in a vegetative state. His medical and perpetual care expenses could run into the millions. We therefore believe that you should be responsible for paying those costs. This is the reason for this lawsuit."

The mediator nodded to Matthew and he began. "Mr. and Mrs. Grayson, Dr. Carney is as distraught as you are about the outcome of the surgery on Raymond. But let's look at this a step at a time. First, just forget about the lack of permission. Florida law states very clearly that in the absence of a competent person to give consent, the doctor is authorized to do whatever he feels is necessary. Next, the idea that Dr. Carney, a trained neurosurgeon, should look at your son, shot in the head, and simply allow him to die is ridiculous. Dr. Carney spent years learning to do brain surgery, he is a leader in his field, and he thought that he had a reasonably good chance to save him. In truth, I very much doubt that, if you had been there when Dr. Carney took Raymond to surgery, you would have stopped him and told him to let your only son die. We think that we could prevail in trial, and we doubt if we would be willing to settle today."

The mediator led the parties to separate rooms. When they were alone, Carney looked at Johnson and said, "That was good, Matthew. I agree, we shouldn't settle."

Johnson responded, "Bob, that was just for show. We want them to think of a low number. But I'm telling you, the insurance company wants to settle today, and that's why the adjuster is here."

The mediator walked in a moment later and said, "Mr. Johnson, their first offer for settlement is 1.5 million. Do you have a counter-offer?"

"Yes," said the adjuster. "Offer them four-hundred thousand."

Within twenty minutes, the case was settled. Carney's insurance company had agreed to give Raymond Grayson and his family seven hundred and fifty thousand dollars to settle the case. Carney couldn't believe it. He had worked to save that kid's life, and yet he was sued, successfully, for over three-quarters of a million dollars for helping the kid. Jesus Christ, he thought, what a fucked up system.

CHAPTER 7

David woke up first; he smiled at Susan's arm draped across his chest. He thought that he might just love her, and figured that this was as good as it could get. What else could a guy want: she drank beer, loved sex, and even liked football. Besides, she was pretty, and let him have a night with the guys now and again without whining. Yes, he would ask her to marry him soon.

He climbed quietly out of bed so as not to wake her and went into the shower. He still had that annoying feeling whenever he thought of Dr. Franks, but he hoped that it would pass. His conscience would be a real pain in the ass in his line of work if it cropped up too much. Really, this was a personal injury practice, he reasoned. Our consciences need to be checked at the door. But he'd have to mull that one over again before long, he figured.

After Susan got up and they had coffee, they walked to the office together. David went to his cubicle and Susan to the accounting department. David busied himself with two cases he had gotten over the past few days — neither seemed too interesting. He figured that Mr. Howe could probably scare up a few grand for these clients, but that would be about it.

His phone rang. "David Archer, here," he answered.

"This is Nadine Davis, Mr. Archer. I think I need to talk with you."

"How can I help you, Mrs. Davis?"

"My husband died at Middle Florida Hospital last night, and according to Jake Morris' ads, most people who die unexpectedly in the hospital do so because of medical malpractice. I'd like to know if that happened to my husband."

"Mrs. Davis, if you wouldn't mind, I could come to you to get you to sign the necessary papers, then I could go about getting copies of the records. You need to make funeral arrangements and be with your family. I could do the leg work. Then, once things are a little less stressful for you, we could spend some time together."

"Thank you. That would be fine. I'll give the directions to my house to your secretary."

Two hours later, David was sitting at the Davis' kitchen table drinking coffee. Nadine tried to keep her composure but couldn't. Davis kept handing her tissues and tried his best to console her.

"My husband had a terrible motorcycle accident. They didn't know if he would make it through the surgery, but he did. Then they thought that he wouldn't make it past the first day, and he did. Finally, when he was doing so well, he up and died. The coroner is doing an autopsy, but Dr. Boxley said that he thinks John died of a blood clot. I don't know any more than that. All I know is that he was alive when I left the room and he was dead before I got out of the front door of the hospital."

David passed her a few papers. "Mrs. Davis, I need you to sign these papers. This one allows me to act on your behalf in obtaining all of John's medical records. This other one is a contract between you and Morris, Cuney and Howe, promising us 35% of any settlement we get, after expenses are paid of course. Finally, this one says that you won't hire any other firm but Morris, Cuney and Howe." Nadine signed the documents and David was gone.

David remembered Jake Morris' words to him when he was hired: "Strike when the iron's hot. When the family is distraught, that's the time to get them to sign on with the firm. If they get a chance to think about it, they may get good feelings about the doctor. We don't want that. We want them to hate the doctor. That's why we go to the hospital or the house to sign them up, before they have a change of heart. Always remember that, David." David called the office on his way to his car. There were no messages. He asked to speak with Susan. She was on another line and he got her voicemail. He turned off the phone and walked in silence.

***

In the normal course of business, a product or service is sold or supplied, and the producer is paid. Not so in the legal profession. Some lawyers bill by the hour, mostly those lawyers in the criminal and business law fields. The lawyers working in the civil courts work in a much different arena and are paid in a much different way than their counterparts in criminal law.

The first, most glaring difference between criminal law and civil law is the burden of proof. We are all taught in grade school that a person is innocent until proven guilty, and that someone who is accused of something unlawful must be proven guilty beyond a reasonable doubt. But this protection is only afforded those in the criminal justice system. The civil system is a bastardization of this principle and allows one party to seek redress from another party under the claim of a preponderance of evidence. So, if it is possible that one party injured the other, that injured party can seek redress. It is the civil system that hears the cases of medical malpractice.

In the medical system, by comparison, the doctor bills his patient by the hour or, as in the case of certain types of critical care treatment and some more basic procedures, by the service — as is the case for physical examinations and office visits and for surgical procedures. In the fields of business and criminal law, lawyers are paid much the same way. But, in the area of personal injury, such as medical malpractice, the attorney shares the winnings with the client. In no other civilized country can an attorney be paid this way. The British system forbids its attorneys from sharing in the winnings and insists instead that the attorney bill his client by the hour. The American system of payment, called the contingency system, makes the attorney a partner with his client rather than his advocate, which some argue provides that attorney with a more than adequate motive to alter the outcome of the case dishonestly, to cheat in other words, for the benefit of his client. Some argue that justice is lost in this arena, and it is in this arena that Susan Parks has chosen to find employment, and the accounting methods used by her employer had her confused.

Specifically, Susan couldn't figure out why the firm booked expenses the way that they did. When a case was taken in, expenses were paid from the firm's general account. When the case settled and money came in, the first dollars were used to repay the firm for the expenses that had been laid out, then the firm took its 35%, and the rest was given to the client. However, Susan kept finding office expenses that had been charged to clients, and she thought that someone in her department was being careless. She found the appropriate files in the computer and printed a list of expenses, and then she printed a list of expenses that had been charged to clients. In the previous 12 months, over $750,000 in expenses had been charged to clients improperly. She thought that she must be wrong, that she had merely made a mistake in terms of which files were for what purpose, so rather than speak with anybody in the firm, she put the printouts in her purse and called her college accounting professor on the phone. It was better to find her error this way than to be embarrassed by her superiors. When David had tried to call her, she was on the phone with Tyler McNab, arranging a luncheon meeting for the next day.

David poked his head into her office when he got back. She blew him a kiss, and he then set to work getting John Davis' records. He felt that this was a case that might bring in a nice settlement, and maybe a bonus for him. He filled out the necessary records requests, addressed them to the hospital and to Steve Boxley's office, and sent them by certified mail. He knew that the certified mail didn't get a response faster, but it got their attention, and occasionally a phone call from the insurance company trying to arrange a quick settlement. Jake Morris always told them that the cost of certified mail was worth it.

***

The morgue has a smell unlike any anywhere else. It is the smell of death, mixed with the smell of rotting flesh and antiseptics and floor wax. If the sign 'Medical Examiner of the Middle Florida District' doesn't intimidate the casual guest, then the smell must. The ME's offices are in a building attached to the jails and across the street from the courthouse. There is an underground tunnel leading from the courthouse to the ME's office, so the medical examiner can walk quickly to the courts to give testimony and the prosecuting attorneys can get their reports in murder cases in an efficient manner. All in all, it was an expedient system.

At the entrance to the morgue, inexplicably, was a metal detector with an armed guard, screening anyone coming in. The visitor needed to identify himself to the guard and was then subjected to a search and a pass through the metal detector. From there, he would walk to the entrance of the ME's offices where an elderly and surly secretary would accost him.

"State your business."

If the visitor couldn't give a good enough reason for being there, the secretary would rise up and begin to shout for the guard to escort the guest back to the street. Those passing the test would be directed to the assistant ME doing the autopsy or research in question. The autopsy room was about the size of a movie theater. The noxious smell that one would notice upon arriving at the building would be magnified many times in this room. In fact, it became obvious that the smell originated in this room. There were four tables in the center of the room, and on one wall was a refrigeration unit with five rows of five doors each, for the storage of up to 25 bodies. There was a slot in each door of the refrigeration unit for a 3X5 card giving the name (if known) and case number of each decedent.

The refrigeration unit had doors on the other side, so each body could be removed from the opposite side as well. On that side was a much smaller room, with curtains around each wall. If a body needed to be identified, the assistant ME would go into the small room and open one of the refrigeration doors, slide the body out of the chamber, and slide it onto a gurney. He would then cover the body except for the face, and then open the curtains. The family would be on the other side of the window and could identify the body from there. This room looked like the tasteful viewing room from a funeral home; the other side of the refrigeration unit looked like something out of a horror movie.

This room was where Steve Boxley stood now. He couldn't get over John Davis' death, and he was at the coroner's office to watch the autopsy. The coroner removed the stitches in John's belly and reopened the abdomen, took out the wires holding the pelvic fractures together, and opened the chest with a Y incision. He turned on the tape recorder and started to dictate.

"Case number 020-98760. John Davis.

"This is the body of a well developed 50 year-old white male who died while a patient at Middle Florida Hospital. There are staples holding an abdominal incision closed. These are removed. There are wires in the hip bones. These are removed. A Y incision is made to open the chest.

"First examined are the abdominal organs. They were weighed, and are normal in weight. Liver is congested, looks healthy. Spleen is absent, and fresh sutures are on the artery and vein of the spleen. There is no blood around the area of the spleen. The pancreas is normal. The blood vessels of the abdomen are normal.

"There is a pelvic hematoma which appears to be resolving, as the blood in it is becoming discolored. There is no fresh blood in the pelvis.

"The chest is examined next. The heart is enlarged, as though it was straining against the lung. The left lung is of normal weight. There is scar tissue around the upper lobe, consistent with the placement and subsequent removal of a chest tube, and a healed tear in the lung, showing evidence of a previous collapsed lung. The right lung is heavier than normal, and appears to contain a large clot. When the lung is cut, a clot is seen. This is consistent with a pulmonary embolism.

"Because of the pulmonary embolism, the legs are examined. The left leg shows evidence of a large clot in the vein extending from the mid-calf to just above the knee. The right leg is normal.

"End of report"

The coroner looked up at Steve and said, "Well, Dr. Boxley, I haven't done the toxicology, and I'll need to look at the tissue under the microscope, but unless I find something earth-shattering, I think I found the cause of death. I should have a final report within a week, but I'm sure it will be signed out as a fatal pulmonary embolism."

Steve thanked the coroner and left. In his car, he powered up his cell phone and took out a slip of paper and called John's wife. "Mrs. Davis, this is Dr. Boxley. Again, I'm so sorry for your loss. I just finished watching the coroner do John's autopsy, and it looks like John died of a pulmonary embolism. He'll have a final report within a week, and I'll make sure you get a copy. Please call me if I can do anything for you. Goodbye, Mrs. Davis." Steve hung up and drove away.

He replayed the lecture that he had given just one day ago over and over in his mind. Could the first year resident have been right, the risk of heparin would be less than the risk of pulmonary embolism? In hindsight, it sure was. But what if he had used heparin and John had bled to death. Wouldn't he be just as dead? Well, that's why he didn't sleep well at night, any night, and why his life expectancy was lower than other men his same age. Doctors have too much stress. Maybe he should find an easier job. No, this was what he loved, and like they said yesterday, shit happens.

CHAPTER 8

Susan had walked across the quad at the Business Institute of Florida and around the fountain behind the administration building, her arms loaded with books on her first day at college. She was finally free, away from home for the very first time. She had decided that she wanted to study accounting and follow in her favorite uncle's footsteps. Her uncle was a CPA, and he had been a major influence in her life. She loved her parents, but her father was a reporter for CNN and was out of the country more than he was at home. Her mother's brother was the male influence during Susan's high school years, and she wanted to be just like him. When she met with her high school counselor and told him she wanted accounting, the Business Institute of Florida seemed like a fine choice. Because she qualified for the 'bright futures' program from the state, Susan would only need to pay about $600 per year for school.

As she crossed the quad, she walked right into a middle-aged gentleman who seemed to be out for a leisurely stroll. Her books were strewn all over the sidewalk; she apologized, and started to pick them up. The gentleman helped her, and then introduced himself.

"I'm Professor McNab."

"Oh, my. I'm in one of your classes, sir." Susan blushed and started to stammer. "I'm so sorry for being so clumsy. I'm not normally this bad. My name is Susan, Susan Parks."

"Nice to meet you Susan, Susan Parks. Let me help you with your books. Where are you headed?"

"To the freshman dormitory."

They split the load of books between them and Dr. McNab walked her to her dorm. There, he handed her the books and left. But since Susan was in the accounting

75

department, she spent a lot of time with Tyler McNab, and she soon was invited to have dinner at his home with his family. She became fast friends with Tyler's daughter, and at graduation, Tyler had raved about her to her parents. Susan and her former professor still corresponded with each other by e-mail almost weekly.

At lunchtime, the day after she contacted Tyler McNab from her new office at Morris, Cuney and Howe, Susan left the office and walked to the Hyatt Hotel on Eastshore Drive. She gave her name to the hostess at the restaurant and was seated immediately. A few minutes later, Tyler McNab walked in. Susan jumped up and greeted him warmly. "Thanks for coming, Dr. McNab." They might be old friends and quite fond of each other, but he was still her former professor and that was the way she thought of him first and foremost.

"Anything for my favorite graduate. And, call me Ty now. You're not my student anymore."

They sat down and looked at the menu, making small talk about their families. The waitress took their orders and as she walked away, Tyler said, "Susan, what is bothering you?"

Susan opened her briefcase and took out a sheaf of papers. "Ty, look at this. I am doing the accounting for Morris, Cuney and Howe, and I keep finding problems with their expense records. I found $750,000 of improper expenses charged to clients, but I can't understand what's going on. I'm afraid I may be missing something and don't want to appear stupid by asking."

Tyler spent the next few minutes locked in concentration. Finally, he tapped the side of his head and asked Susan how the firm was paid for its services. Just as Susan was about to answer, lunch arrived. They ate, and made more small talk, the accounting issue put aside for the moment. Ty had been doing well. His daughter had had a daughter since Susan graduated, and his son was in graduate school studying for his MBA. Ty caught up on Susan's life, and was happy that she and David were starting to settle down together. After lunch, Ty suggested that they go to his office at the college. The two of them walked to the school, and while they walked, Susan called the office on her cell phone to tell her boss that she'd be late.

In Ty's office, they spread the papers across the conference table.

"Susan, how does your firm get paid for their work with these types of cases?"

"We work on a contingency basis"

"Explain what that means specifically at Morris, Cuney and Howe, please."

"Well, we don't charge the client for anything that we pay for, unless we win the case. Then we pay expenses out of the settlement award and what ever is left is split sixty-five percent for the client and thirty-five percent for the firm."

"Do you consider the staff attorney's work as an expense?"

"No, absolutely not. The firm's fee is the thirty-five percent, which covers the wages of anyone who worked on the case. The only expenses we pass on to the client are those that we need to lay out. In fact, if we charged the client for our wages, that would be illegal."

Ty asked Susan to pick a case that had brought in a nice amount of money. She immediately chose *Dunn v. Ebert*. Ty asked her to give him a brief synopsis of the case.

"Leonard Dunn was a gentleman who saw Dr. Ebert because of abdominal pain and bleeding when he had a bowel movement. Dr. Ebert asked him to have a barium enema, and Mr. Dunn cancelled the test three times. The next time he saw Dr. Ebert was one year later, now with severe pain and 35 pounds lighter. Dr. Ebert again asked him to have a barium enema and this time he agreed. The test showed a very large tumor, and when the surgeon went in, he found that the tumor had spread everywhere. Mr. Dunn died three months later. His wife and children sued Dr. Ebert for delayed diagnosis of the cancer. Dr. Ebert's lawyer wouldn't settle and we went to court. Mr. Cuney got a surgeon to lie through his teeth and say that Dr. Ebert should have sent Mr. Dunn a registered letter, or even gone to Dunn's house to pressure him into going to the hospital. The jury awarded the Dunn family 1 million dollars."

"Ok, Susan, now let's look at the income and expense register for that case. Would you go through it with me, please?"

"Sure, Ty. We laid out money here, $2550 for various experts. We paid three doctors to review the records before we could find one who was willing to say what Mr. Cuney wanted him to say. There's another $3500 for deposition fees, and another $2000 for travel expenses. Finally, here's another $8500 for trial expenses. That totals, let's see, hmm, $16,550 in expenses. Subtract that from one million dollars, and we get 35% of what's left and the client gets the rest."

Ty did a quick calculation and found that the payouts didn't equal 1 million dollars. Instead they totaled $950,000. That left a total of $50,000 unaccounted for. Susan looked over the numbers and was flabbergasted. There was no mistake — someone had not accounted for that money, or should she be starting to think that someone had stolen that money?

She asked Ty for advice. He told her that she was in danger with this information. She had found mistakes totaling three quarters of a million dollars, and someone she worked with had apparently embezzled that much this year alone! Ty suggested that she go to the police, but she refused. "I'll think about it and talk it over with David," she decided.

"Well, be very careful, Susan," Ty pleaded.

"I will." She did agree to leave a copy of the papers at Ty's office, just for safe keeping. They copied the file, and Susan got ready to leave. She gave Ty a kiss on the cheek and returned to her office, lost in thought.

***

The Central Florida Medical Society met on the third Thursday of each month. Steve was chairman of the insurance committee, and he reported to the society president. The insurance committee would meet the night before the Thursday group meeting. That particular meeting was quite distressing. Malpractice insurance rates were set each July and January, and the new rates had just been published. Steve thought, "Nothing like a bill you can't pay to rally the troops." Just about every specialist in Central Florida showed up at the insurance committee meeting. Steve thought that if any of them were armed and a lawyer walked into the room, there would be blood on the walls.

"My new rates are $120,000," shouted one of the more vocal obstetricians. "I'm paying $95,000," said one of the dermatologists. Steve called the meeting to order. "Look," he said, "everyone had a major increase. I spoke with FIC, Florida Insurance Company, earlier today. My own rates are going from $50,000 per year last year to $110,000 per year this year. I've had only one suit, and it was frivolous and settled for only $6,000. They said that I'm rated as a higher risk because I do trauma surgery. They also said that the average rise was 45% over last year. I know that I can't afford that kind of increase, and I doubt if any of you can, either. We need help. Any suggestions?"

"I'm leaving the area," said Bob Carney. Here, my malpractice rate was $35,000 this year, and my malpractice insurance company wanted to raise it to $75,000 — and that was before my recent case. After that settlement, they told me they were dropping me. The only insurance I could find will cost me $185,000 per year. To hell with that. I'm moving to New Mexico. It will be $30,000 per year there. And screw the attorneys. If any of those bastards get a brain tumor, there won't be anyone for 50 miles to operate on them." Steve knew Bob had a point. He was the only guy in the area who did brain surgery, but lawyers would not be the only ones without a brain surgeon within 50 miles if Bob made good on his threat and left the area.

"I'm giving up obstetrics and doing only gynecology," one of the OBs said. "I was at our OB-GYN group meeting recently, and of the eight obstetricians in the area, five are giving up OB. Sadly, there just won't be enough obstetricians to deliver all of the babies in Central Florida. But money is money, and until we get relief, that's that."

Steve saw his opening and attempted to move the meeting in another direction. "How can we get relief?"

"We need tort reform."

"We need caps on non-economic damages."

"What does that mean?" asked one of the residents.

"When a patient claims malpractice, there are economic damages and non-economic damages. The economic damages are easy: lost wages, medical bills, that type of thing. The non-economic damages are the big bugaboo. That includes things like pain and suffering or loss of ability to have sex due to pain – and can you believe that shit? Like anybody gives up sex due to a pain anywhere but in the affected area, so to speak. Mental trauma due to injury is a big one. Those are the awards that kill us, because there is no limit to what the lawyers can get for so-called non-economic damages.

"We need new rules. When a doctor testifies in a case in Florida, he needs to be licensed and practicing in Florida. When he talks about community standards of care, he needs to be from that community. If he lies on the stand, the Medical Society needs to take away his medical license."

Steve closed the meeting. "These are good thoughts. I'll pass them on at the general meeting, and also to the legislative committee. Meeting adjourned." A bitch session might make everyone feel better, but his colleagues weren't likely to get beyond that stage tonight, with everyone still stinging from the rate announcement.

Steve drove home substantially more depressed than he had been before the meeting. He had always thought that this area had a very high quality of medicine and that it was a great place to live. He wasn't so sure anymore. Franks was dead. The police called it an accident, but Franks was a close friend and Steve knew he was despondent over the lawsuit. Steve suspected suicide, and even if it wasn't, the death was related to the trial anyway, because at the least, Franks was distracted. Now Carney was leaving town, and the OBs were closing shop. Steve knew that if he got sued again, and with his high-risk clientele that seemed likely, he would need to leave, too. Many years ago, Steve thought, the medical malpractice system worked. Occasionally, a doctor does deviate from the standard of care, or as it is described, 'deviates from the manner a prudent physician would have behaved in a similar circumstance.' So, what had happened to change the system so much?

There are many influences making the system the mess it was, he said out loud. First, there has been an explosion in the number of lawyers and a simultaneous decrease in the reimbursement for legal services, a simple supply and demand correlation. Add the exploding media presence to that, network television competing with all-news stations, and there simply was not enough news to fit the time slot, which meant that news had to be created. Medical errors used to be between the doctor and his patient, or at worst between these parties and the members of the legal profession, but now these cases became newsworthy. Add in cable stations that covered the courts 24/7, and the result is heightened awareness of a medical world previously shrouded in mystery. Now these issues between doctors and their patients were part of the daily entertainment and seemed epidemic to anyone with a TV or radio.

The final nail in the coffin of the medical profession was a court decision allowing lawyers to advertise. Previously, the bar association felt that it was undignified for an attorney to advertise, but a lawsuit against that ethic changed the face of law and the media forever. Now, law firms could advertise and even solicit patients while they were recovering from surgery by running commercials on daytime television that exhorted them to consider suing.

As medical malpractice became a hot-button item, lawyers began to publicize their verdicts and settlements, thereby alerting the public to the lottery that the civil court system had become. Got a postoperative infection? Call Morris, Cuney and Howe, maybe we can make you rich. Steve almost laughed at the thought as he switched on the car radio. The news came on for a few minutes, a story about a fire, and then Steve sneered when the anchor told him that the news was sponsored by Morris, Cuney and Howe, 'For the Little Guy.' Steve hit the power button and drove the rest of the way in silence.

***

Steve Boxley got on the chartered bus with a few of the other physician leaders from Central Florida. They were going to Tallahassee, the state capital, to have some quality time with their legislators. Along the way, they would be stopping to pick up more doctors to finish the trip with them. They were hoping that they could get some legislative relief for the medical malpractice mess. They had lost doctors already, and others were grumbling that they might need to leave. No one could recruit any new doctors to the area.

None could afford the malpractice rates. The crisis had exploded to the point that the state representatives were now willing to listen to them.

Steve was the unofficial spokesman, so he talked with each of the doctors in turn. He heard the same horror stories from some of the doctors he was meeting with from other parts of the state. Some of the specialists from South Florida, especially the Miami area, were hit the worst, with insurance costing up to $200,000 for the lowest level of coverage — if they were lucky enough to get coverage at all. While things had not gotten that bad in Central Florida, he knew that the crisis was like a runaway train and would spread to the entire state in a year or less.

They arrived at the state capital at 11:00 in the morning and were met by a few aides. They were shepherded to a conference room, and after getting coffee and doughnuts, three legislators stepped in to speak with them. Steve was standing to one side, listening to Alex Daniels, one of the local Tallahassee doctors whisper to him a small dossier on each of the three legislators who walked in. "That's Mike Bloch. He's from Palm Beach. They are pretty close to Miami, and Bloch is a trial lawyer. He made a fortune doing plaintiff law, and has sued his share of doctors. He'll be nice and friendly, but he's not your friend. No matter what he says, he'll vote against any kind of tort reform. The next one, the lady, is Marcia Pitts. She's from this area, and was a businesswoman before being elected to office. She'll probably be somewhat sympathetic to us, because she had about 200 employees and knows how much medical insurance costs. She knows that the cost of health care is directly proportional to the doctor's and hospital's costs, and that those costs are proportional to malpractice rates. That's Bob Hugoll. He'll be our best bet to help. He is a health care attorney; his firm arranges joint ventures between hospitals and group practices, and he's made it clear that he hates malpractice attorneys. In fact, he uses the name of that group in your area — Morris, Cuney and Howe — all the time when he speaks about the issue, uses it pejoratively of course. He's from your area, near Tampa I believe."

"Ladies and gentlemen, thank you for coming," said one of the aides. "Please be seated. Let me introduce the three representatives, the Honorable Mike Bloch, the Honorable Marcia Pitts, and the Honorable Bob Hugoll. Mr. Bloch will speak first."

"Thank you, Scott, and thank you all for coming today. We here at the capital are well aware that there is a problem with malpractice insurance carriers, and rest assured that we are working diligently to help you folks. The major issue is one of poor investments by the insurance companies. They collected your premiums in the 1990s, and the investment income during that time generated phenomenal returns. The investment returns were large enough that the insurance companies never needed to raise rates, and in fact, took premiums from doctors that they otherwise wouldn't have insured because they knew that they would earn enough from the investments to cover any payouts in the lawsuits. Now that the stock market is not doing well, the insurance companies see their profits dwindling, and they need to raise premiums to catch up. So, I will be proposing a bill to make the insurance companies lower their rates."

"Mr. Bloch," said one of the doctors from West Florida, "if you do that, more of the insurance companies will leave the state. I doubt very much if that will help with anything. We need tort reform."

"That's your opinion, Doctor," said Bloch bluntly.

"Ladies and gentlemen, I'm Marcia Pitts. I represent the good men and women from Tallahassee, and I sympathize with your problem. As a businesswoman, insurance was a very real cost to me, and I understand what the cost of malpractice insurance is doing to your practices. I agree with the doctor who just spoke. We need real tort reform and in the form of a constitutional amendment, so the legislature can't play with it year after year."

"Thank you, Mrs. Pitts. Next to speak will be Mr. Hugoll."

"Thank you. I represent Central Florida, and I see the loss of doctor after doctor from our area. In fact, my daughter was sick last week, and my wife needed to go to the emergency room instead of our pediatrician's office to have her checked because one of the pediatricians in that practice left the area. He couldn't afford his malpractice insurance. So, for me at least, this is hitting home. I'm open to all suggestions and ideas as to how we can beat this thing."

"Thank you all for agreeing to meet with us," Steve Boxley said. "We have a terrible situation on our hands. We are losing doctors left and right, and with no end in sight. These predatory malpractice attorneys need to be stopped, and we need to be able to help our patients without constantly looking over our shoulders. I'm handing out a position paper from our local Medical Society, and I'd like to review it with you.

"We have a number of suggestions for legislative relief for our troubles. The first issue revolves around plaintiff's experts. Currently, anyone with a medical degree can testify against a doctor. Here in Florida, fully 80% of the plaintiff's experts are living and working out of the state. By importing these paid mouthpieces, the state has no control over them. They can literally lie through their teeth, and we — the Medical society and the state regulators in the Board of Medicine — can't touch them. We propose that only physicians licensed in Florida be allowed to testify in Florida malpractice cases.

"Next, we think that doctors should be practicing in the field that they are testifying in. This may seem intuitive, but over 50% of the expert testimony given for the plaintiffs is given by doctors who are retired or who practice outside of the field in which they are claiming to be experts. We think this needs to be corrected.

"Another issue is accountability. A plaintiff's expert can literally say anything that he wants in court, whether it's true or not. If that expert testimony was reviewed by the Medical Society, and the doctor's license was suspended in the interest of public safety if he testified to incorrect medicine, these whores would think twice before lying in court. But, of course, this could only work if we restricted experts to doctors actively licensed and practicing in this state.

"Finally, we need a cap on non-economic damages. Too often, one of the lawyers convinces the jury that his client needs a million dollars for pain and suffering when in fact that figure exceeds common sense, and he gets it. These outrageous amounts are killing our ability to find insurance.

"Thank you for listening."

Steve could see that Alex was right. Bloch just smiled and shook his head from side to side head while Steve was talking. Hugoll, on the other hand, was nodding vigorously the whole time. "This is the guy who can help us," Steve thought.

The meeting was quickly adjourned. The legislators needed to get to an important vote on the floor. The doctors were ushered into a souvenir shop and were on their way back to the bus shortly thereafter. All but Steve Boxley.

***

Susan tried to explain the numbers to David that night after dinner. He didn't seem to understand the problem, and he told her just not to worry about it. In fact, he suggested that she drop the issue. But it bothered her all night, and by the morning she decided to talk to Jake Morris about it.

She walked into the building and went directly to Jake Morris' office. She spoke with Morris' secretary, who penciled her in for a private conference at 11:30 that morning. Two hours later, Susan was sitting in Jake's office. "Yes, Susan, what can I do for you?" Jake asked.

"Well, Mr. Morris, I think I found a problem with the accounting of expenses, and I wanted to talk with you about it," she replied.

Susan laid out the papers on Jake's desk that she had shown to Tyler McNab, and reviewed her calculations with him. Jake asked her if she had gone over the papers with anyone else. She thought about Ty and David, but said no, she hadn't discussed it with anyone. Jake asked her why she didn't discuss it with her department head. Susan explained, "I'm concerned that she may be skimming money from the client settlements, so I wanted to come directly to you."

"I think I understand your concerns, Susan. Thank you. I'll keep these papers and go over them with my personal accountant." Jake smiled and thanked her again as he guided her out the door.

Immediately, Jake called Stan Large on his private phone. Again Stan answered on the first ring.

"Yes, Jake."

"Stan, I need you here, now."

Stan could hear the urgency in Jake's voice, and he knew that he shouldn't ask why. "I'm on my way. I'll be there in a few minutes."

Jake hung the phone up and walked to the picture window overlooking the bay. The weather was beautiful, and from the 32nd floor, the boats looked like small dots in the water. The view calmed him, and as he waited for Stan to arrive, he thought about their first meeting.

Jake had just scored his first big settlement and changed his practice from criminal law to personal injury law, specializing in medical malpractice. Stan had been a criminal law client of Jake's. He was a small time numbers runner, a foot soldier for the mob. For his day job, he worked as a private eye.

Jake had started to increase his spending after the first big case, and had purchased a Jaguar XJ-6. He also started to travel in fast circles, much to the chagrin of his first wife. More ominously, Jake began to use cocaine, and he fell in with a dangerous crowd. Within six months of his famous first case, Jake had a $500 per day habit. With a problem like that, it's quite easy to make more than a few enemies.

Stan had been arrested for running numbers and used his one phone call to reach Jake. "Mr. Morris, I saw your ad on the TV, and I know that you specialize in medical malpractice, but I remembered your name from your old office, and I figured that I'd call you if I ever got arrested. Can you help me?"

Jake went to the courthouse and bailed Stan out. They discussed the case, and Jake decided to represent Stan. Jake was able to get Stan's charged dropped, and the two men began to develop a relationship. Jake started using Stan for investigations and Stan boasted about Jake to the mob. For the next few years, Jake handled a few big cases for the mob, and was well paid for it.

Along the way, Jake's cocaine habit got out of control. One evening, Jake and Stan were at Ormond's, the local club to be seen in at the time. Jake had done a few too many hits of coke and was a bit wild, talking too fast and too loud and spilling everybody's drinks. He was with one of the local hookers, and the two of them slipped out for a quickie in Jake's Jag. Stan was at the bar when Jake pulled him aside and hustled him out to the parking lot. In the backseat of Jake's car was the hooker, stone dead and half naked. Stan could see that Jake and the hooker had had sex and that Jake had beat the shit out of her. Stan told Jake that he would take care of things. He gave Jake the keys to his Chevy pickup and told Jake to go home. Stan brought Jake's car back the next day, picked up his truck, and never told Jake what he had done with the girl. But Jake wasn't stupid. He knew that he had left enough semen in her that if she were found, the DNA evidence could convict him. He watched the news and read the papers for days, but there was no story about the death of the hooker. Jake figured that she was five miles out at the bottom of the Gulf of Mexico.

If nothing else, Jake and Stan shared the knowledge that one of them had killed this girl and the other had disposed of the body. So the two men remained in this unofficial arrangement together, each doing for the other within his given capacity, bound by a terrible secret they both shared. Each knew that he could trust the other more than he could trust his own wife.

Jake's thoughts were interrupted by the intercom's beeping. "Mr. Large to see you, sir," said Jake's secretary.

"Send him in."

"What's the matter, Jake?" asked Stan.

"One of my employees, Susan Parks, was just in here. She is in the accounting department, and found a $750,000 accounting error. If our books were to be audited, they would find that we have embezzled somewhere around $6,000,000 over the years. We need to do something about her."

"Does anyone else know about this?"

"No, I asked her and she said that she thought that the CFO might be embezzling, so she didn't speak with her. Instead she came directly to me. In fact, she gave me the proof." Jake showed Stan the papers that Susan had left in his care.

"I'm no accountant, but I know that you are allowed to file an amended tax return. Why don't you just say you found a mistake and file an amended return?"

"Because, we didn't embezzle from our company. We embezzled from our clients. If we were to be caught, we would lose our law licenses and go to jail."

"Christ. Who is this 'we' that you're talking about?"

"All three of us; me, Sam Cuney and Jay Howe and me. All of us were involved."

"Do they know about this stuff the Parks girl brought in?"

"No, they don't."

"Good. Don't tell them. We can make this go away. Just give me a day or two to think this out."

"Sure. Thanks Stan."

CHAPTER 9

Bob Hugoll had motioned for Steve to stay behind as the other doctors were leaving. He asked if Steve would stay in town for a day or two, and told him that he would arrange for his return to Central Florida. Steve made a few phone calls and arranged for coverage. They went into Hugoll's office and sat down.

"Well, Dr. Boxley, we have a big problem. Morris, Cuney and Howe are a major problem in our neck of the woods, Central Florida, but there are at least 20 of these same predatory firms in Florida, doing the same thing as Morris, Cuney and Howe. These law firms are huge, and they are funded with a lot of money from the tobacco settlements. The Medical Society can't touch them when it comes to money and clout. These firms own the legislature, and organized medicine isn't even close when it comes to access with the representatives. Do you remember Mike Bloch from earlier today?"

"Yes, he was one of the speakers. I understand that he is a trial lawyer and not at all sympathetic to our cause."

"You underestimate him, Doctor. He is expressly antagonistic to your cause, and he, personally, has donated over one million dollars to political action committees that have access to politicians. All of his pet causes, the things that he donates money to, are all legal lobbies, fighting just the sort of legislation that you want to pass."

"Well, Mr. Hugoll, what can we do?"

"First, call me Bob. Steve, we need a *cause celebre*. We need a story of a patient who couldn't get medical care because of the crisis, and then we need to get the media to eat it up. That's the only way we can get this issue into the papers, and we will need to have the populace sympathetic to your problem if anything is to change via legislation.

Otherwise, this issue is just going to be perceived as bellyaching by a bunch of rich doctors."

"Rich doctors!" Steve exploded. "We have doctors declaring bankruptcy and others leaving the state because they can't pay their malpractice insurance bills. How is that a sign of wealth?"

"It's not, Steve, but 'Joe six-pack' isn't going to be sympathetic to you. He will, however, be sympathetic to a patient who can't get care. Do you know of any such case that we can exploit?"

"Yes, I do. There was a woman who came to one of the local hospitals in labor. The only OB group that worked there has lost two of its five members because they couldn't afford their malpractice insurance. The remaining three doctors closed their office at that hospital because they couldn't cover it with only three doctors. This woman showed up anyway, and she was in the late stages of labor and the baby was in trouble. Of course, there was no one there who could do an emergency Cesarean-section delivery, so she needed to be transferred to another hospital. A few years ago, any surgeon would have been willing to do a C-section for her in an emergency, but now, because of the malpractice crisis, not one would even consider it. She was transferred immediately, in an ambulance going 'lights and sirens,' but the baby died. I'm sure that Morris, Cuney and Howe could find someone to sue, but really there was no one available to help her. Maybe they should sue themselves; it's their fault that there are not enough obstetricians in Central Florida."

"That's our case. What's the woman's name?"

"Anita Smith. Her husband Peter is a carpenter. They have one other child, a boy. He's four years old. The baby who died was a girl. It's really tragic; they named the baby Angel after she died."

"Well there you have it. We'll push through legislation for tort reform and call it the Angel Smith Act. Those trial lawyers will look like a group of uncaring bastards if they decide to fight this law."

Steve and Bob Hugoll left the capital grounds and walked a few blocks to a nice restaurant. They sat outside and enjoyed the night air. Steve thought that he could get used to this, the politics, the wheeling and dealing, and he did notice that Bob didn't need to wear a beeper.

The next morning, Steve was ushered into Bob Hugoll's office and was introduced to four representatives and about 15 aides. They spent the next six hours drafting legislation that would address the malpractice insurance issue. Their hope was that it would be ready to go before the Legislature just as the story of Angel Smith was hitting the newspapers. Towards the end of the meeting, a man was brought in. He was introduced as a reporter for the Central Florida Times. Steve spent the next hour giving him all of the details of the Angel Smith case, then he called the Smith family to get permission to use their names in the story and for the legislation that would have their daughter's name attached to it.

***

Susan walked home with David, feeling pretty good. She told David about her meeting with Jake Morris, and she was happy that her boss seemed quite concerned. She figured that he was annoyed because he thought someone was embezzling money from his company. David always thought that Jake was a fair man, and if Susan was right, she might be in line for a promotion. They both guessed that it was the CFO who was skimming money from the firm, and if she got fired, maybe Susan would move up to CFO in her place. All the more reason to stay with those CPA review courses.

The sex was great that night. Susan was thinking about her promotion and David about his new case, the John Davis case. Maybe soon, David thought, he'd go out and get an engagement ring for Susan.

CHAPTER 10

Central Florida Times

Tampa Bay, FL
By Mark Rodriguez

Anita and Peter Smith were ecstatic to find out that Anita was pregnant with their second child. Four year old Carl was praying for a sister, and it seemed that he was going to get his wish. Anita showed up for prenatal care at the offices of Central Florida OB/GYN Associates regularly, and an ultrasound proved that the baby was going to be a girl; everything looked perfect. Another four weeks and the family would be larger.

Last month, OB/ GYN Associates got their bill for malpractice insurance. They had been paying about $60,000 each for the five members of the group. The bill showed a rise to $145,000 for each of the members. Now, OB /GYN — Obstetrics and Gynecology - is a high risk field in terms of malpractice insurance, but this was unbearable. The two newest members of the group left. They could not afford to pay that bill. This left only three doctors in the group. They were unable to cover both of the hospitals where they were on staff, so they notified Middle Florida Hospital that they were leaving the institution. They also notified all of their patients that they would only be working at Samaritan Hospital, and they directed their patients to go only to Samaritan Hospital for their care.

When Anita went into labor, she knew something was wrong. With Carl, the contractions were about five minutes apart, and when her water broke, the water was clear. This time, there really were no contractions, just pain, and when her water broke, she saw blood, a lot of it. Peter put her in the car, they dropped Carl off at a neighbor's house, and then headed for Samaritan Hospital. But the pain and bleeding worsened, and Peter went to Central Florida Hospital because it's closer. That mistake may have cost their daughter her life.

As soon as Anita got to the ER, she was surrounded by doctors and nurses. Peter heard a stat call paged over the loudspeaker. "Any available OB / GYN doctor, come to the ER stat." A few minutes later, he heard, "Any available surgeon come to the ER stat." Later, the ER doctor told them that there were no obstetricians in the hospital, and the surgeon who was in the hospital refused to see her because of the liability. She would need to be transferred to Samaritan. They put oxygen on her, gave her something for the pain, and sent her on her way by ambulance. The baby died on the way to Samaritan Hospital. The baby's name was Angel Smith.

This reporter interviewed the president of the Medical Society. I have learned that these two OB / GYN doctors are not the only doctors to leave the area. The only Neurosurgeon who does brain surgery is leaving in December, and about 25 percent of our specialists are thinking about leaving too. This is a grave crisis in health care, and we need to do something about it. The Medical Society feels that the threat of malpractice suits is unbearable for all doctors, and the rise in insurance premiums has driven many doctors to bankruptcy. Last year, there were 29 insurance companies providing insurance for malpractice in this state. Now there are three. It's estimated that if nothing changes, the wait to see your family doctor will increase to four weeks or more, the wait for elective surgery will go up to seven months, and as many as 1,000 people will die waiting for procedures and hospital treatment because of a lack of doctors.

Bob Hugoll, a state representative from the Tampa Bay area, will be introducing legislation that will go a long way to ease this crisis. We need to give him our full support.

CHAPTER 11

Jake Morris threw the newspaper down and yelled for his secretary. "Get me the editor of this rag, now!" he screamed.

A few moments later, the editor was on the phone. "Yes, Mr. Morris, what can I do for you?"

Jake replied, "Mr. Crandall, my firm spends $600,000 a year advertising with you, do we not?"

"Yes, you do, Mr. Morris."

"Well, what the hell are you trying to pull with this page one story about Angel Smith? Malpractice reform will kill us, and if it does, it will kill your advertising revenue from us. Is that what you want?"

"No, sir, but I can't muzzle this reporter. This is a good story, and we're going with it. If you'd like, I'll send Mark Rodriguez, the reporter, over to your office, and you can reply to the article."

"Not yet," said Jake, "but soon."

An hour later, Jake and Stan Large were huddled together. Stan told Jake that he had thought his accounting problem through, and the only solution he could come up with was to kill Susan. He told Jake that he needed to find out everything there was to know about Susan Parks.

"I think that the best way to kill her is to get her into the hospital and make it look like an incidence of medical malpractice. You can make such a big stink about her death that it would deflect any attention away from you as a suspect."

"That's great, Stan. But, how can you get her into the hospital?"

"I need to get into her house. If I can search her medicine chest, I can find medications that would point to, say, a heart problem or lung trouble. At the very least, I could get her personal physician's name off the label of a pill bottle, and then I could break into the doctor's office to look at her records. If there are any conditions we could exploit, I should be able to find them. But, if I do, I'll need help with killing her, somebody who knows medicine so whatever we do looks believable."

"Great, get moving. When will you know something?"

"Tomorrow, at the latest."

***

Stan loitered outside of the office at 5 p.m., waiting for the employees to start streaming out of the building. Susan and David walked out together, and Stan followed them, being careful to stay about a block behind. They led him to their home, and he stood outside for a while, then the two of them left. As they passed Stan, he heard the girl playfully arguing about where they should go to dinner. He knew that he'd have a good hour or two alone at their home.

After waiting about 15 minutes, he went to the front door. The lock was a cheap one, and he had it open in about 10 seconds. He banged on the door before he opened it, just to make sure there was no dog. He heard no sound at all coming from inside. He walked in and latched the door behind him. He took a tour of the entire house because Jake had suggested that he look for any financial papers from the firm. If he found any, he was to set fire to the house to destroy the papers. He found none, and then set out to learn something about Susan Parks. In the kitchen, he found nothing. There was a basket in one of the cabinets, and in it he found a few pill bottles, but two were for David and the one for her was for Percodan. The label said to take one pill every six hours for pain in her shoulder; the date on the pill bottle was 2 years ago. This didn't help much, but Stan wrote down the name of the prescribing physician. He could get Susan's records at his office if he needed.

He hit the jackpot in the bathroom. There he found a bottle of pills that the label said was 'Glucophage,' and the prescription was for Susan. Stan remembered that this was a drug for diabetes. He also found a wallet next to the pill bottles. In the wallet was a machine to test blood sugars and a small envelope of needles to prick Susan's skin for that sugar tests. This was what Jake wanted, and it had only taken him a few hours to get it, but he walked around the house for another half hour just in case he had missed anything important, then he left.

Stan went directly to Jake Morris' home, and the housekeeper led him to Jake's study. Jake got up from dinner and closed the door to the room.

"Well?"

"I think I got what you wanted. It seems that she's diabetic. She has medicine for diabetes, and a machine that tests her blood sugar."

"Perfect, Stan. Thank you. Stop by the office tomorrow and we'll cut you a check for your work."

Jake smiled. He fully intended to charge Stan's $2000 fee to one of his client's accounts, so Stan's work was actually free. How great was that?, he thought. He led Stan out, and before he went back to the dinner table, he placed a call to rural Georgia.

***

J. Marcus Semben always wanted to be a doctor. But, he had a problem throughout school. He just wasn't good enough. He graduated college with a C average, and no US medical school would even consider him. He finally got accepted to a medical school in the Bahamas, but only after a payoff from his father to the governor of New Providence Island. He completed a residency at Pickett Hospital in central Georgia, a program well known to be substandard. In fact, he was the second person ever to take that curriculum in twenty years. Semben was one of those people who could not rise above his situation; his residency was terrible and he did nothing to improve on the status quo. So, he became a second-rate urologist, something that was glaringly apparent to his colleagues in rural Georgia. Despite the fact the Semben was the only urologist for 20 miles around, the majority of the urology work was referred out. This left Semben with a small practice made up of patients referred by doctors too ignorant or uncaring to realize that Semben was dangerous.

As inferior a doctor as he was, Semben knew that he needed to do something to supplement his income. Medicine was out; he was a dismal failure at that. However, medico-legal case reviews piqued his interest. One day, while in his office, he received a phone call from a lawyer in Florida, Jake Morris. Mr. Morris had asked Dr. Semben if he would be interested in reviewing a file for him, to see if he, Semben, could develop a theory as to whether or not malpractice had occurred. When Semben asked how he had located him, Morris hedged and told him that he had heard about him from a mutual friend, the name now having fortuitously slipped his mind, who suggested that Semben might be interested in entering the field of medical case review. In truth, what Morris didn't tell him was that he had actually gotten his name from an old friend who was a member of the Georgia State Board of Medicine. The board was meeting and considering action against Semben's license. Jake guessed rightly that a doctor who was that bad was ripe for recruiting for a career of lying for profit.

Lying under oath is perjury, and perjury is a crime. Repeated criminal acts such a Semben's could cause him to be indicted under the RICO statute, which was originally designed to trap organized crime figures but now used to trap repeat offenders. Semben had lied under oath enough times to put him away for two centuries. Now, a few years after that initial phone call, Semben was beholden to Morris for almost ninety percent of his income. He had sold his soul, and the devil was about to demand his due.

J. Marcus Semben, M.D., was sitting in his study, reviewing charts for a plaintiff's attorney in Pennsylvania. He had been trying to think of a theory that would allow a claim of medical malpractice to be brought against an obstetrician in suburban Philadelphia. The obstetrician had delivered a "bad baby" about six months ago, and the parents had gone to a few of the more "reputable" Philadelphia malpractice attorneys, as oxymoronic as that term sounded even to Semben, and they had all turned the case down. Now, a less honorable attorney had the case, and Semben was his hired gun. The doctor had done all of the routine prenatal screening, and everything was normal. The labor had been uneventful. At the delivery, there were no problems, but the baby came out blue and needed to be worked on for about 5 minutes before it started to breathe. There was brain damage, and now Semben's job was to see if he could come up with a plausible reason why it was the doctor's fault. The attorney figured that if he could get the case into court, once the jury saw the kid, he'd get a million dollars or more. The records looked good, and the fetal monitor tracings looked normal. He had just realized that about two minutes of fetal monitor strips were missing when the phone rang.

"Yes."

"Dr. Semben, this is Jake Morris."

"Hello, Jake, what do I owe the honor of a call from the boss?"

"I need your help. I'd like you to speak with a friend of mine. His name is Stan Large."

"Sure, Jake, no problem."

Semben smiled. Jake needed him, and he had just figured out the way to get this case into court. Even though the two minutes of missing fetal monitor strips were in the middle of hours of normal strips, the attorney could claim that they were abnormal and that the obstetrician should have done an emergency C-section. The lawyer could maintain that when the doctor saw the complications of his actions, he destroyed the evidence. "Of course it's bullshit," he thought, "but it will get that kid into the courtroom, and then the doctor's dead. If we get lucky and the jury believes that the doctor destroyed evidence, we could get punitive damages, maybe another million."

He fired off a fax to his Pennsylvania employer outlining his thoughts, and then he went to bed and fell sound asleep. A short time later, the phone rang.

"Hello."

"Dr. Semben?"

"Yes."

"My name is Stan Large. I believe that Mr. Morris told you to expect my call."

A shiver ran down Semben's neck. The voice on the other end of the line was frightening. There was something in Large's tone that sounded threatening, and Semben began to realize that whatever Jake Morris wanted him for, it wasn't for something good.

"Yes, Mr. Morris called me."

"Good. I'll be there tomorrow."

"Where do you want to meet me?"

"Don't worry, I'll find you."

For the first time since Semben was a child, he had nightmares that woke him up every 30 minutes for the rest of the night.

***

Mark Land had finished seeing the patients by 6:30, and Steve Boxley showed up a few moments later to start another day. They had a cup of coffee, then gathered up the students and saw their patients together. Mr. Kane was doing splendidly, and he would be able to go home in a day or two. His tumor was malignant, and the cancer specialist had recommended that he start chemotherapy whenever Dr. Boxley felt that it would be safe. Steve spent a few minutes speaking with him about that, and then recommended that Mr. Kane allow Steve to implant a port, a device under the skin that would make the chemo treatments easier. If he didn't have the port, every time the oncologist wanted to give a treatment, the nurses at the cancer center would have to start an IV. This port was like an implanted IV line, always ready to be used. Mr. Kane agreed, and Steve told Mark to add him to the OR schedule for the next day.

Rounds finished, the team headed for the operating room to start the day. The first case was a carotid endarterectomy. Steve asked the first year resident to give the group a short talk on the operation.

"Carotid disease is one of the many ways that arteriosclerosis manifests itself, otherwise known as hardening of the arteries. The plaque builds up in the carotid artery, which is the artery in the neck running up to the brain. When the buildup is too much, it can cause a stroke. We try to intervene before that happens. Generally, we try to clean out the artery when the buildup exceeds 60% of the diameter of the artery."

Steve asked Mark to comment on the operation itself.

"There are many ways to do the operation, but Dr. Boxley likes to do it under general anesthesia. He asks for the patient's brain to be monitored during the operation with an EEG, an electroencephalogram, which monitors brain waves. With this, we can tell if the patient's brain is getting enough blood while we're working. Next we expose the artery. We then clamp it and open it up. We scoop out the plaque and close the artery again."

Steve covered the complications himself. "The operation is not difficult, but it is very demanding. Everything must be done perfectly. Any deviation from perfection can lead to a stroke; remember that we are operating on the blood supply to the brain. Despite the best, most perfect procedures during the operation, about three percent of all patients undergoing this operation will have a stroke during the surgery, and we don't know why. What we do know is that without the operation, up to twenty percent of these patients will have a stroke. So, it certainly seems worthwhile to do the surgery."

The nurse called to Dr. Boxley and his team, "It's show time, Doctor." Mark and one of the students scrubbed, and Steve told them to call him when Mark was ready to clamp the artery.

Steve went to the lounge and sat down to watch TV while he waited. Two things happened simultaneously that sickened him. The first, not surprisingly, was a commercial from Morris, Cuney and Howe. This ad made the ludicrous statement that only three in one hundred cases of medical malpractice were ever brought to an attorney, and then gave the punch line: "if you think that you or a loved one were the victim of medical malpractice, please call Morris, Cuney and Howe immediately." The second thing was far more ominous. The hospital administrator poked his head into the lounge looking for Steve and showed him two certified letters. One was addressed to the hospital, and had already been opened; it contained a request for the medical records of John Davis. The other letter was unopened and addressed to Steve. He ripped it open and saw an identical letter to the one that went to the hospital, only addressed to him. He crumpled it up, muttered "shit," and threw it into the trash.

Steve didn't speak with the administrator. He simply walked out and headed for the operating room.

***

Semben awoke with an awful premonition. He felt like there was a great weight on his chest, and he kept looking over his shoulder everywhere he went that morning. He went to the hospital to do his rounds and completed them quite quickly. He had one procedure to do, a cystoscopy, and he managed to complete it without much difficulty. Next stop was the office. His secretary was off, and the phones were forwarded to the answering service. Semben unlocked the door to his office and walked in.

The door opened into the waiting room, which was large enough for about six people to sit. Sadly, he thought, he had never had the pleasure of seeing the waiting room filled. There was a sliding glass window opening into the front office where his secretary sat and answered the phone. A door to the left of the window opened to a hallway. Semben walked along the hallway in darkness. He knew that he would pass three examination rooms on his way to the back of the office, where his private consultation room was located.

He flipped the lights on and gasped as he saw a burly, unshaven man sitting behind his desk. Lying on the desk was a gun, pointed in the general vicinity of Semben.

"Holy shit," he shouted. "What's this about?"

"Quiet, Dr. Semben, or you'll end up with an extra hole somewhere. I'm Stan Large. I told you I'd find you. Please sit down."

Semben did as he was told.

Large got up and put the gun into a shoulder holster. He walked over to the corner of the room where he had placed a suitcase, hoisted the suitcase onto the desk and opened it.

104

"Do you know what I have in here, Dr. Semben?"

"I have no clue, sir."

Large slowly removed documents, actually small books, bound in blue covers. "These are court transcripts, Dr. Semben. Since I had to travel here by plane, and I needed one suitcase to carry my clothes, I could only bring a few of your masterpieces. However, if you need me to, I can get all of them."

"Masterpieces, what are you talking about?"

Large opened one of the transcripts and began to read.

"Question: Dr. Semben isn't it considered a routine complication to develop an infection following this type of surgery. Answer: Not at all. These types of operations should not cause infection, ever. Question: Doctor, are we not speaking about surgery for a ruptured appendix? Answer: Yes we are. Question: Well, isn't a ruptured appendix by definition infected? Answer: Counselor, this type of infection will only occur if the surgeon is incompetent.

"Dr. Semben, Morris, Cuney and Howe recovered $200,000 in damages for this patient. Of course, you know that your testimony was an out and out lie, a complete fabrication."

"So what?"

"Let me continue, then," Large said. "Question: Dr. Semben, isn't mental retardation of this type, so-called Down's syndrome, due to genetic abnormalities? Answer: Occasionally. Question: Occasionally, how about always? Answer: No, it is occasionally caused by bad prenatal care, as was given to the plaintiff. Question: So it is your testimony that the defendant doctor caused this baby's Down syndrome? Answer: Absolutely.

"This case won $300,000 for Jake Morris' firm.

"So, you have lied under oath well over one hundred times. Mr. Morris has asked me to explain to you just how tenuous your position is. You could be tried under the RICO statutes and put away in jail for decades. Shall I go on?"

"What do you want?"

"We need your help. Give it to us, and we will burn these transcripts. These particular masterpieces are your most wild lies, Doctor. These cases were settled because of your depositions, so there is no court record of these lies. Help us, these never see the light of day. Refuse to help, and these go to the State Attorney.

Semben flopped down in the chair facing his desk and analyzed his situation. He knew that Large was right. He had lied so many times under oath that he couldn't even remember all the deception. He also knew that perjury was a crime, and he was perhaps the most prolific perjurer in Georgian history. He really had no choice but to help Large.

"Fine. What do you want from me?"

"I want your help in arranging the murder of one of Jake Morris' employees."

"Why, if I may ask?"

"You may not ask. It is none of your business."

"Mr. Large, I am not a murderer."

Large went on a first-name basis with Semben. "Marcus, you are a murderer. You have killed people, even if you've never committed premeditated murder. You are about the most incompetent physician in all of Georgia. So, murder is something I'm sure you're quite comfortable with."

Semben glared at him. "How do you propose to kill her?"

"That's your job, to figure out the method. We need to make it look like medical malpractice occurred. I have information that may help you, though; she's a diabetic."

CHAPTER 12

Bob Hugoll stood before his colleagues in the rotunda of the State House.

"Gentlemen and ladies, thank you for listening to me today. We face a grave time for healthcare in our fair state. As you have heard, we are losing many of the finest of our physicians. The 'brain drain' is terrible. You see, the experienced doctors, because by definition they are the ones who've been in practice the longest and thus exposed to the most risk, are the ones who are most likely to have been sued a few times in our overly litigious times. They, then, are the ones who are finding the most trouble getting malpractice insurance, which is not only absurd but a recipe for disaster. This forces experienced doctors to pack up and leave Florida, and the result is not only fewer doctors, but less experienced doctors treating the good citizens of Florida. This is obviously now a crisis.

"The causes of this crisis are many. The insurance companies will have you believe that the main reason for the prohibitive rise in premiums is the explosion of lawsuits and the ridiculous settlements and judgments for the plaintiffs. These companies will tell you that the contingency fee arrangement with plaintiff attorneys and their clients, wherein the lawyer gets up to 40% of the settlement, is obscene and leads to the filing of many frivolous cases. This is, of course, not a wholly inaccurate assessment.

"The plaintiff attorneys feel that the medical community is simply not providing adequate care for the citizens of our state, and they, the attorneys, are the only hope for injured people. They say that the rise in insurance premiums is due to poor returns from the stock market for the insurance companies. This, too, is not a wholly inaccurate assessment.

"The medical community sees things differently. They feel that these lawsuits are generally groundless, and that the lawyers file them to see if the insurance companies will send them a few bucks to drop the case. The human body is not a machine, and doctors can not predict with 100% accuracy the way any given patient will respond to any given treatment. However, when the response is not perfect, the patient consults an attorney. The medical community's assessment is not inaccurate either, but there is more than enough blame to go around."

There was an audible murmur at this point that spread among the crowd of legislators gathered before him, and for the moment it took Bob Hugoll to take a sip of water to clear his throat before proceeding, he looked as if he was not sure if there would be a communal outburst at his hubris, his gall to take on some of these men and women's most prized campaign contributors or a chorus of polite amens. After all, these people would not want to look like they were *not* in favor of quality healthcare for their constituents, no matter who was giving them money. He quickly took up where he had left off:

"The sad part of all this is the effect on healthcare. Angel Smith died because her parents couldn't find an obstetrician to care for her. Doctors are leaving our state, the quality of the doctors who remain is decreasing, and there are fewer doctors available. More insidiously, this crisis is affecting research, as more attorneys are suing researchers, claiming that their clients would have had a better outcome had they not participated in the studies. Some experts predict that, in a few years, medical research will be non-existent if something is not done soon to ameliorate this crisis."

Another murmur spread through the crowd that Hugoll could not read.

"Further, the effect on medical education is devastating. Experienced physicians allow doctors in training to participate in the treatment of their patients in order to

108

further the educational process and create the next generation of qualified physicians. However, the complication rate when trainees are involved is slightly higher, and as malpractice suits rise in number, the willingness of our physicians to teach declines. Already, I'm told by the Medical Society, the number of doctors in my home district, Central Florida, who teach students and residents, has dropped from 175 to 68. The result of that drop is terrible. Students tend to go into practice where they've trained, and as the number of students in our area falls, so too will the number of trainees who set up practice in our area.

"This crisis does not occur in a vacuum. Doctors are beleaguered, and government regulation and lawsuits have demoralized the profession. In past times, physicians would urge their children to go into medicine. Now they forbid them. At one time, 80% of doctors said they would be honored to have their children go into medicine. Now only 25% of doctors say that. The medical schools no longer have the 'best and brightest' applying. Those students are going to business school. So, the applicants are not as good as they were 15 years ago. Therefore, as time goes on, the quality of the people who will be caring for us will suffer."

The murmur was growing in intensity now, and the politician sensed that this was the point he had been aiming for, something just short of a frenzy, and he got to the reason for his oration.

"I am proud to say that, along with three of my colleagues, I am introducing the Angel Smith Act. This act will go a long way toward giving our doctors much-needed relief. I hope that you will join me in passing this most important legislation."

He took another drink of his water and let the moment ride, let his colleagues' apprehension and curiosity mingle a bit. Then he cleared his throat gently and continued.

"The act will accomplish the following: The maximum contingency allowable to the attorney will be regulated. It is unfair to think that if a settlement is one million dollars, the attorney would deserve 40%, or $400,000, after expenses. That is ludicrous. Therefore, this bill allows for a 40% contingency only for the first hundred thousand dollars of a settlement. After that, the contingency falls to 10%, and after $500,000 in settlement, it would fall to zero."

At this announcement there was now deathly silence.

"All expert witnesses for the plaintiff and defense must reside within 100 miles of the defendant doctors' office or hospital. In addition, all experts must be licensed in, and actively practicing in, the state of Florida."

More silence that was somehow growing in intensity, a malevolent quiet all aimed at the dais.

"All expert witnesses must be actively practicing in the field that they claim they are an expert in. I know this sounds obvious, but in Florida, most of the plaintiffs' experts do not practice in the field that the case involves.

"All expert testimony must be reviewed by the Florida Medical Board. If the testimony is fabricated, or an out-and-out lie, the license of the doctor giving the testimony will be suspended. If there is a pattern of deceptive testimony, the doctor will be charged with perjury and prosecuted."

More quiet, and instinctively the legislator held up his hands as if to quiet a boisterous crowd, but this was as if to hold off the anger that was aimed at him from so many eyes.

"Non-economic damages will be capped at $250,000. You would be amazed at the ludicrous awards given to plaintiffs for these fabricated damages. If the plaintiff loses, the plaintiff's attorney must pay the defendant-doctor's legal expenses. This clause alone will probably stop half of the frivolous lawsuits."

The crowd was now as sullen as drunks at a prayer meeting, angry but also clearly not sure of what to make of this bill, how to deal with either the fallout in the press of opposing it or with those angry contributors, the trial lawyers and their associations.

"There will be a committee of legislators, doctors and attorneys convened to try to create a no-fault type of system to replace the current system. If a patient feels he or she was injured, that patient would submit a claim. If the no-fault board agreed, money would be paid without a trial. There would be no legal grandstanding, and injured parties would be compensated.

"Please join me in overwhelmingly passing this most needed bill. Thank you."

The legislature erupted into applause, the kind of applause these men and women reserved for *seeming* to be in favor of something they would nevertheless fight to the death, and Bob Hugoll was smart enough to know that this meant that he was in for the fight of his political life.

CHAPTER 13

Semben was summoned to the office of Morris, Cuney and Howe the following week. Morris told him that he would have his limousine meet the doctor at the airport. Semben had to leave his house at 5:00 am to get to Hartsfield International Airport in Atlanta in time to catch an 11:00 am flight to Orlando International. He headed for the baggage claim area in Orlando and noticed a proper looking gentleman holding a white card that read "Dr. Semben." He identified himself to James, and James helped him with his bag. Semben was impressed with the car, a vintage Bentley. James told him to help himself to a drink and to feel free to use the phone. The first stop was the Hilton Hotel by the airport. James waited while Semben checked in and dropped off his bag, and then they headed into downtown Orlando. Traffic was heavy on I-4, but they arrived at the office by 3:30 p.m. Jake was waiting for him in his private office; Semben got a chill when he saw Stan Large sitting on a sofa.

Jake began, "I believe that the two of you already know each other. I know that you both are aware of the job, and Marcus, I trust that I will have your complete confidence and discretion. You can trust Stan as you would me. The only people who know about this situation are the three of us. Let's keep it that way. Now, please get going and get this thing taken care of."

Semben and Large went to a local pub and found a quiet back booth. After a few drinks, Semben could begin to talk about the murder they needed to plan without his voice trembling. Large asked him how they could cause Susan to go into a diabetic coma.

Semben said, "I have a plan. We can make her quite sick, sick enough for her to need to go to the hospital. Once we get her into the hospital, we can inject insulin into her IV and drive the hospital nuts, thinking she has some kind of insulin-secreting tumor. She'll eventually die from the lack of sugar in her bloodstream."

"Sounds ingenious. I know that I can get into her house at will. She lives with David Archer, one of the staff attorneys at Morris, Cuney and Howe. He knows nothing about this, and we'd need to get him out of the house."

"I'll need you to somehow substitute her diabetes pills for a sedative. What medication does she take?" Semben asked.

"Glucophage."

"OK." Semben started writing something on a small pad. "Take these prescriptions for Valium and Glucophage to the pharmacy, and bring the drugs to me. Meet me at my hotel tonight."

The prescription for Valium cost Stan Large $23.80, and the Glucophage was $63.90. He strolled around the center of town wasting time until he was to meet with Semben. At the appointed time, he went into the Hilton Hotel and took the elevator to the 15th floor; Semben was waiting for him in the room.

Large gave Semben the medications and the two men sat down at a table in the hotel room. While Large had been shopping for the medications, Semben had been to an apothecary supply company. He had purchased a mortar and pestle, an old-time grinding bowl and grinder that pharmacists once used to actually make, or compound, drugs. The men set to work grinding up the Valium, and once the pills had been reduced to a powder, they pushed the bowl to the side. Next, they took the prescription bottle of Glucophage and carefully opened up the capsules, disposing of the medication down the toilet. Finally, the Valium powder was carefully packed into the Glucophage capsules. Now, the capsules that were supposed to contain medicine for diabetes were actually sedatives. Semben knew that

Susan took three Glucophage capsules each evening for the treatment of her diabetes, and he had packed a huge dose of sedative into each counterfeit pill. So, with one dose of three phony pills, she was taking a major overdose of Valium.

Semben put the doctored Glucophage pills into the pill bottle and instructed Large to go to Susan's house and exchange these new pills for her regular prescription. Large was to flush her medication down the toilet and put the same number of these new pills in the bottle.

***

Steve Boxley left the hospital after his surgeries and went to his office. There, he collected his papers pertaining to his care of John Davis and asked his secretary to make two copies of them. He mailed one set to Morris, Cuney and Howe, to the attention of a staff attorney named David Archer. The second set he put in an envelope that he addressed to his malpractice insurance carrier. Next, he placed a phone call to the carrier and spoke to one of the adjusters, who told him that he would be put in touch with an attorney to represent him and asked if he had a preference. Steve suggested that he be represented by Matthew Johnson, the attorney who had represented Dr. Franks. The adjuster gave him Mr. Johnson's phone number and asked that Steve contact the attorney as soon as possible.

Steve called Matthew Johnson immediately. The two men had met before, and after exchanging pleasantries, they began discussing the case. Matthew asked Steve to summarize the medical facts.

"Well, Matthew, basically Mr. Davis was an unfortunate 50 year-old man in a terrible motorcycle accident. He sustained a ruptured spleen, pelvic fractures, a collapsed lung and significant blood loss. Miraculously, we were able to save him, but sadly, he suffered a pulmonary embolism and died. We of course took all due precautions to prevent that, but obviously, these were not good enough. He actually did quite well through the surgery and was out of the ICU and getting ready to go home when it happened. His wife was devastated, and from the amount of time between his death and my getting the letter, I suspect she must have called Morris, Cuney and Howe within a day or two of his death." Steve was obviously getting agitated. His voice was rising, and he was talking faster and faster. His fist was clenched so tightly around the phone receiver that his knuckles were bloodless.

"Steve," said Matthew, "try to calm down. I know that, to you, this seems like the end of the world, but for Morris, Cuney and Howe, it's just another day at the office. I need to tell you that 'it's nothing personal,' but of course I know it's very personal for you. Just try to put this behind you, and let me do my job. Send me a copy of the records, and we'll talk in person in a day or two."

The two men hung up, and Steve sat alone in the dark for an hour before heading home. He knew that things would never be the same for him. He would now look at every case as a potential lawsuit, every patient as a potential litigant. He began to fantasize about leaving medicine; under these conditions, the profession that had been his life, that had cost him his family, would no longer be any fun at all.

***

The following morning, Stan Large sat in his car outside Susan and David's home for about an hour. He watched as the occupants of the house started to stir, the window shades opening, lights flicking on and off; and finally, he watched as the two of them walked out and strolled hand in hand towards work. After another half-hour, just for good measure, to make sure they did not forget something and have to return, he again broke into the house.

This time, he knew exactly where he was going. The bathroom medicine chest still housed the Glucophage bottle. He took the bottle off of the shelf and counted the pills; there were fourteen of them. These he flushed down the toilet. Then he reached into his pocket and pulled out the bottle with the homemade pills in it and put fourteen of them into Susan's pill bottle. Next, he went to a lamp in the bedroom and placed a wireless bug into the fixture. He repeated the action in the living room. Now, he'd be able to hear whatever was said in both rooms. It was only a matter of time before the plan would be enacted.

Large then returned to Semben's hotel room and set up the receiver for the listening device he had planted in Susan's rooms and made himself comfortable.

***

Matthew Johnson's office was in a high-rise in the center of town. Steve rode the elevator to the 53rd floor, where the offices of Johnson and Freed were housed. The secretary got Steve a cup of coffee and led him to Matthew Johnson's office. Steve shook Matthew's hand and sat down. Much to Steve's embarrassment, his eyes suddenly misted up. This whole situation was painful to his ego and demoralizing to his soul. He was an excellent doctor, and he always prided himself on his professional ethics. He did not cut corners or half-step anything he did in his life, except perhaps his marriage. That thought made him even more morose, but then he got angry. He had not sacrificed his marriage to walk out of this profession because some moronic lawyer thought he could make a buck off of his misfortune.

Matthew asked Steve to give him the copy of the chart, which Steve did, then asked that Steve recount the entire case as it happened. Steve recalled the beep from the hospital and the phone conversation with the resident. He remembered the surgery, the aftercare and the fateful night when John had suffered a fatal pulmonary embolism. Matthew listened without saying a thing. Finally, when Steve finished, Matthew said, "Steve, do you honestly think you did anything wrong in this case? I need to know before we face these people."

"No, Matthew, I do not. I believe in my heart that we did everything right, and if I had it to do over again, I would not do one thing differently." Steve shook his head sadly and said, "Of course, if I had it to do over again, I wouldn't have taken him as a patient."

"Well, Steve, that's water under the bridge. You did accept him as a patient, and now we need to deal with it. I need you to help me defend you. First, we'll need you to tell me any weaknesses in your treatment of Mr. Davis, any judgment calls that Morris, Cuney and Howe can exploit. Next, I'll need you to explain to me how we can defend those weaknesses. Finally, we'll need to secure a medical expert in your field who can testify that your treatment of Mr. Davis was appropriate."

"The only possible weakness in my care of Mr. Davis was my decision not to use heparin to prevent blood clots in his legs. If we had used heparin, he probably would not have gotten the clots, and if he hadn't gotten the clots, he would not have had a pulmonary embolism."

"Can you justify not using heparin?"

"Yes, I can. Mr. Davis had suffered major trauma and one of the reasons I was called in on such an emergency basis was that he was unstable from bleeding. The bleeding was from many sources, but after the surgery that I did, he was no longer bleeding from anywhere but his pelvic fractures. Had we used heparin, he would have continued to bleed from those fractures. By not using heparin, the bleeding stopped, and Mr. Davis became stable."

"Well, the opposition could say that your initial decision to withhold heparin was a good one, but once he was stable and the bleeding had stopped, maybe you should have started it. Would that be a good argument?"

"Maybe, but studies have shown that clots form at the time of surgery. Once they form, it's too late. But, looking at the arguments from the other side, I suppose that they could convince a jury that I should have started the drug."

"Then it's our job to show that you did the right thing. Between us, client to lawyer, do you have any doubts, now that Mr. Davis died?"

"Of course I do. That's the problem, Matthew." Steve started weeping openly now, all his momentary anger turned to utter despair. "Shit, Matthew, I haven't cried in years, and here I am, blubbering like a baby. From now on, I'm going to second-guess everything I do, every decision I make, every operation I start. Am I going to be a basket case now?"

"No, you're not. But I'm sure that you will be second-guessing yourself for awhile. That's a normal response. The plaintiff's attorneys will tell the public that that reluctance to act protects them, now that you will be questioning your every move. But the reality is that that's total bullshit. That self doubt on the part of doctors results in more patient injuries. At least for awhile, you'll find yourself turning away difficult cases, and you'll be paralyzed by your own indecision. I always advise my clients to consider psychological help."

"I'll think about it," Steve said and he dried his eyes, his resolve returning. "Now, you said that you'd like an expert in my field. For trauma surgery, or do you want an expert in pulmonary embolism?"

"Both, if you can think of one for each."

"Actually, Vernon McPeak is a trauma surgeon at the National Trauma Center in Washington, D.C. He wrote an article on the prevention of deep venous thrombosis and pulmonary embolism in the March issue of *Surgical Treatment of Trauma*. I know Vernon; I think he'd be able to help us."

"Good. Call him and ask if he'd be willing to work with us."

Matthew and Steve rose, shook hands, and Steve left. Matthew felt sorry for Steve, and he knew he'd be carrying these demons for a long time to come. They all did, every doctor he had defended, and whether he defended them successfully or not. These suits simply shattered the confidence of normally supremely confident men and women. What a waste, he thought.

***

Susan and David returned home at about 5:30 p.m. Susan set about making dinner while David worked on some briefs that he planned to file the next morning. He had to find an expert to give a deposition about the care of John Davis, and he planned to look at the ads in the back of the most recent edition of *The American Trial Lawyer* for someone willing to sell an opinion. He'd need a surgeon who would be willing to ignore the pelvic bleeding and still testify that the surgeon should have used heparin. "Well," he thought, "If all else fails, Semben will say anything we need him to say for a price."

Susan came into the living room and sat down. "Dinner will be ready in about thirty minutes," she said. "What are you doing?"

"I need to get some things ready for tomorrow, and I need an expert in the John Davis case. This case is big, because Mr. Davis died. However, it's not a slam-dunk because he died of a pulmonary embolism. That could have been prevented by heparin, a blood thinner. The issue is that if the doctor had used a blood thinner, Mr. Davis may well have bled to death." David smiled and said, "I guess, no matter what the guy did, we'd get a lawsuit to file, huh."

"Do you have any experts in mind?"

"Not right now, but I'll look around. Worse comes to worst, I can always use Semben."

"I know that he gets a lot of money from the firm. I guess he's the 'expert of last resort,' a man who will say anything for a fee," Susan said.

Unknown to David, J. Marcus Semben and Stan Large were listening to their conversation. Large chuckled a bit under his breath, but Semben seethed. "It will be my pleasure to kill that bitch," he said.

After dinner, Susan dutifully took her medicine, three of the Glucophage capsules, and sat down to watch television. The pills tasted rather bitter in her mouth, but she swallowed them anyway. David started working on his briefs, and shortly after that, Susan started to get very tired. In fact, she was so tired that she started slurring her speech and almost fell on the floor when she got up to go to bed. She kissed David and said, "I'm exhausted, honey. I'm turning in now. Wake me when you come to bed."

By midnight, David turned off the lights and went to bed. He snuggled close to Susan and tried to wake her for a quickie, but she wouldn't budge. Her breathing was slow and regular, and there was obviously no way he was going to get lucky that night. Semben and Large had a snicker over David's attempts.

The next morning, the alarm rang, as it always did, at 6:30 a.m. David got up and showered, and when he was done, he tried to wake Susan. She stirred, but she was still slurring her speech and told David she didn't feel well. She said that she was going to stay home today. David kissed her goodbye and left.

Large listened to Susan's regular breathing for a while, then he and Semben left the hotel room. He drove directly to Susan's house. This time he didn't wait. He picked the front door lock, opening it for the third time, and the two men entered. They went directly to Susan's room. Semben put on surgical gloves and took out a small syringe and a vial of medication. The syringe was an insulin syringe, and the vial contained long acting insulin. Semben filled the syringe completely and walked over to Susan. He asked Large to turn her on her back and open her mouth. When Semben reached into Susan's mouth and pulled on her tongue, exposing the tissue below the tongue, she struggled ever so slightly, but she was too drugged to have any strength and was only semi-conscious at best. Semben injected the full dose of insulin directly into the large web of blood vessels under the tongue. The absorption was instantaneous at this location, and there was no needle mark to be found in case foul play was suspected.

They rolled Susan, who was now completely limp, onto her side and left.

***

Steve Boxley was in the office seeing postoperative patients when his beeper went off. He called the hospital immediately, and the operator told him that Mark Land was looking for him. She connected Steve to the trauma room.

"Hi, Dr. Boxley, hold for Dr. Land."

"Sir, I have a 39 year-old lady who was shot in the abdomen at a bar this afternoon. Her vitals are stable at the moment, but the X-rays suggest that the bullet may have hit her liver. In addition, she is paralyzed from the waist down, so we suspect that the bullet has lodged in her spinal cord. She needs to go to surgery. Can we proceed?"

121

Steve knew that at any other time, on any other day, he would say yes and head to the hospital. But the recent visit with Matthew Johnson made him miss a beat and he hesitated, but only for a second. Mark asked if something was wrong. "No, Mark, I'm fine. Go ahead and call the OR. I'm on my way."

Steve asked his office nurse to finish the post-ops without him and headed to the hospital. Not surprisingly, the ball game being broadcast on the radio was sponsored by Morris, Cuney and Howe, 'For the Little Guy.' Steve turned the car into the doctors' parking lot and headed for the emergency department.

When he arrived, he put on a gown and walked into the trauma room. He saw a pale woman, shivering with cold, blood leaking out of a small hole in the upper right side of her abdomen. He introduced himself to her and started to examine her. Steve looked around the room. All of the support personnel were waiting for instructions from him. He took his time with the examination, far more time than he would normally take. It wasn't that the assessment was particularly difficult; it was that he found that he could not be decisive. The decisions that, before, would come automatically, now didn't come at all. If he decided to transfuse blood, would she get an infection and sue him? If he told Mark Land to place an invasive central venous monitoring line into one of the veins leading to her heart, would Land inadvertently puncture her lung, leading to a lawsuit? And, what about an operation? Right now she was stable. If he thought that the best course of action was surgery, to identify any injuries and treat them, and if it turned out that there were no injuries other than the spinal damage, which he couldn't fix anyway, would some paid witness, some whore of a doctor, testify that the exploratory surgery was unnecessary and that Steve had further injured this already wounded woman unnecessarily?

Steve excused himself and walked into the bathroom. He barely recognized the reflection in the mirror, this shaky, pale, sweaty man standing before him. Who was this? Certainly not a board certified surgeon seasoned by more than fifteen years of surgical practice. This guy looked like a sniveling newcomer to the profession, one who would be washed out by the rigors of a residency. He knelt on the floor before a toilet and vomited twice, splashed cold water on his face at the sink, took a deep breath and walked out of the lavatory. He strode up to the side of the stretcher and started barking out orders. "Mark, place a central pressure IV line, please. Someone, call the OR and tell them we need to bring this lady up for surgery. Start transfusing two units of uncrossmatched blood, and tell the blood bank that we'll need another ten units of blood available. Call the neurosurgery department and ask them to send down someone who can get the bullet out of her spinal cord." Steve remembered that Bob Carney, the hospital's only neurosurgeon was leaving town. "If Dr. Carney can't help us, call orthopedics and get us a spinal surgeon. Let's go, people!"

Steve took a deep breath and exhaled, somewhat shakily. That had never happened to him before, and he certainly didn't like it at all. How would he react in the operating room? He got a chill and headed for the phone. He called Dr. Nan Freedman's office and asked Nan's secretary to put her on the phone; when she came on the line he asked for her help. "Nan, this is Steve Boxley. I know that this is a terrible imposition, and it certainly is painful to be asking, but something happened to me this morning, and I need your help." Steve went on to explain his recent lawsuit, his paralysis at the patient's bedside in the trauma room, and told Nan that he was afraid that his inability to act might happen again in the operating room. He knew that he could lose his patient if that happened, and he was far too cautious to take a chance. Nan told him she'd be right there, and Steve headed for surgery.

The woman lay naked on the operating room table with a body warmer taped to her chest and legs. Her abdomen was exposed and was being washed down by the nurses. Steve, Nan, and Mark Land stood at the scrub sinks preparing to operate. Mark couldn't understand what was happening. Earlier, Dr. Boxley was indecisive about treatment, and now Dr. Freedman was scrubbing at his side. In the years that Mark knew Dr. Boxley, he had never been so unsure of himself. What was happening to his mentor?

The surgery was rather straightforward. Dr. Boxley, with Dr. Freedman's help and guidance, fixed the hole in the liver and removed a portion of the small intestine that had been injured. They packed the intestines out of the middle of the abdomen and stepped back as Dr. Carney moved in to remove the bullet from the spinal cord. The injury to the cord was rather impressive, and Dr. Carney was pessimistic about her recovery. "Maybe she'll be able to put some weight on her legs, but she'll never be stable enough to walk on her own," he told the others. "But, I'll do what I can and pray for a miracle for her."

Carney finished, and Steve helped Mark close the abdomen. After the case, Steve excused himself from Mark and walked with Nan to another room. "Thanks Nan. I could not have done it without you." Steve welled up with tears. "I don't know what I'm going to do now. I can't keep asking for help from you and the other department members, and now I'm going to look at every patient as a potential litigant."

"You need help Steve," Nan replied. This happened to me two years ago, and I'm still bitter. I saw a shrink, and I must say that he helped me. I know that I didn't do anything wrong, and that the paid hacks who testify against good doctors are lying. You're one of the best surgeons that I know, and I'd hate to see you fade away. Please get help." With that and a gentle touch of reassurance to his forearm, Nan turned and walked away.

CHAPTER 14

David had taken a keen interest in Susan's diabetes when they started to get seriously involved. He was not sure why this was exactly, but he suspected that he feared being involved with someone he might lose at a relatively young age, or maybe some part of him knew even early on that he wanted to have children one day and he wondered what effect her condition would have on her ability to make babies. He felt stupid when he thought this way, but he eventually realized that he merely cared more about Susan than all the other women he had known put together, that his curiosity was an act of love, a word that made him both smile and shudder. A new pamphlet he had ordered from a medical information clearinghouse somewhere arrived just today and he had read it at his desk:

The pancreas is an organ that is located in the back of the abdomen, behind the stomach and intestines. It is quite difficult to expose in surgery, and rather silent as organs go. Most people have never heard of the pancreas.

Despite its obscurity, the pancreas is fairly important. It makes enzymes for digestion. Without it, malabsorption occurs; the patient will lose weight and suffer chronic diarrhea. Despite the magnitude of that problem, malabsorption pales in importance to the loss of the other function of the pancreas: the manufacture of insulin. Insulin is a vital hormone that regulates glucose, or sugar, metabolism. A diabetic's pancreas either doesn't make enough insulin or can't make any. Those who can make insulin, just not enough, may be able to be treated with pills that, in effect, stimulate the pancreas to work harder. Those who make no insulin need insulin injections.

When a patient eats a meal, the body is able to gauge the amount of sugar that's been eaten, and insulin is secreted into the bloodstream by the pancreas. Insulin forces the sugar into the cells, thereby keeping a steady level of sugar in the blood. If the sugar level is too high, symptoms occur, too low and symptoms occur too. For that reason, very tight control of diabetes is mandatory for good health.

When the sugar level falls too low, the brain is starved for sugar and the patient begins to act abnormally. The best description is that the patient begins to act drunk. Speech gets slurry, motions are off-kilter, and the patient gets sleepy.

These were the words that he was recalling as David rushed home from work and called for Susan. When she didn't answer, he went into the bedroom and saw that she was still sleeping. He sat down on the side of the bed and tried to wake her. But she wouldn't wake up. In fact, she couldn't wake up with her blood sugar bottomed out. She was in a coma, and nothing David would do could change that. Foam came out of the side of her mouth, and her eyes wouldn't open. David panicked at first but finally thought to call an ambulance.

"9-1-1, what is your emergency?"

"My name is David Archer. My girlfriend, Susan Parks, is unconscious. We need an ambulance."

"I've dispatched one to your address. They should be there in four minutes."

"Hurry," shouted David as he hung up.

As promised, about four minutes later, David heard the wail of sirens, and a moment later he heard the paramedics running up the walkway to the house. He let them in and led them to the bedroom. One of the paramedics asked David if Susan had any medical problems. "Yes, she's diabetic. She takes pills for it; not insulin." David was asked if she had been sick recently. David recalled that she had gotten quite sleepy after dinner last night and went to sleep early. He also told them that she was groggy that morning and had skipped work.

The paramedics skillfully hooked her up to a heart monitor, started an IV line, and put an oxygen mask on her face. She looked so helpless that David started weeping. "Help her, please." One of the attendants led David out of the bedroom and helped him sit down in the living room. "Stay here, sir. We need you out of the way to be able to help her."

In the bedroom, one of the paramedics told the other, "If she's diabetic, she may be hypoglycemic; her sugar may be too low. I'll draw a tube of blood now, so we can confirm her blood sugar level when we get to the hospital." He then injected an ampoule of D-50 into her IV. This would provide Susan with a large dose of glucose and help her if the problem was a low blood sugar. About 30 seconds later, Susan started to stir, but she didn't regain consciousness. She was given a second dose of the D-50, and this time she woke up.

"What happened?" she asked, and glanced around the room.

David heard her speaking and ran into the room, almost bowling over one of the paramedics. "Baby, you're awake. You gave me quite a scare." She smiled up at him serenely, but she was still very pale and not herself.

Susan was loaded onto a stretcher and transported to the hospital. David followed behind the ambulance to Middle Florida Hospital and parked in the emergency room parking lot. As he walked through the electric doors, he had a strange feeling in the pit of his stomach as he read the embroidered jacket of one of the doctors walking out of the hospital. It read, "Dr. Steve Boxley, General and Trauma Surgery." David knew that this was one of the doctors he would be suing on behalf of John Davis. The queasiness in his belly worsened considerably as Dr. Boxley gave him a warm smile and told him to have a nice night.

The emergency room physician was speaking to Susan when David walked into the cubicle. He asked her about the previous evening, and between Susan and David, they were able to piece together the details. They decided that she had been fine until she took her nightly dose of Glucophage. Susan commented to the doctor that the pills were unusually bitter that evening, and the doctor noted that in his record. She also told him that shortly after taking the medication, she felt very sleepy, as though she couldn't control her drowsiness. She went to bed, and the next thing she remembered was waking up with the paramedics tending to her. David filled in a few pieces; he told the doctor about how he couldn't wake her up when he went to bed, and how she was slurring her speech that morning. He finished up with her situation when he came home from work and needed to call 9-1-1.

The doctor left the room for awhile, and after a bit, returned with a sheaf of papers. "Susan, we have a significant problem. Now, a normal blood sugar in an otherwise healthy person is between 80 and 110."

Susan interrupted, "Doctor, every time my doctor checks my blood sugar, it's always 105."

"Good," the doctor continued. "However, the paramedics drew a vial of blood from you before they gave you the infusion of glucose in the IV. Your sugar was 21. That is almost fatally low. Considering that you don't take insulin, just pills, there is no chance of a dosage mistake. So, we need to consider a tumor called an insulinoma. Basically, it's a tumor that secretes insulin into your blood stream. Left untreated, it can cause a coma, like you had today; if you had not been found, it could have killed you. Susan, we need to admit you to the hospital to control your blood sugar, and you need to be seen by a surgeon to see if you have an insulinoma."

Susan, visibly shaken by this news, agreed to be admitted, and David, who was now feeling like he had to be strong for her but feeling on the inside like he wanted to weep like a child, went to the admissions office to take care of the paperwork. In about an hour, she was tucked into a bed in room 311. Her arm bracelet said that she was a patient of Dr. Jay Ireland. Her nurses fussed about the room, making sure that she was comfortable and telling her what to expect. She had a visit from the charge nurse, who said, "Susan, the doctors are concerned with your dangerously low blood sugar. They will keep you on an IV drip of glucose because it's safer to have a blood sugar level that's high than one that's low. We'll be checking in on you frequently, and we'll be checking your blood sugar every four hours."

She gave Susan a push button that was wired to the wall. "This is your call button. If you need anything, and I mean anything, push this button and we'll respond immediately. By the way, Dr. Ireland will be in to see you very early in the morning, and he's asked that our chief surgeon see you tomorrow to evaluate you for an insulinoma."

"Oh, who would that be?" Susan asked.

"Dr. Steve Boxley," was the reply. "He's excellent. I think you'll like him."

David started getting nauseous again when he heard this news. He knew that this man would soon be an adversary, and he did not want that fact to complicate Susan's treatment. He kissed Susan and told her that he needed to be on his way. Susan turned on the TV and tried to fall asleep.

***

A burly man entered Middle Florida Hospital by the loading dock at about 10 p.m. He located the maintenance area in the basement of the hospital, and entered. The on-duty maintenance man was out in the hospital somewhere working, but there was a series of hooks on the wall, and on a few of the hooks were coveralls for the day crew. Stan

Large looked at each of the ID badges attached to the coveralls and chose one that looked a little like him on a pair that would more or less fit him. He put the coveralls over his clothes, found a bucket and mop, filled the bucket with detergent for the sake of authenticity and headed for the elevators. While on the elevator, he made a call on his cell phone. "Meet me on the 3rd floor," he told Semben. Once the elevator opened at three, he pushed the bucket out and started to mop the floor of the A-wing outside Susan's room. Moments later, Semben arrived, wearing a shirt and tie, a white coat without any name on it, and a stethoscope slung over his shoulders. The two men nodded at each other, and Large said, "No one has been down this hall for a while. We should do it now."

Large knocked gently on the door to the room and pushed his way in immediately after. He quietly told Susan that he would be mopping the floor and he'd be done in a minute. Shortly after that, Semben walked in and said, "Hi, Ms. Parks. I'm your intern tonight. I'm just looking in on you. Do you feel alright?"

"Yes," Susan replied, "I'm fine."

Semben listened to her lungs, took her pulse and took a vial out of his pocket. He smiled at Susan and said, "Just flushing your IV with a bit of saline, nothing more than salt water." The vial contained insulin, and Semben injected her IV with a large dose. He smiled again, told Susan that he'd look in on her again, and left. After a moment or two, Large announced that he was done mopping and wished Susan a good night.

When Large left the room, he saw that Semben had been holding open the door to the elevator and stepped on. The doors closed and the two men rode in silence to the 11th floor. They got off and strolled down towards the C-wing, which was closed for renovations. There they found a supply closet. Large stashed the coveralls, mop and bucket in it for later. They returned to the elevator and left the hospital.

Once they were safely in Large's car and on their way, the men relaxed. They headed to a local bar, and only when he was sitting down and looking at his beer did Semben notice that he was shaking. But he felt exhilarated at the same time. He actually enjoyed injecting insulin into Susan Parks' IV line. Maybe he was a killer after all, he thought, and the notion was not as unpleasant as he had assumed it might be.

"We'll do this same thing for another day or two. Get these doctors all confused with Susan's condition, then we'll kill her," Large said.

"Sounds good to me," replied Semben. "But you'll need to learn how to do the injections, too, Stan. If I keep going in there myself, they'll get suspicious. I've been thinking that maybe we should inject the insulin into her IV bag, that way she'll get a constant infusion of insulin when we're not there."

Susan was watching television as the insulin entered her bloodstream. The insulin began to cause sugar to leave her blood and enter her cells. Despite the sugar infusion she was receiving, her blood sugar plummeted. As she got dizzy, she pushed the call bell to alert the nurse. "Yes, can I help you?" came the reply through the intercom. No reply. "Hello, do you need help?" Again, no reply. The charge nurse shook her head and walked down the hall to Susan's room. Susan was sleeping soundly, the call bell in her hand. The nurse shook her to wake her and was unable to rouse her. A few firm slaps on the face and the nurse realized something was very wrong. She yelled for help and ran to the nursing desk to get the supply cart. Like the paramedics earlier in the day, she quickly drew blood, and then she injected 2 ampoules of D-50 into Susan's IV. Within three minutes, Susan was awake. "What happened?" she asked.

"I think your blood sugar dropped again," the nurse told her. The IV drip of sugar was turned up, and the nurse vowed to keep a closer eye on Susan. Later, she found out that the blood test showed that the blood glucose test was 26.

The charge nurse spent the rest of the shift keeping an eye on Susan, and she now checked her blood sugar hourly. "Funny," she thought out loud as she gave the report to the next nursing shift, "the sugar was 105 the whole rest of the night."

***

Dr. Jay Ireland walked into Susan's room at 7:15 the next morning. "Good morning, Susan," he said. "I'm Dr. Ireland."

"Hello, Doctor. Nice to meet you."

Dr. Ireland spent the next thirty minutes at Susan's bedside, carefully listening to her explanation of the events of the previous day. He told her about the precipitous drop in her blood sugar the previous evening, and he explained that he was very concerned about her.

"This is not the typical presentation of someone with diabetes. Yes, occasionally, people who use insulin come in with an overdose, or if they are ill from other causes, they may come in with a dangerously low blood sugar, but Susan, you're perfectly healthy, and your blood sugar readings are among the lowest I've ever seen.

"Before yesterday, your blood sugars have been great. I've already called your family doctor, and since you've been stabilized on Glucophage, your lowest blood sugar was 86 and your highest was 123. These current values make no sense.

"The only explanation that I can see is that you have an insulinoma. That is a small tumor in the pancreas that secretes insulin, which runs amok in your body. Such a condition doesn't respond to the normal controls that cause your body to stop making insulin. Instead, the tumor just keeps on secreting insulin, and if left untreated, it could kill you."

"Is this a cancerous tumor?"

"No, generally not."

"How can you diagnose this tumor?"

"We can usually find it on a CT scan of the pancreas. But, sometimes, we never see it, and we ask a surgeon to go in and look for it in surgery. Sometimes, they can't find it either, especially if it's quite small, but if it's there, they usually can locate it."

Dr. Ireland went on. "I've asked Dr. Boxley to come see you. He's an excellent surgeon, one of the best. He has a lot of experience, and if you need to have surgery, he's your man. I am going to ask that the CT be done as quickly as possible, so Dr. Boxley can review it before he comes in to see you."

Dr. Ireland said goodbye, and left. A while later, an x-ray technician came in with two glasses of a white liquid and asked Susan to drink both glasses as quickly as possible. She told her that she would be headed downstairs for a CT scan very soon.

About one hour later, a wheelchair rolled into the room, and an orderly helped her into the chair. She was rolled to x-ray and left in a waiting room with about five other scantily clad patients. A few minutes later, the orderly wheeled her to the scanner, which looked like a giant doughnut with a stretcher in the middle of it. She was swallowed up by the scanner. The technician told her to lie quietly while she got the doctor, who would be injecting something into her IV. Immediately after the technician left, the door opened and the same nice intern who had seen her the previous evening walked in. He said hello to her, then injected a syringe-full of a clear fluid into her IV bag, smiled, and left. A moment later, the technician returned, accompanied by one of the radiologists. The radiologist started to inject a liquid into her IV line and Susan said, "I was already injected, Doctor."

"I don't know what you're talking about," the radiologist replied. "I'm the only radiologist here now, so I'm the only one doing the injections." Susan shrugged and assumed that the intern was just checking her IV again. But why had he injected into the bag this time rather that the IV line? "Oh well, another medical mystery," Susan thought, and then the noise of the CT machine running drowned out her thoughts.

The insulin dripping into Susan's veins from the IV bag caused her blood sugar to drop very slowly this time. It dropped to about 60, and then stabilized. At 60, Susan was awake, but she started to slur her speech and act abnormally. The people in the x-ray department hadn't met Susan before, so the change was not apparent to them. It was only when Susan got back to her room that the change was noticed. As before, blood was quickly drawn for a blood sugar level and an ampoule of D-50 was injected. Also as before, Susan responded to the glucose and woke up. The blood test showed a sugar level of 63.

David came to visit Susan during his lunch break. He looked terrible, Susan thought, probably from worrying about her. David was thinking the same thing about her; she looked terrible. As they were chatting, a man strode into the room.

"Good afternoon, Susan. I'm Dr. Boxley. I'm a surgeon. Dr. Ireland has asked me to come see you about a possible insulinoma."

"Good afternoon, Dr. Boxley," Susan said as she shook hands with him. Steve shook hands with her, and turned to David. "Who is this, Susan?"

"Oh, excuse me, Doctor. This is my boyfriend, David Archer." Steve had been in the process of extending his hand to David just as he heard his name. He froze for an instant and then continued to shake David's hand, but he glared at David and could only nod his greeting.

Steve turned back to Susan and continued, "Susan, I have reviewed your CT scan with the radiologist. Neither of us sees a tumor, but with your roller-coaster blood sugar levels, there is no other explainable cause for this. For now, I will give Dr. Ireland a day or two to finish his work-up, and I will get an MRI scan of your abdomen – maybe it can see the tumor that the CT can't – but I think that you'll need surgery to find the tumor."

While Steve was talking to Susan, she started to drift off to sleep. Steve called for the nurse and asked her to check Susan's blood sugar and then to give her an ampoule of D-50. The nurse complied, but said, "I'm sure she's just tired. It can't be her blood sugar; I just gave her D-50 not two hours ago." But, as she injected the glucose, Susan perked up, and the sugar level was found to be 48. Steve was very concerned by Susan's odd combination of symptoms and made arrangements to transfer her to the Intensive Care Unit where her condition could be more closely monitored.

***

At precisely 5 p.m., Steve Boxley arrived at Matthew Johnson's office to meet with the lawyer and Dr. Vernon McPeak. Steve was excited to get started on his defense, and he was quite pleased that Vernon had agreed to testify on his behalf. The two doctors shook hands warmly and exchanged pleasantries. Vernon's family was doing quite well, thank you, and Vernon was sorry to hear that Steve was now divorced. After a few minutes of reminiscing, they got down to business.

"Thank you for participating on my defense team, Vernon," Steve said.

"My pleasure, Steve. I reviewed the records that Mr. Johnson sent me and flew down here a few hours ago. Matthew and I have been talking about your treatment of Mr. Davis, and I think that this is a very defensible case.

Matthew began, "The plaintiff's attorney will try to make it seem that Mr. Davis was stable and doing so well that he could have been given heparin, and if the drug had been administered, he will claim, the pulmonary embolism would have been avoided. He's claiming wrongful death and asking for damages. So, we need to show that any prudent physician acting on behalf of Mr. Davis would have done the same thing that you did. That's a tough burden of proof, because he'll have an expert testify that he, the expert, would have started heparin, and it will be up to us to convince a jury that this option would have been bad medicine."

"Do we know who their expert will be?" asked Vernon.

"Well, they will likely use their routine, paid hack: J. Marcus Semben," replied Matthew.

Vernon continued, "What are his credentials? Does he teach residents? Has he been published in any journals or did he write any books or chapters on this issue?"

"No to all of your questions," replied Matthew. "And in fact his credentials are terrible. He's a urologist in a rural part of Georgia, and he needs to testify as a plaintiff expert to make ends meet. Here in Central Florida, he is admitted to the court as an expert, despite the fact that he is not an expert in any of the fields he testifies in, except urology. And, to tell you the truth, I really don't think he's much of an expert in urology either."

"Well," said Vernon, "then it will be our job to try to get him to say something stupid about Steve's course of treatment and then destroy what he's said with a quote from a journal or book that I wrote. That will allow me to hang him for you. So, Steve, tell me about this case."

"John Davis was in a terrible motorcycle accident. He had a collapsed lung, and his breathing failed; he had a ruptured spleen and a fractured pelvis. We took him to surgery, and after we finished with him, the orthopedic service stabilized the pelvic fractures. After a few days, we transferred him out of the ICU, and a day or two later, he had a fatal pulmonary embolism."

"Did he have any risk factors that may have predisposed him to deep venous thrombosis?"

"Well, at the time, we really couldn't talk with him because we had to put in a breathing tube. But the truth is that he didn't have any of the classic risk factors, like smoking or obesity."

"Did you discuss whether or not to treat him with heparin?"

"What difference does that make, Vernon?" Steve asked.

Vernon deferred the answer to Matthew. "Steve, if you thought about giving heparin and decided not to do it because of the risks, and if you documented that decision in the chart, that could help us immensely. You see, that would show that you weighed the risks and felt that it was in Mr. Davis' interest not to give the drug. If you didn't document your choice, then the plaintiff attorney could simply say that you didn't even consider it and that you are just a bad doctor."

"Actually, Matthew, we had a lecture on deep venous thrombosis and pulmonary embolism a day after we operated on Mr. Davis, and we did discuss our decision at that lecture. Would that help?"

"Yes," said Matthew. "We could use one of the people at the lecture as a witness. Who might we be able to use?"

"Sandy DeStefano. She's the hospital risk manager. In fact, I asked her to speak to the students and residents about this very issue. She commented that we would be screwed no matter what we had decided; if he had a complication, we would have to defend our decision. The lecture and her little speech addressed just this issue."

Vernon spoke next. "Good. When we begin to defend this case, we'll need to call her as a witness. What treatment options did you discuss in the lecture?"

"Well, we commented that he was having ongoing bleeding from the pelvic fractures, so we elected not to use the heparin. I specifically said that we chose to use TED hose and that we hoped that this option would be enough to protect him." Steve's voice dropped. "I guess that option wasn't enough, huh?"

After a few moments of silence, it appeared that the conversation had reached its end, and Steve changed the subject. "So, Vernon, how are things up in Washington? We're having a devil of a time with this malpractice insurance issue, and we're getting no real help from the state politicians or the feds."

"We have a tough time, too, but not nearly as bad as here in Florida. It's my understanding that you're losing doctors from the state. Is that true?"

"Oh, yes. They're leaving in droves, especially in South Florida. Here, we're just starting to see that happen. The first to take flight from our hospital for this reason is a neurosurgeon. Once he leaves in a few months, there will be no one doing brain surgery for more than 50 miles. We've also lost a few of our obstetricians. Let me tell you, if I had a good offer, I'd leave in a heartbeat."

The conversation drifted to small talk, and the three men eventually said their goodbyes. Steve headed home and Vernon headed for the airport to return to Washington. Steve just couldn't shake the dread that he felt. Was it from this lawsuit, or was it something else, he wondered, but certainly this suit was enough to make anyone this uneasy.

***

Susan looked around the Intensive Care Unit. The sensory stimuli were amazing. There was the constant *beep-beep* of the heart monitors, the whirring sound of the ventilators, the occasional alarms of the medical machines, and of course, the antiseptic smells. She didn't know how she was going to sleep with all of the noise; maybe that's why everyone got sleeping pills in a hospital.

A gurney rolled up next to her bed and one of the transporters asked her to slide onto it. She was headed to x-ray once again, now for an MRI scan. She was rolled to the scanner, which, it was explained to her, was a huge magnet. The technician quizzed her for a minute. If she had any metal implanted in her body, the magnet would make the metal move, and Susan could suffer grave injuries. So, she was asked if she had a pacemaker, *no*, any metal joint replacements, *no*, any previous brain surgery, *no,* or was she wearing any jewelry, *no again.* Susan was helped into the scanner, and now she understood why her friends who had undergone MRI scans said that they felt like they were going into caskets. The "tube" was only slightly larger that Susan's body, and when she was in it, she agreed that she felt like she was buried alive. She felt a claustrophobic tightening in her chest.

"I'll be talking to you during the scan," the technician said, as if he read her mind or perhaps sensed her fear; or maybe patients had actually lost it in this tube, gone mad, she thought. "And when I'm not saying anything, you'll hear music coming out of the speakers. That will take your mind off of the claustrophobia. Feel free to doze off if you can. If you speak, I can hear you — the intercom is always on."

A minute later, Susan heard a loud bang, and the technician said, "OK, Susan, that noise is the scanner at work. Just try to ignore the noise. Now, hold your breath for a few seconds. Good. Here we go."

For the next twenty minutes, the machine would turn on, and the banging would be intense, followed by absolute silence, the silence of the grave, thought Susan. The soft music did help when it came on, however, and eventually, the scan was done. Susan was placed back on the gurney and put in a waiting room with some other patients who were also waiting for transportation back to her room. While she was lying there on the gurney, a muscular man wearing a white coat walked into the waiting room. Susan thought that he looked out of place, especially when he walked over to her and started fiddling with her IV line. He was clumsy; she thought that he must have never done this before. He uncapped a syringe and injected a few drops of a clear fluid into her line, told her to have a nice day, and walked out. Soon, she was on her way back to the ICU.

As Susan was put back into her bed, her nurse noticed that the side of her face seemed paralyzed, and Susan didn't respond when the nurse talked to her. As before, blood was drawn, and D-50 was injected. When Susan awoke, she saw a crowd around her, and the first face that she recognized was that of Steve Boxley. She smiled weakly and said good morning to him. The head nurse whispered something into Steve's ear, and Steve said, "Susan, your blood sugar was 42. I've already reviewed the MRI with the radiologist, and it was completely normal. But, with your blood sugar plummeting like this, it has to be an insulinoma. I'm recommending surgery. I'll come back later today and discuss it with you."

David came in to visit Susan at lunchtime, and Susan told him about her morning as he turned pale with fear. She recounted the MRI scan and the man who had flushed her IV line in the waiting room. She commented that he had seemed so out of place there, almost as an aside, as if it were merely tangential to the actual story but something that just occurred to her. David was worried for her, and he tried to figure out a way to tell Susan that he was participating in a lawsuit against Dr. Boxley. He decided that he just couldn't tell her.

David had stopped at a fast food place on his way to the hospital, and he unpacked the greasy feast for the two of them. They ate quietly, and as they finished, Dr. Boxley came into the ICU.

"Good afternoon, Susan," he said and smiled, but he glared at David for a second, then said hello to him as well. "Susan, we have a problem. While all of the imaging tests we've done have failed to find the tumor, we believe that you have an insulinoma, and we believe that it needs to be removed. I've spoken with Dr. Ireland, and he is finished with the testing. He has no other diagnostic ideas, and he feels that we should proceed with exploratory surgery. The only other suggestion that I have would be for another opinion, by an endocrinologist. That's a doctor who specializes in medical disease of the endocrine glands, like the pancreas and thyroid. I've reviewed your case with one of our staff endocrinologists, and he says that he'd be happy to meet you if you'd like, but based on the CT scan and MRI, as well as your symptoms, he would have no recommendation but to operate on you. Would you like him to come to see you?"

"No, Doctor, I trust you. I'd like to get better and get out of here. When do you want to operate?"

"Tomorrow, if that's OK with you."

"Let's do it, then."

That night, Susan had a lot of problems falling asleep. She asked for a sleeping pill. The nurse gave her one, and twenty minutes later, she was almost asleep. She heard a metal pan clanging near her bed and struggled to open her eyes. A janitor was mopping the floor around her bed, and she caught a glimpse of his face. How funny, she thought. The guy mopping the floor looked just like the man who had flushed her IV line earlier in the day. She drifted off to sleep just as the janitor furtively looked around and realized that he was alone in her cubicle, pulled out a syringe and unloaded it into her IV line.

Thirty minutes later, Susan's nurse came to check on her. She was snoring, but the nurse was concerned. The corners of her mouth were at odd angles, and when she tried to wake Susan up, she couldn't. She shouted for help and blood was drawn. After three ampoules of D-50, Susan started to stir, and the blood sugar test showed a level of 32. The nurse couldn't understand what Susan was talking about, something about the janitor flushing her IV line in the X-ray department.

Dr. Boxley's beeper went off at midnight, and he called the ICU immediately. "Doctor, Susan Parks had another spell. Her blood sugar was 32. We gave her three ampoules of D-50, and now she's awake and lucid. I know that you're planning to operate on her tomorrow, but we're afraid for her. Do you have any ideas?"

"Yes. I want you to inject three more ampoules of D-50 directly into her IV bag, so she gets a constant infusion of high-dose glucose. I think that will protect her until we operate on her." Steve thanked the nurse and tried unsuccessfully to get back to sleep. Just before the alarm went off, he fell into a deep slumber and dreamed of things he did not want to remember, especially the terrible darkness that he could not see through in his dream, and he awakened with a start when the radio came on.

CHAPTER 15

Central Florida Times

Tampa Bay, FL

By Mark Rodriguez

Dr. Bob Carney is a world-class neurosurgeon. He has published research articles in many journals, and he is widely respected. In a field that is already shorthanded, Dr. Carney provides neurosurgical services to the entire Central Florida area. He stopped doing spinal surgery about six years ago, preferring to leave that to the orthopedic doctors, which allowed him to concentrate on the area where the need for his services was greatest, brain surgery. You see, he is the only doctor doing brain surgery in the entire area, for fifty miles around. Dr. Carney announced last week that he will be moving to New Mexico at the end of the year. He was willing to disclose his reasoning.

"The decision is quite painful: my family is here, and our roots are here. My son attends the University of Central Florida, and my daughter goes to business school at Florida Academy. We've lived here for 18 years. But this decision was purely economic. Last year, I paid $35,000 for malpractice insurance. That seems like a lot of money, but I was willing to accept that rate to protect my patients. However, I was notified by my insurance carrier that they would not renew my policy, and when I was finally able to locate a new policy, it cost me $185,000. Now, you tell me how I can make a living with an insurance premium like that."

I asked Dr. Carney if he would be willing to share his malpractice suit history with us. He was willing to do so, and continued, "I have been in practice for 18 years in this area, and as time went on, I began to limit my practice to brain surgery. I do about 150 major brain operations a year. So, in those 18 years, I have done more than 2500 operations. I have been sued four times. Three have been dismissed. The last one went as far as the discovery phase, the stage at which each side is able to question the other under oath. The case involved a gunshot wound to the head. The patient was shot outside of a bar; I was called and responded immediately. I could not speak to the patient because he was unconscious. His parents had been notified by the police and were on their way to the hospital. There was no way to reach them and no time to wait. We took him directly to the operating room. After hours of surgery, we were able to save his life, but unfortunately, he had permanent brain damage. He required weeks of therapy and will always need attendants on a daily basis. His parents sued me for 'wrongful life.' Their attorney said that I should have let him die, and by operating on him, I had exposed them to tremendous medical and chronic-care bills, and that I should pay for those costs.

"Their expert witness was a paid liar and agreed with the parents' attorney that I should have let him die. They wheeled this poor boy into the deposition, and my insurance company panicked and settled for seven hundred and fifty thousand dollars.

"I don't think that's the way the system is designed to work. So, I'm going to New Mexico, where the malpractice system is not broken, and I'll be paying $30,000 per year for insurance. Maybe there, my work will be appreciated."

State Congressman Bob Hugoll has met with the State House and has sponsored, along with three of his fellow representatives, the Angel Smith Act. This legislation will serve to reform our badly broken medical malpractice system, and it is gaining steam in the legislature. This paper stands firmly behind reform of this system, and stands with Representative Hugoll in his efforts to salvage the quality of medicine practiced in Central Florida.

There are multiple parts to the Angel Smith Act, and in summary they will control the runaway payments to the attorneys who represent plaintiffs in malpractice cases, limit the expert witnesses for the plaintiff to doctors who live and work in the geographic area where the patient care took place, limit expert witnesses to doctors who actually practice in the field about which they are testifying, cap non-economic damages, make the plaintiff's attorneys responsible for the defense costs if the plaintiff loses, and finally, try to create a no-fault type of system to replace the current one.

Since the start of this crisis, Central Florida has lost at least twenty five doctors who have either retired prematurely or left the state. When a doctor retires early, he does not try to replace himself with a new doctor, and the community suffers.

Please contact your representative and voice your support for the Angel Smith Act.

CHAPTER 16

Steve stopped into the preoperative holding room to say hello to Susan. He took her hand and gently told her that everything would be alright. He let her give David a kiss goodbye, and then Steve and the anesthesiologist wheeled Susan into the operating room. The anesthesiologist gave Susan an injection of Versed, and she was asleep in seconds. Two minutes later, she had a breathing tube in her trachea and a machine was breathing for her. The nurses wasted no motion. Susan was undressed, a urinary catheter was placed into her bladder, and the entire abdomen and chest area was washed with an antiseptic scrub. Meanwhile, the anesthesia team placed a large tube into her jugular vein, and through that tube they inserted a balloon-tipped catheter and let the blood flow carry it gently into her heart. This allowed the doctors to measure the pressure in the chambers of Susan's heart. That way, if she got into trouble from bleeding, there would be plenty of warning. Electrocardiogram leads were attached to various places on Susan's torso so that her heart could be monitored during the surgery. A pad was fixed to Susan's thigh to act as a ground for the electrosurgical unit that Steve would use in the surgical dissection. Finally, sterile surgical drapes were placed over Susan's abdomen and chest to create a sterile area for Steve to work in.

Steve and Mark Land burst into the room with their arms and hands held high. The sterile nurse gave them towels to dry their hands, and then she put gowns and gloves on both of them. Mark made an incision that ran from one side of Susan's body to the other, just under the ribcage. He asked the nurse for the electrosurgical knife, and the fat, muscle and peritoneum fell away. A special retractor was placed into Susan's abdomen; it was fixed to the operating table so it wouldn't move. The intestines were moved to the sides, and the colon was moved to allow the doctors to see the pancreas. Steve took over and began systematically evaluating the entire pancreas. When he was finished, he told Mark that he could find nothing: no masses, no tumors, not even any irregularities. He let Mark explore the pancreas as well, and likewise, Mark felt nothing abnormal. Steve next called the x-ray department and asked the radiologist on-call to come to the operating room with an ultrasound machine and an ultrasound technologist. They were there within five minutes. Steve then evaluated the entire pancreas with the ultrasound; but again, nothing amiss. The x-ray people left the room, and Steve completed his abdominal evaluation by checking all of the intestines, the major blood vessels in the abdomen, both kidneys, the liver and gallbladder, the spleen, and the female organs. All were normal. Steve stripped off his gloves and told Mark to close.

Steve walked into the waiting room and looked for David Archer. He was sitting at the back of the room with an older man and woman, to whom Steve introduced himself. They in turn told Steve that they were Susan's parents. Steve was relieved; he could talk to them and avoid looking at David, the lawyer whose fingerprints were all over the suit against him.

"As you probably know, your daughter was admitted here at Middle Florida Hospital because of a very low blood sugar. She kept having episodes of unexplained hypoglycemia. It was our feeling that the only explanation would be an insulinoma, a tumor that manufactures insulin and secretes it whether the body needs it or not. Her CT scan and MRI were both negative for a tumor, but the final test is exploratory surgery. We just did that, and fortunately or unfortunately, we found nothing to explain the low blood sugars. Her examination was normal. Regarding the surgery, she should do just fine; but regarding the blood sugar problem, I have no suggestions. It will be up to her attending physician, Dr. Jay Ireland. I suspect that Dr. Ireland will call in an endocrinologist to help." Steve gave Susan's parents his card and told them to call him if they had any questions.

"I'm going back now, so I can be in the recovery room when Susan wakes up."

Susan was brought to the recovery room shortly after Steve finished speaking with her parents. She began coming out of the anesthesia and moaned in pain. The recovery room nurses gave her a pain shot, and as Dr. Boxley had ordered, checked her blood sugar. It was 85, perfect. After about twenty minutes, Susan began to awaken and Steve was there to speak with her. He told her about the absence of any findings to explain her low blood sugars, and he told her that he had spoken with Dr. Ireland and that they would have an endocrinologist come to see her the next day. Susan became rather distraught because she had gone through major surgery only to find out that there was still no plausible explanation for her problems. She began to cry softly as Steve left to make his rounds.

About an hour after Susan got to the recovery room, she was awake and comfortable enough to return to her room. As she was wheeled into the ICU, she was greeted by her nurse and helped back into her bed. The nurse scurried about, rehooking Susan's monitor leads, straightening out her IV lines, and setting up the self-directed infusion pump for her pain medications. "Susan, this is called a PCA pump; PCA stands for patient-controlled-analgesia. This push button that I've placed in your hand will allow you to give yourself a shot of morphine directly into your vein to help with the pain. Be careful not to lie on the tubing of the IV or to crimp it in any way, because that will stop the flow of the IV and prohibit the morphine from entering your bloodstream." The nurse intentionally crimped the tubing, and the machine let out a shrill alarm. "Do you hear that? That is the alarm that tells us that your IV is blocked. If you hear it, check around yourself and make sure that you're not blocking the tubing yourself. Now, push the button." Susan pushed the button, heard a *beep-beep* from the pump, and in a moment, felt the pain relief of the morphine hitting her bloodstream. The nurse smiled as Susan began to drift off to sleep, patted her on the head and walked out of the room.

***

Jake Morris was at a meeting with his two partners, Sam Cuney and Jay Howe, as well as their lawyer, Craig Sharp. Jake had a copy of the most recent article from the Central Florida Times on his desk, and he was pounding the desktop. "We are in deep trouble if this continues. We need our own cause that will deflect attention away from the malpractice crisis. Right now, with the Angel Smith Act, and this most recent article about a malpractice crisis, I think we could lose if an amendment regarding tort reform to the Florida Constitution was proposed. We need to find something to strike back with."

Jay Howe spoke up. "You know Jake, if we had a malpractice case that was so horrible, and the doctor's hands were so bloody that we could cause the public to be outraged, we could counter the actions of the doctors."

Jake smiled. He had led Howe right to the trough. "Yes, Jay. I agree. If we take in a case like that, let's use it in the media."

Jake dismissed the meeting, and a few minutes later he was sitting with Semben and Large. "Gentlemen, it's time to move our schedule ahead. Stan, how are things going with your project?"

Large grinned at the thought that murder could be referred to as a project. "Fine, Sir. Ms. Parks was admitted to Middle Florida Hospital a few days ago with a very low blood sugar. We have managed to cause a number of episodes of dangerously low sugars, so much so that they did an exploratory surgery on her to see if she had a tumor in her belly. She is recovering from surgery, and we plan to cause a few more episodes before we terminate this project."

Jake asked Semben if the cause of her spells could ever be traced to foul play. "I don't see how, Jake," Semben replied. "In order to do that, someone would need to suspect foul play in the first place. There is no reason to suspect it because Susan is a diabetic, and diabetics have problems controlling their sugars. It's the nature of the beast. Furthermore, we're injecting the insulin directly into her IV line, so there are no needle holes on her body to make anyone, especially the coroner, suspicious. Finally, the one time we did inject her, we did it under her tongue, and that injection is untraceable."

Jake looked around the room. "We need to move quickly and terminate Susan tonight."

The men around the table nodded. Susan's fate was sealed. She would die tonight.

***

Susan awoke about 8 p.m. and looked around. She was in her ICU bed at Middle Florida Hospital. The lights were turned down, and the soft luminosity from the fluorescent fixture above her head gave everything in the room a yellow glow. She heard the muffled beeping of her heart monitor and the quiet voices and occasional laugh coming from the nurses' station. She reached up and touched her belly, and the sharp pain of the incision reminded her that she had vowed not to touch there again. She pushed the button for the PCA and felt the welcome rush of the morphine into her veins. Just then, her nurse slipped into her room and noticed that Susan's eyes were open. "Good evening, honey," the nurse said. "How do you feel?"

"Not bad, thanks," Susan replied.

"Well, honey, I need to draw your blood to check your sugar." Susan gritted her teeth and extended her arm. The nurse skillfully drew a vial of blood on the first try. "Your boyfriend called. He said he'll be here to visit you in about an hour. He needed to work late. He said to tell you he loves you." The nurse smiled broadly and left the room. All was quiet again.

The door of the elevator opened on the 11th floor and two men got out. One was wearing a shirt and tie with a white coat. A stethoscope hung from one of the oversized pockets of the coat. He waited while his partner walked down the closed C-wing and retrieved the coveralls he had stolen days before, the bucket and mop that were stashed with the clothing completed the outfit. Semben and Large then returned to the elevator and went directly to the ICU.

Large walked toward the utility room and filled the bucket with warm water, then started leisurely mopping the floor of the ICU. Fortunately, everything was quiet and the nurses were all behind the desk, watching the monitors and chatting.

Semben headed over to the nurses' station and sat down in front of the chart rack. He knew that he couldn't get away with this during the day shift because all of the nurses knew the doctors, but on the night shift, the nurses rarely knew who the doctors were. Generally they dealt with them by phone. He guessed right. None of the nurses challenged his right to be there. He reached for the first chart that he saw and busied himself reading it. Suddenly, he looked at the assembled nurses and started shouting, "Why wasn't I called about these lab values. Who's in charge here?"

One of the nurses identified herself as the charge nurse, and the others cowered. Semben demanded that they call the x-ray department for a chest x-ray report and call the laboratory for the most recent lab results. In doing this, he managed to get all of the nurses scurrying around. This left no one to watch the patients, and that left Large time to slip into Susan's room. Susan was still groggy and watched in horror as the maintenance man took her IV line into his hand and flushed a full syringe of liquid into it. The man stepped out of the room and Susan tried to scream, but in her state, it only sounded like a whimper. The nurses couldn't hear her over the noise that Semben was making.

The maintenance man smiled at the nurses and the obnoxious doctor and pushed his bucket out of the ICU. Semben suddenly got up and told the nurses to call him with the results of the tests, and he, too, left the ICU. The nurses looked at each other: who was this doctor, and how could they call him with results when they didn't even know who he was? They started to giggle, and suddenly, everything was back to normal.

Susan's nurse wandered into Susan's room and spoke immediately. "I checked your blood sugar result, and it was 90, perfect." She saw that Susan was distraught and asked what was wrong.

Susan tried to speak, but couldn't. She slurred her speech and muttered, "The cleaning man...my IV," and lapsed into unconsciousness. The nurse shrugged her shoulders — assuming that Susan had just given herself a dose of morphine — making the perfectly reasonable assumption that her babbling was the result of drug–induced hallucinations, and left the room.

Semben and Large stashed the mop and bucket, the coveralls, the stolen ID and the white lab coat in the closet on the 11th floor. They knew that it would be months before they were found, and by then, there would be no suspicion, just supplies stored in the wrong place. They headed for the parking lot.

About 45 minutes later, David walked into the ICU and said hello to the nurses. He walked into Susan's room and saw her sleeping. After a few minutes of trying to awaken her, David called for the nurse. "Help in here. I think something's wrong. Help." The nurses all came running and quickly realized that something was terribly wrong. They drew blood and began injecting D-50 into her veins. One ampoule, then another, then another. No response. The monitor began to show a very slow heart beat, then a flat line. One of the nurses called a code and another placed a breathing tube into Susan's lungs. A third started to do CPR. Susan was young, and her heart started beating again, but the damage was already done. Her brain had been without oxygen for too long, and this time she wouldn't wake up. A stat page was placed to Dr. Boxley, and he was told to come to the ICU immediately. Susan was placed on a ventilator, and medications were started to support her blood pressure and pulse. Soon, her vital signs were stable, but there was no sign of consciousness.

Steve rushed into the ICU and went immediately to Susan's bedside. "What happened here?" he asked.

"We don't know," the charge nurse responded. "I checked on her and she seemed upset, babbling something about the maintenance man and her IV, then she drifted off to sleep. I thought that was from the morphine. A few minutes later, her boyfriend arrived and found her comatose. We ran a code, and restored her vitals, but she hasn't awakened."

Just then the computer printer came to life and printed out Susan's blood sugar test that had been done just before the code was started. The result was 6, arguably the lowest value anyone in the room had ever seen.

Steve walked to the desk and called Susan's parents to give them the terrible news. Then he sat in the dark weeping silently.

***

At precisely 7 am, Steve sat down in the ICU conference room with Susan's parents and David Archer. He began by expressing his deepest distress over Susan's condition, and then started to explain the hopelessness of the situation.

"We do not know how long Susan was unconscious due to low blood sugar. What we do know is that 45 minutes before David found her; the nurse checked the blood sugar and it was normal. So, in that short time, the blood sugar plummeted. None of us has ever seen anything like this happen before. A short time ago, I asked one of the neurologists to do an electroencephalogram, or EEG; this would determine whether or not Susan has any brain wave activity." Steve spread the printout of the EEG on the table, and even the untrained eyes of those assembled could see what Steve was about to point out. "As you see, the EEG is flat line. There's no easy way to say this: Susan is brain dead. The only thing that I can offer you now is the comfort of knowing that she felt no pain, and ask if you'd be willing to give the gift of life to other people. When a person is admitted to the hospital, they are specifically asked if they are organ donors. Susan said that she was and signed the appropriate forms. If you would allow us to do so, we could proceed with organ donation."

Susan's parents were inconsolable, but David spoke up. "If we allow organ donation, will we still be able to do an autopsy?"

"Yes, absolutely," replied Steve.

Susan's parents thought about it for another moment or two and agreed. "Yes, Dr. Boxley," said Susan's mother. "We would like for Susan to live on in another person. Please arrange for organ donation."

Steve stood up and walked away. He called the coroner's office and the Center for Organ Sharing, a nationwide system for organ harvesting and transplantation. He returned to the conference room and told Susan's parents that the organ harvesting team would be in to meet with them in about an hour, and that the coroner's office would send a medical examiner to be present for the operation. After the procedure, the coroner's office would take Susan's body and complete the autopsy. They could have the body in about two days for the funeral.

Later that evening, a surreal operation took place. Susan was wheeled into the operating room, and four surgeons scrubbed. The anesthesiologist turned on the gases. "I know that she's brain dead, and therefore can't feel anything, so I really shouldn't need to use anesthesia gas, but I'd feel guilty if I didn't," he said. Her abdomen and chest were prepped for the procedure, and the abdominal incision was reopened. Then, the chest was opened. The kidney transplant team started first, carefully removing first the right then the left kidney. The arteries and veins were carefully tied to prevent bleeding. Because the admitting diagnosis was possible insulinoma, a tumor of the pancreas, even though Steve had found no tumor, the team couldn't take a chance on transplanting a pancreas with a tumor into a recipient. Therefore, the pancreas was not removed. Next, the liver was taken. Two of the surgeons took the organs to a sterile table in the back of the room and started flushing the organs with saline solutions. When they were done, the organs were packed into coolers and the two men left the room. The cardiopulmonary transplant team moved forward and carefully removed the lungs and heart from the chest. Finally, when they were done, the anesthesiologist turned off all of his machines and looked at his watch. "Time of death, 11:54 p.m." The surgical staff stepped away from the table, and the medical examiner wrote a note in the chart attesting that he saw nothing to explain Susan's death during this procedure. He then took over, and the assistants from his office placed Susan's body onto a stretcher and took it to a waiting hearse for transport to the coroner's office.

Steve and the transplant coordinator went out to the waiting room and spoke with Susan's parents and David. They both expressed their condolences, and the coordinator told them what was to become of the organs. "I know that you are grieving, but you and Susan have given the greatest gift of all to a number of people. We've already found matches for the organs. One of Susan's kidneys will be going to a fifteen year-old boy in Kansas and the other to a forty-three year-old woman in New York. Susan's heart will be transplanted into a thirty-one year old man who suffered from a viral infection of his heart last year and has been in ICU here at Middle Florida Hospital for the past two months. Susan's lungs will be transplanted together in a fifty year-old woman in Alabama. I hope the knowledge that you have given the gift of life to so many people helps you find some comfort at this time."

***

David walked into the offices of Morris, Cuney and Howe the next morning and went straight to Jake Morris' office. Jake was aware of Susan's death and offered David his condolences. David thanked him and told him about the funeral arrangements. Then he continued. "Mr. Morris, I think that we need to take a good, hard look at Susan's care at Middle Florida Hospital. She was young and healthy, and she shouldn't have died. I think that there may have been some medical malpractice involved in her death. I'd like to find out for sure."

Morris smiled inside. His plan was working. "David, I can't say that you're wrong. I've never heard of a similar case, and you may be correct. Why don't you get Susan's mother and father to come to the office as soon as they're willing, and we can all discuss it."

"Mr. Morris, her parents are so angry that they are willing to come in now."

David left Jake's office and called Susan's parents. They came immediately, and shortly all of them were seated in Jake's office.

"Mr. and Mrs. Parks, first let me express my deepest condolences," said Jake. "Susan was one of our finest employees, and we always thought that she'd go far here.

Why, in fact, just the other day, my partners and I were discussing Susan's future in the accounting department. This is a tragic loss."

Mr. Parks tried to speak. "Mr. Morris," he said, but Jake cut him off.

"Please call me Jake, sir."

"Jake, my wife and I are very concerned that Susan did not have to die. The doctors spoke to us and said that they had never seen a case like this. Certainly, if they were better doctors, they would have known what they were looking at. Furthermore, that Dr. Boxley did an operation that clearly was unnecessary. Then, while she was in the intensive care unit, the intensive care unit for christsake, she died while the nurses were not watching her. David thinks that we may have a case, and he suggested that we speak with you. He said that even though he handles cases for your practice, that you might be willing to take this one yourself."

"Mr. Parks, I would be honored to help you." Jake thought that this would be a good time to malign Dr. Boxley. "As a matter of fact, I think that this Dr. Boxley is a butcher. We are suing him now because of the death of a man in a motorcycle accident. I would be pleased to hurt Dr. Boxley as much as he hurt your daughter. I will be sure to have David sit second chair to help me every step of the way. Now, if you would go with David, he'll have you sign the necessary papers, and we can get started."

David took Mr. and Mrs. Parks into the conference room that he shared with the other associates and had them sign the contract for Morris, Cuney and Howe to be the exclusive law firm representing their interests, and the medical record release and the form authorizing Morris, Cuney and Howe to take thirty five percent of any settlement that would be reached. Then, David returned to his office and Susan's parents left for home.

A flight left from the Middle Florida International Airport at 10:55 that night. On it were J. Marcus Semben and Stan Large. Semben was returning home for awhile. He had his work cut out for him — he needed to prepare to testify against Dr. Boxley on behalf of Nadine Davis — and Large just needed to get out of town for a few weeks until Susan Parks was safely six feet underground.

***

Susan's funeral three days later was a mob scene. She was a recent graduate from the Business Institute of Florida and had made many friends there. It seemed that all of them came. Many of the professors cancelled class to attend as well. Morris, Cuney and Howe was a large company, and Jake Morris closed the office for the morning to allow the employees to be there. Finally, Susan was part of a large family, and they came from all over the country. Steve Boxley felt drawn to the funeral, and sitting there, he estimated that about 250 people were in attendance.

After the opening remarks from the minister, David was asked to give a eulogy. He stood behind the lectern, visibly shaken, and began: "Susan was my best friend. I have known her since college, and we lived together. We were just starting to discuss marriage and children. We already had bought a home together, and I thought that our lives were just beginning. It seemed that we would have so much time together. How wrong could I be? In a few short days, she went from a vibrant, healthy young woman, to an ill, sick and finally dead young woman.

"For now, we are comforted to know that Susan gave the ultimate gift of life to four other people, and I was told this morning that all four of the organ recipients are doing quite well. Susan's mother and father have already received notes of gratitude from the families of the recipients, and I'm sure that when they are able, the beneficiaries will write to them themselves.

At this point David broke down crying and needed a few moments to compose himself. He looked out over the crowd and saw Steve Boxley, and the hate that he felt for Steve was enough to clear his head and let him continue.

"We don't know what happened to Susan, but I vow that we will find out." He shot a menacing look in Steve's direction. "I hope that we can all learn from Susan that every day is precious and that we must love one another with all our hearts. We never know when our lives will end, so we need to live each day as if it's our last. Goodbye, Susan, I love you." Then David broke down again and was helped off of the pulpit by the funeral director.

Steve looked at the gentleman next to him, an older gentleman who looked somehow out of place, neither resembling the family members or like a lawyer or student. "How did you know Susan?" Steve asked, because he felt compelled to ask when the man looked at him and smiled wanly, as if lost in thought and wondering what Steve was doing here too.

"Susan was in a number of my classes at the Business Institute of Florida, and we became friends, she was friends with my daughter and the rest of my family too. I felt very close to her and David, and was stunned to hear that she died. In fact, I saw her just a week or two ago, and she looked great. How did you know her?"

"I was one of her doctors at the hospital. I only knew her for a short time, but I really liked her, and I was devastated when she died. I came here today to pay my respects."

The teacher held out his hand, and introduced himself. "Tyler McNab. Call me Ty."

Steve responded in kind. "Steve Boxley. Call me Steve."

"Steve Boxley, you say? I recognize your name. Does your daughter attend school at University of Central Florida?"

"Why, yes, she does," Steve replied. "She's a business major. Do you know her?"

"Yes Steve, I do. I teach there on occasion, the upper level business classes. She's in my Accounting 404 class. She's quite bright; I think she'll make a fine accountant.

"Well, you must be the Dr. McNab that she raves about all the time. She says that all of her successes are your fault."

Ty got a serious expression on his face and looked Steve in the eye. "Steve, why did this lovely girl have to die?"

"I wish I knew, Ty." Steve misted up again, and then he brushed away the tear. "I truly don't know. I've never seen a case like this before. She seemed so healthy, and I have absolutely no explanation for her blood sugars to be so unstable. In fact, just 45 minutes before she had a blood sugar value of six, it had been quite normal. In my entire medical career, I've never seen a blood sugar fall that fast. I don't even know if it has ever been recorded that it could plummet that fast. Huh, well I guess it can."

After another eulogy by a family friend, the service ended. The crowd walked the short distance from the chapel to the gravesite, where the minister said a few words, then Mrs. Parks untied a rope that allowed the casket to slowly descend into the ground. Mrs. Parks fell to her knees and needed to be helped up by her family. The crowd slowly dispersed, and as they left, they filed past Mr. and Mrs. Parks and gave their condolences. Steve and Ty walked up to them together and said their goodbyes. They headed to their cars and shook hands, each going his own way.

Steve drove slowly back to the hospital, a place that he was quickly learning to dread, the place where people died inexplicably or where a good medical decision could be turned around on a whim to look like the worst decision in the world. His hands trembled on the wheel, and they would not stop.

CHAPTER 17

The hearing room at the Florida state capital building is quite imposing. The committee sits up on a raised platform, on executive chairs behind a polished cherry wood table. They look out over the assembled audience from on high, giving a sense of the power they hold over those who come before them. The witnesses sit at a table on the ground level, on uncomfortable stackable chairs, and the audience sits on wooden benches, like penitents who must be reminded to pay attention with discomfort. Members of the media sit on the floor in front of the witness table, with microphones and cameras pointing towards the committee. The members of the committee each have name plaques in front of them, and the state cable television cameras are trained on the committee members at all times. The members had learned long ago to preen for the cameras, as their constituents may be watching, so they came dressed in expensive suits and all seemed to be Shakespearean actors in a tragedy as they sat on high in serious consideration of all matters that passed before them, a kind of heightened sense of themselves spewing out over the audience. Some of the members really don't care about the nature of the testimony they are hearing of course, but the important thing is the opportunity to get on camera. If they can berate and embarrass the witness and hence enhance the notion of their own importance, power, and grave intelligence, so much the better.

"Hear ye, hear ye, the House Committee on Medical and Energy Issues is now in session, the Honorable Michael Bloch presiding. Come to order, please," hollered the page to open this particular session.

Bloch banged the gavel a few times, and the room quieted down. He looked directly into the cable news camera, barely looking at the people in the audience or at the witness stand. "Good afternoon, ladies and gentleman. Welcome to the House Committee on Medical and Energy Issues hearings on malpractice issues. We have heard that there is a malpractice crisis brewing in our state, and while I must say that I am unaware of any significant problems, the insurance companies and the doctors have demanded that we explore this issue. The speaker of the house has referred this issue to this committee, and it will be taken up here. Now, I need to establish ground rules for our hearings. First, I will tolerate absolutely no outbursts from the audience. Any noise, and I will clear this room. Second, each witness will be limited to three minutes, and then each member of the committee will have the opportunity to ask questions of the witness. No witnesses will be allowed the opportunity to speak again after the question and answer period. Understood? Good, then let's begin. First witness, please identify yourself."

A tall man with silver hair and an impeccable gray suit stood up and walked with a certain elegance to the witness stand. "Mr. Chairman, members of the committee, I am Robert Landmark. I am the CEO of the Florida Specialists Insurance Trust. We are a malpractice insurance company that specializes in insurance for surgical specialists. As such, we recognize that we cover high risk doctors, and our underwriters charge a premium to cover these doctors. While each specialty is different, the average policy that we wrote last year cost $41,000. Because of the crisis that is underway, we have had to drop about one third of the doctors that we cover, and the average policy for the rest has risen to $73,000. The doctors who were dropped are having a difficult or impossible time getting insurance now, but that is something that I'm sure you'll hear about from other witnesses. My concern is the terrible rise in insurance premiums that these doctors face. Furthermore, the premium that we have charged really is not enough to cover our costs, but we think that if it's any higher, the insurance commissioner of the state will refuse to allow us to continue to offer insurance. So, we actually take a loss on every policy we write. Our biggest concern is the runaway settlements that have been occurring. At this point, we can't even begin to estimate what we will need to pay for any given case; juries simply seem to be throwing money at the plaintiff without regard for the actual injuries or expenses. Thank you for the opportunity to be heard."

Bloch began, "Mr. Landmark, if your insurance company can't calculate the risk, how can you stay in business? The fact that you are remaining in business means to me that you are lying to this committee, that you are actually using this crisis to get us to allow you to further raise your rates. I think that your insurance company got caught with your pants down when your investments lost value in the stock market, and now you want to recoup your losses by blaming the lawyers."

"Mr. Bloch, with all due respect, that is ludicrous. We are a professional company, with certified underwriters. They simply can't predict the risk because every settlement makes no sense when compared to the last one. We need a system that gives us stability."

Bob Hugoll spoke next. "Mr. Landmark, I respectfully disagree with Mr. Bloch. I agree that the legal climate in Florida is terrible, and that fact is evidenced by the mass defection of insurance companies from the state. I would like to thank you for not leaving, and I will do everything in my power to make it profitable once again for insurance companies to work in Florida."

"Will the next witness please step forward?" The chairman smirked ever so slightly as he said this, but it was not lost on Bob Hugoll.

Jake Morris stood up and made his way to the stand, looking something like a gangster in blue pinstripes. "Gentlemen, my name is Jake Morris. I am a partner in the law firm of Morris, Cuney and Howe, and, as you may know, we represent people injured by doctors and hospitals. We serve a very necessary function in society. Without us, the doctors would be free to hurt patients without any oversight. Please don't take offense, but the legislature has not passed any meaningful legislation to stop bad doctors, and if it were not for firms like mine, they never would be taken out of practice. By filing lawsuits against those doctors who injure unsuspecting patients, we are getting restitution for those who have been hurt."

"Mr. Morris, I'm Bob Hugoll. I must ask if you really believe what you just said. Can you really sit there with a straight face and ask me to believe that when you take up to forty percent of the settlement, you are helping anyone but yourself?"

"Mr. Hugoll, you must understand that I work on a contingency basis. If I take a case and lose, I will pay all of the expenses and not make one cent. This is a tremendous risk, and, therefore, if I win, I must be able to reap a significant reward. That's only fair. Remember that the lawyers who defend the doctors get paid by the hour, and they get paid whether or not they win."

"Mr. Morris, I'm Marsha Pitts. I'm a businesswoman, and all I know is that these ridiculous, frivolous lawsuits are driving the cost of business for healthcare providers through the roof. At our recent hearings, we heard a nursing home owner testify that two years ago, the cost of liability insurance was about $60 per bed per month. Now, he's paying $400 per bed per month, and the cost is so high, that he can't pass it on to the residents of his nursing home. It is my belief that rapidly rising insurance premiums are directly related to the flurry of lawsuits that your firm has filed against nursing homes. Thanks to you and your colleagues, most of the nursing homes in this state will likely close within the next three years."

"Ms Pitts, I see things differently. To my view, these nursing homes are dangerous, and if we cause some of them to close, we are doing the unsuspecting public a service."

In closing out Jake Morris' testimony, Mike Bloch, being careful not to look in Bob Hugoll's direction, said, "Mr. Morris, we appreciate your input, and I, for one, deeply appreciate your position on this matter. Thank you, sir." He then looked at the witnesses and asked Peter Smith to be seated at the witness stand. "Mr. Smith, thank you for coming. Please begin."

A man who looked out of place among all the expensive suits in his off the rack sports coat and tie rose self-consciously and made his way to the stand and sat down.

"Thank you Mr. Chairman. I am Peter Smith, my daughter Angel died as a direct result of the medical malpractice crisis in this state. Had there been no crisis, two of the five doctors at my wife's OB/GYN office would not have left town. Then, when we rushed to Middle Florida Hospital, she would have been cared for properly. Instead, there were no obstetricians available, and no surgeon was willing to help out because of the malpractice risk. Florida is a great state, and offers much to entice people to come here. If we wanted to, we could lead the country in medical excellence. Instead, we let parasites like Mr. Morris," and he pointed at Morris as he said this, "sue the medical profession out of existence, and my daughter died because of that. These doctors need relief, and they need it now."

Mr. Bloch responded in a clinical tone, "Mr. Smith, if I'm not mistaken, you were notified by letter that the obstetric group that your wife used was no longer working at Middle Florida Hospital, and that, even in an emergency, you were to go to Samaritan Hospital. Don't you feel that you were, at least in part, responsible for your daughter's death?"

Bob Hugoll jumped to his feet, his face deep red with rage. "Don't answer that, Mr. Smith. Mr. Chairman, you should be ashamed of yourself. This man has lost his daughter, and regardless what he read in a letter, this is the United States of America. Something is terribly wrong if a woman in labor can go to a major hospital and be denied obstetric care because of a lack of doctors; especially if that lack of doctors is due to frivolous lawsuits filed by out of control lawyers."

The onlookers had previously only murmured politely, quieting immediately when the participants in the hearing spoke, but now the noise from the audience in the gallery was deafening, and despite the banging of his gavel, Mike Bloch could not get the room quiet. "This hearing is adjourned," he yelled in frustration, the slightest hint of fear crossing his face, and he rose to his feet and strode out of the room.

CHAPTER 18

Things slowly began to get back to normal for Steve Boxley, except that he was now researching the pulmonary embolism issue for his impending trial regarding the death of John Davis. He started seeing a psychologist about the panic attacks, and a low dose of Prozac along with some psychotherapy seemed to be the perfect combination. He was even dating once in a while, the sister of a colleague he met at a party or the waitress at the deli where he ate lunch sometimes.

The trial date for the Davis case loomed ahead, and he dreaded the daily mail delivery, knowing that eventually he would be getting papers regarding the death of Susan Parks. To make matters worse, the malpractice crisis gloom was settling over the medical community and his fellow medical professionals were growing nearly as morose as he was at times. It was the only topic of discussion in the doctors' dining room and the surgeons' lounge. The predicament was definitely going national. Ten states in addition to Florida had a bona fide crisis situation, and just one week before, Nevada University / Las Vegas Trauma Center, the fifth largest trauma center in the nation, had closed its doors. When the trauma team was interviewed, the only reason for the closure was the malpractice situation. Over half of the surgeons could not obtain insurance, and the hospital could not afford to pay its policy bill. Unbelievably, when the president of the Nevada Trial Lawyers Association was interviewed, his response was to blame the doctors, saying that they were greedy and were simply not willing to pay premiums that would protect their patients. Of course, that gave the doctors a good laugh, however bleak the joke, while they were packing up and moving out of the state — many had been thrown into bankruptcy because of the situation.

Finally the date for the Davis trial came. Steve had scheduled himself to be off for two weeks, hoping it would all be over in that amount of time, and he had arranged for Nan Freedman to cover for him during his absence. This way, he could devote all of his time and effort to his defense.

Steve walked into the courtroom and sat down next to Matthew Johnson at the defense table. Across the aisle was the plaintiff's table. Mrs. Davis sat between Sam Cuney and David Archer. The judge walked in as the bailiff cried, "All rise, District Court for the Middle District of Florida is now in session. The Honorable Judge Melvin Martin presiding."

"Be seated," said Martin as he sat down behind the bench. "Please call the case."

"The next case is *Davis v. Boxley*, a claim of medical malpractice. The plaintiff, Davis, is seeking damages in the amount of two million dollars."

Cuney rose and said, "Sam Cuney for the plaintiff, your honor. With me is David Archer, my assistant."

Matthew Johnson spoke next. He stood and said, "Matthew Johnson for the defense, your honor."

The judge spoke to all of the assembled: "Gentlemen, good morning. I expect that this case will last two to three days. I will not tolerate any stalling. I do expect that, at the end of each day, both of the attorneys will meet briefly to see if an out of court settlement can be reached. I must admit that I abhor medical malpractice cases and would very much like to see them settled in an arena other than my court.

Judge Martin looked at the two attorneys and asked if they were ready to proceed. They both replied in the affirmative. "Mr. Cuney, please proceed with your opening statements."

Matthew leaned over to Steve and whispered, "Steve, this opening statement is what we call a 'free shot.' Cuney can say anything he wants to say about you, and I can't object. I want you to bite your tongue and keep your mouth shut while he talks." Steve squirmed in his seat, knowing full well what would come next, the outright lies that would be deemed slander in any other venue.

"Thank you, your honor." Cuney looked at each member of the jury in turn and began. "Ladies and gentlemen of the jury, I thank you for your attention. You are about to hear the case of Davis vs. Boxley. John Davis was a nice, fun-loving, middle aged man who made the mistake of enjoying the pastime of motorcycle riding. One evening, he was involved in an accident, possibly of his own making. John had no idea of the details of the accident, other than remembering a car speeding by and a cigarette being flicked at him; the police can not reconstruct the incident with any accuracy. So, let's blame John for the accident. There were no other vehicles involved. No one else was injured. Admittedly, John was near death when he arrived at the hospital, and only with the tireless work of dedicated nurses, technicians and, yes, even doctors – including the defendant, Dr. Steve Boxley – did he survive. But, survive, he did. John was stabilized and within a day or two, was released from the intensive care unit and transferred to the general surgical postoperative floor. It was there that Dr. Boxley dropped the ball. Dr. Boxley allowed John to develop a large blood clot in the back of his left leg, and as he continued to ignore John, Dr. Boxley allowed that blood clot to break loose and travel to his right lung. That blood clot killed John, but the only reason that blood clot developed and broke loose was because Dr. Boxley was asleep at the wheel.

"Ladies and gentlemen, I have no doubt that Dr. Boxley is a fine surgeon, but, clearly, his interest in his patients does not extend beyond the operating room. Did you know that a surgeon is only paid for the operation? The insurance companies expect the surgeon to provide the postoperative care for free. I suspect, but of course I can't prove, that Dr. Boxley simply doesn't care about the patient after he leaves the OR, because there is no more money to be made.

"Over the course of the next day or so, I will lay out our case of medical malpractice against Dr. Boxley. You will see how Dr. Boxley lost interest in Mr. Davis after the surgery was complete. He had done his work in the operating room and would be paid for that work, but now came the free care, and Dr. Boxley just wasn't willing to expend the effort. As he ignored John, the clot was quietly forming that ended up killing John. Or, should I say that Dr. Boxley killed John with the help of the clot?"

Cuney nodded towards the jury. He had identified two of the jurors who had been smiling at him; he was sure that by the end of the case he would have them eating out of his hand, and he knew that they would try to sway the other jurors towards his side during deliberations. He smiled at the two sympathetic jurors and sat down.

"Mr. Johnson, would you like to address the jury?" asked Judge Martin.

"Yes, thank you. Ladies and gentlemen of the jury, I want you to do me a favor. Mr. Cuney is a very theatrical attorney, and he will make many grandiose statements during this trial in an attempt to convince you that Dr. Boxley did something wrong in his treatment of Mr. Davis. He will try to convince you that you should award Mrs. Davis a lot of money. All I ask is that you follow this trial with an open mind. I ask that you remember that medicine is an art as much as it is a science, that there is more than one opinion as to the correct treatment of a patient. What is good for one patient can be lethal for another; what may help one patient may hurt another. A doctor can not treat a patient with a recipe book, but instead he needs to make decisions instantaneously, based on his clinical judgment. Sometimes, patients don't do what their doctors want them to do, and complications occur.

"I also ask that you consider this case with this fact in mind: to find a doctor guilty of malpractice, you must find three things to be true. The first is a deviation from the standard of care. The question is, 'Did this doctor do what another, prudent doctor would have done in the same situation?' Remember that an error in judgment is not malpractice, that only a deviation from the standard of care is malpractice. Second, there must be an injury. Even if the care deviated from the standard, it is not malpractice if there is no injury. And, finally, there must be damages. If a doctor behaved horribly and injured the patient, the only way that you can find that he committed malpractice is if that care caused damages. Otherwise, you can not find that malpractice occurred.

"With these standards in mind, I intend to show you that, while Mr. Cuney will have a supposed expert tell you that Dr. Boxley's care deviated from the standard, Dr. Boxley's care did not deviate from that standard at all. If you agree with me, then you can not find that malpractice occurred. This was simply a tragic motorcycle accident in which a good man died. Again, please keep your ears and your minds open, and I'm sure that you'll agree with me."

Matthew took his seat, and the judge looked at Cuney.

"Mr. Cuney, are you ready to proceed with your case?"

"Yes, Judge."

"Go on, then."

"I call Mrs. Nadine Davis to the stand."

Mrs. Davis was sworn in and seated in the witness box. With Sam Cuney's help, she identified herself for the court and began to recount her memory of the days surrounding John's death. "I remember the phone call from the police. I ran down to the hospital. I remember speaking with the surgical resident and finally with Dr. Boxley." She said his name with a sneer, and continued, "Dr. Boxley told me that he suspected that John would not last through the night. He told me that they had taken out his spleen and that John had a collapsed lung; he had put a tube into the lung to re-expand it. He told me that the orthopedic surgeons were with John after he finished, stabilizing his fractured pelvis. I remember that Dr. Boxley's main concern was the bleeding from the fractures, and he said that John might bleed to death."

"What happened next, Mrs. Davis?"

"Well, John stopped bleeding. In fact, I remember Dr. Land — he's one of the surgical residents — telling me that John had stopped bleeding, and he, Dr. Land, was starting to be optimistic that John might make it. They even transferred him out of the ICU to a regular room a day later."

Nadine started to cry and Cuney patiently waited for her to gain control, a look of compassion on his face as he looked sidelong at the jury to see if he could gauge their reaction. A couple of the jurors were obviously moved by her loss, by her grief. "Go on, please," he said in a soothing voice that was just short of overacting.

"I was visiting John, and I had a pleasant conversation with him and his roommate, a nice boy who had had an appendectomy. I left for the evening, but before I even left the hospital, I heard the operator page a code blue for John's room. Well, of course, I ran back to the room. Dr. Boxley didn't let me go in the room, but he came out a few minutes later and told me that John was dead."

"Did you ever find out why he died?"

"Yes, Dr. Boxley called me after the autopsy and told me that he died from a blood clot in his lung, a pulmonary embolism."

"Thank you, Mrs. Boxley. Judge, I have nothing further."

The judge responded, "Mr. Johnson, do you have anything to ask this witness?"

"Yes, thank you. Good morning Mrs. Davis. I am Matthew Johnson. I represent Dr. Boxley. I am sorry for your loss, but we need to determine in this courtroom whether or not Dr. Boxley made any medical decisions that may have contributed to your husband's death. Do you believe that Dr. Boxley did anything wrong?"

"Mr. Cuney told me that the medical expert he hired thinks that Dr. Boxley should have given John a blood thinner called heparin."

"Do you agree with that?"

Cuney jumped to his feet. "I object, your honor. That question requires Mrs. Davis to have medical knowledge that she does not possess."

"Sustained. Mrs. Davis, you do not need to answer."

Johnson continued, "In that case, I have no further questions of this witness."

"Mr. Cuney, call your next witness."

"I call James Danielson."

Mr. Danielson was sworn in, and Cuney began questioning him. "Mr. Danielson, what is your occupation?"

"I am an economist. My job is to calculate the potential earnings of disabled and deceased people, to help determine damages."

"And have you had the opportunity to do that for Mr. Davis?"

"Yes, I have, sir. Mr. Davis was an electrician, and he earned $45,000 per year. He was 50 years old, and statistically would have worked for 15 more years. Simple mathematics tells us that $45,000 per year times 15 years equals a lost wage of $675,000. By calculating an inflation rate of 4% and interest rates of 8%, and giving Mr. Davis cost of living increases each year, I believe that his earning potential would have been one million dollars if he had lived."

Cuney smiled subtly at the jury and thanked Danielson for his opinion. "Your witness, counselor."

Matthew walked up to the witness stand and introduced himself. "Mr. Danielson, what degrees to you have in order to do your job?"

"I have a bachelor's degree."

"In what field?"

"In fine arts."

"So you don't have a degree in mathematics?"

"No."

"Statistics?"

"No."

"Are you an actuary – someone who does this type of calculation for a living?"

"No."

"So, if I understand, you are not trained in this field, and you have no degree in mathematics."

"You are correct, but..."

Matthew cut him off. "Yes or no, sir."

"No, I don't have any formal training in mathematics."

"Without a degree in mathematics, how can you be admitted to the court as an expert?"

"Well, when I finished college, I was unable to find a job in my field. My uncle is an accountant and he gave me a job helping him at the office during tax season. I did well with him, and one day an attorney called for my uncle to help him determine someone's potential earnings. My uncle was out of the office so I offered to help. I did a good job for the lawyer and he started using me regularly. I took a few economics courses at the Junior College and starting working with more and more lawyers, working as an economist."

"Have you ever worked for the defense?"

"No, sir, only the plaintiff."

Matthew sneered at him, "Now, with your fine arts degree, did you take into account the fact that Mr. Davis was severely injured in the accident, and may not ever been able to work again?"

"No."

"Did you deduct the disability payments he would have received, had he survived?"

"No."

"Just out of curiosity, in order to be an expert at this field, would I be correct in assuming that all I would need is a sympathetic attorney for the plaintiff and a two dollar calculator.

Cuney jumped up again. "Objection, your honor, badgering the witness."

Before Judge Martin could rule, Johnson said "Question withdrawn. I'm done with this witness."

Cuney responded with just a hint of anger remaining in his voice, "The plaintiff calls Dr. J. Marcus Semben."

Semben took the stand and was sworn in. Cuney questioned him to establish his credentials. Steve Boxley whispered to Johnson, "He's not trained in my area of surgery, nor is he an expert in pulmonary embolism. Why don't you try to get him disqualified?"

"Steve, this guy is a liar, and I've seen him testify before. I'm not going to object to his testimony. He'll probably screw up. If we make Cuney get another expert, he may get somebody half decent next time."

"Dr. Semben, have you had the opportunity to review the records of this case."

"Yes, I've reviewed the hospital chart and the autopsy report."

"In your expert opinion, did Mr. Davis have to die?"

"Not at all. He had a successful surgery, and he was on the mend. Unfortunately, he had a terrible complication, a clot in the veins of his left leg, and the clot broke off and traveled to his right lung. This could have been prevented by placing Mr. Davis on heparin."

"Dr. Boxley will have us believe that the heparin would have made Mr. Davis bleed, and that he didn't use heparin for that reason. What do you think of that logic?"

"I strongly disagree. Yes, Mr. Davis could have bled, but Dr. Boxley would simply have had to stop the heparin, maybe give some plasma to the patient, and it would have stopped. And, if it didn't, he could have operated to stop the bleeding. A small price to pay to prevent this terrible catastrophe.

"So, you see no scenario in which Dr. Boxley could have been correct in his care?"

"None at all, sir."

Cuney looked at Johnson with a modest sneer and said, "Your witness."

Matthew walked towards Semben and said, "Good morning, doctor. Nice to see you again. I see that you are spending a considerable amount of time here in our Florida courts. Do you work for Morris, Cuney and Howe?"

"No, I do not. However, I am an excellent doctor, and that firm chooses to use my services to help rid the medical profession of incompetent doctors."

"As an excellent doctor, perhaps you'd like to tell the jury about the vast, extensive experience that you have in the field of trauma surgery."

"I am not a trauma surgeon, Mr. Johnson."

"How many patients in the past year have you treated for a ruptured spleen and collapsed lung, along with pelvic fractures?"

"None, sir."

Cuney jumped up once more. "I object, your honor. Dr. Semben has already told Mr. Johnson that he is not a trauma surgeon. Yet Mr. Johnson is continuing to badger him about his experience in that field."

Judge Martin glared at Cuney and said, "Counselor, this is your expert in a trauma case. I would say that if he can't take the heat, he shouldn't be in the kitchen. I'll allow this line of questioning, but Mr. Johnson, let's move along, please."

Cuney grumbled and sat down. Johnson continued, "So, sir, are you telling us that even though you have never treated a patient like Mr. Davis, you still can formulate an opinion about the care that was rendered by Dr. Boxley?"

"Absolutely, sir," Semben replied with a smile.

"Dr. Boxley did use TED hose on Mr. Davis. Would that not have helped prevent the DVT?"

"Obviously, it didn't, counselor."

"Dr. Semben, have you ever read the journal called *Surgical Treatment of Trauma?"*

"Yes, I have. I read it frequently."

"Do you consider that journal to be authoritative in the field of trauma surgery?"

"Yes, I do."

"Are you familiar with the work of Dr. Vernon McPeak?"

"No, I'm not."

"Doctor, that is discouraging, because Dr McPeak is on the editorial board of the *Surgical Treatment of Trauma*, and he is considered one of the country's experts on pulmonary embolism. I must call into question your statement that you are a frequent reader of the *Surgical Treatment of Trauma*, as Dr. McPeak publishes, on average, one article each month in that journal. However, let's move on. Would you say that you read this journal every issue, every month?"

"Yes, I do."

"That's interesting; my secretary called the publisher and told them that she was your secretary, and asked about your subscription. They checked their records and said that you don't have a subscription."

Semben opened his mouth to speak, but Johnson held up a finger, then said, "Before you perjure yourself and tell me that you read it in the library of your hospital, you need to know that we asked the publisher about that, too, and your hospital doesn't subscribe, either. Now, are you still such an avid reader of this journal?"

"Well, I do look at it from time to time."

"Your honor, I'm handing the bailiff a document that I've designated 'Defense Exhibit 1.' It's a copy of an article from the *Surgical Treatment of Trauma*. I've highlighted the summary." Johnson turned to Dr. Semben once again. "Dr. Semben, will you please read the highlighted portion of the article for the court."

"In summary, it is our opinion that the risk of pulmonary embolism increases with the duration of anesthesia and the severity of the trauma. While the ideal treatment for the prevention of deep venous thrombosis and pulmonary embolism remains anticoagulation with heparin, it is virtually impossible to treat every patient due to the risk of bleeding, especially in those patients with pelvic fractures. Therefore, we recommend that all trauma patients be fitted with support stockings and be subjected to early physical activity. We further recommend that only selected patients without pelvic fractures be treated with heparin. It is dangerous to place each and every patient on heparin simply because they have suffered trauma. In fact, our study leads us to the conclusion that the mortality rate is higher in the treated group than in the non-treated group."

"Doctor, you just said a mouthful. Whether you agree with this or not, would you please translate this passage for the benefit of the jury."

"This summary basically says that the researchers would not place patients with pelvic fractures on heparin, because the risk of bleeding is too great, and they felt that the risk of dying from bleeding actually is greater than the risk of dying from a pulmonary embolism."

"So, based on this article, it would seem reasonable to conclude that Mr. Davis should not have been heparinized, is that correct?"

"Yes, but you must understand …"

Johnson help up his hand and said, "Doctor, I asked you a question. Please just answer it; yes or no."

"Yes, it is correct, based on that article."

"Now doctor, I understand that even though you have never treated a trauma patient like Mr. Davis, you consider yourself to be an expert in this field. So, I would like to allow you to show the jury any articles you may have written that disagree with this position taken in the *Surgical Treatment of Trauma*. Have you written any?"

"You know that I have not."

"So, can I assume, even if you don't agree, that Dr. Boxley was following the suggestions laid out in this highly respected journal. Doctor, I remind you, just answer the question yes or no."

"Yes, that is correct." Semben shifted nervously in his seat, the look of the embattled on his face, the look of the outmatched.

"Doctor, I'd like to point out that this article was written by Dr. Vernon McPeak, the doctor we discussed just a moment ago. As I told you, he is on the editorial board of this authoritative journal that you claim to read monthly. Would you look at the byline under the article title and confirm for the jury that this was written by Dr. McPeak."

"Yes, it was."

"Thank you, doctor. I have nothing more, your honor."

Judge Martin spoke next. "We will adjourn for lunch. Be back by 1 o'clock p.m."

***

Steve and Matthew sat in a booth in the back of the London Pub across the street from the courthouse. Matthew was eating a hearty lunch: quarter-pound cheeseburger, steak fries and a bowl of soup. Steve had ordered a salad, but he was playing with it rather than eating. "I'd much prefer a beer to this," he said.

Matthew responded, "Me too, but we can't. We both have to be sharp. Our defense starts this afternoon. How do you think the morning went?"

"I'm happy," Steve said. "You seemed to chew up their economist, and Semben looked like a dammed fool on the stand."

"Yes, it did seem to go our way, but remember that a jury does things we lawyers can't explain, that seem to be utterly unrelated to either the law or even common sense sometimes. They may just feel sorry for Mrs. Davis and rule in her favor, regardless of how good our case is. That's why we will meet with Cuney after the day's over and see if we can reach a settlement that is acceptable to both of us. Cuney must be telling Mrs. Davis the same thing. No matter how good it may look for them, the jury may decide in your favor and give her nothing. So, they have a reason to want to settle out of court as well."

Steve sighed and said, "Matthew, this is why people hate lawyers. The issue is not whether I'm right or wrong, just how much money will make this go away, right?"

"Yes Steve, that's completely right."

Steve looked away so the lawyer would not see the disdain in his eyes, not for this man but for his profession, and he fixed his gaze on the television on the wall over the bar. He was far enough away from the TV that he couldn't hear it, but the closed captioning was on and he could read the words. He saw Jake Morris' smiling face, and read his words as Jake said, "You only have a short time to have your case reviewed by one of our experienced attorneys, so call us if you suspect medical malpractice. We're Morris, Cuney and Howe, 'For the Little Guy.'" Steve almost choked on the single bite of his salad he had just managed to get as far as his mouth and told Matthew that he would meet him in court. He wanted to take a walk around the block before going back.

***

The courtroom slowly filled after the lunch recess, and the court was again called to order. Judge Martin took his place and asked Sam Cuney to call his next witness. Cuney told him that the plaintiff rested. Martin looked at Matthew and told him to begin to present his case.

"The defense calls Daniel Hawkins."

Mr. Hawkins was sworn in, and Johnson welcomed him. "Mr. Hawkins, would you please tell the jury about yourself."

"I am an economist. I have a bachelor's degree from the University of Pennsylvania, and a Master of Business Administration, that's an MBA, from the Wharton School at the University of Pennsylvania. I have passed all of the required tests and am a certified actuary. My job as an actuary is to work for an insurance company and predict risks and expenses."

"We will be asking you to help decide the earning potential of Mr. Davis, had he not passed away recently. The plaintiff's expert, Mr. Danielson, has testified that Mr. Davis could have earned up to one million dollars had he not died. We will be asking you your opinion of his potential earnings. But first, I'd like to review your credentials, and compare them to Mr. Danielson's. Mr. Danielson has a bachelor's degree in fine arts, and yours is in economics, correct?"

"Yes, that's correct."

"Good. You have an advanced degree, an MBA, and he has none, correct?"

"Yes, correct again."

Cuney rose. "I object, your honor. Mr. Danielson was accepted by the court, and this is unfair. Mr. Danielson is not here to defend himself."

Martin countered, "Mr. Cuney, Mr. Danielson is your witness. You hired him. Has Mr. Johnson said anything that is untrue yet?"

Cuney looked glum. "No, sir."

"Good, then. Mr. Johnson, you may continue. Objection overruled."

"Thank you, your honor. Mr. Hawkins, you work full time in the mathematics field, as an actuary, and Mr. Danielson says he's an economist. Is that true?"

"Not really. Mr. Danielson is known well in the court system for his ability to give favorable testimony for plaintiffs, but he most certainly does not work in the field of mathematics. In fact, I believe that he works in a restaurant when he is not testifying."

Johnson looked at Cuney, expecting an objection for his treatment of Danielson, but Cuney said nothing. A wise choice, because it was all true.

He continued, "How do you calculate the earning potential of someone, Mr. Hawkins?"

"We start with his yearly earnings, of course. Then we calculate his life expectancy. Hazardous behaviors are taken into account. We also consider any retirement accounts; you see, if he had considerable retirement money put away, we assume that he would have retired earlier than if he had nothing saved. Finally, we put this into a big picture and calculate his lost earning with that information."

"Have you come to a conclusion about Mr. Davis' potential earnings?"

"Yes, I have."

"Please tell the jury, what is your opinion regarding what his earnings would be?"

Hawkins got out of the witness chair and walked over to an easel with a white board sitting on it. He picked up a marker and began to speak.

"We first interviewed his wife and his employer. Mr. Davis had told the company that he planned to retire as early as possible, and funded his retirement account with the maximum allowed by law. He set a retirement date for when he turned 55 years old. He had $400,000 in his retirement account already, and with the current inflation and interest rate, that would be worth $575,000 when he retired at age 55. The Davis' house is paid off, and their expenses were minimal. I firmly believe that Mr. Davis would have been able to retire at age 55, and that he would not have had a financial problem in the world."

Hawkins wrote '5 years to retirement, $45,000 per year, equals $225,000' on the whiteboard.

He continued, "Next, we looked at his insurance. He had a policy that paid $500,000 as a death benefit. Mrs. Davis was the beneficiary. The policy had a double indemnity for accidental death. That means that if Mr. Davis were to die accidentally, as he did, the policy would pay double, or one million dollars."

He wrote '$1,000,000 in insurance payments' on the board.

He went on, "Mr. Davis was a motorcyclist. We have actuarial tables that predict life expectancy based on health and lifestyle. He was healthy, but his life expectancy was reduced by an average of 5 years because he rode motorcycles. Therefore, his life expectancy was 68 years. Considering his retirement funds and social security payments, Mr. Davis would never have run out of money."

He wrote 'Life expectancy 18 years after death in hospital. Total retirement funds plus interest plus social security equals $945,000' under the prior entries on the whiteboard.

Finishing up, he said, "If we look at these numbers, and add the life insurance payment to the retirement funds and the social security payments, then subtract 5 years of lost wages, Mrs. Davis still comes out $1,720,000 ahead. Now, I can make no judgment regarding medical malpractice, but it is clear that there are absolutely no economic damages to Mrs. Davis resulting from the death of her husband."

"Now, Mr. Hawkins, have you assessed the economic damages to the Davis family if Mr. Davis had survived?"

"Yes, I have. Mr. Davis had no disability insurance. Unfortunately, because of his injuries, he never would have been able to return to work, despite what your opposition would like the jury to believe. Therefore, he would have had no employment income, and would have been unemployed. His only income would have been social security. To continue their lifestyle the same as before the accident would have cost the Davises about $3,000 per month, after social security income. Had he lived for 18 more years, to the life expectancy of 68 years of age, he would have needed to come up with $640,000, not even considering inflation."

Johnson wanted to make his point to the jury, so he asked, "Mr. Hawkins, could you please summarize for us?"

"Certainly, counselor. The financial effect of Mr. Davis' death on his wife was to make her one million, seven hundred and twenty thousand dollars richer than she would be if he had survived. Furthermore, had he survived, the family would have had to pay $640,000 to maintain their lifestyle. Therefore, the net effect of Mr. Davis' death was a profit of two million, three hundred sixty thousand dollars to Mrs. Davis. Now, I know that this sounds heartless, but this is strictly mathematics. I'm making no comment on the value of the life of John Davis, just on the economics of his death."

"Thank you, Mr. Hawkins," said Matthew Johnson, as he turned to Cuney. "Your witness."

Cuney knew that there was nothing that he could make Hawkins say that would help his case, so he just wanted him off the stand and out of the jury's mind. "I have no questions, your honor."

Judge Martin looked at Johnson. "Call your next witness, Mr. Johnson."

"The defense calls Ms. Sandy DeStefano."

Sandy was sworn in and was seated in the witness stand. Matthew asked her to tell the jury a bit about herself and her job.

"My name is Sandy DeStefano. I am the risk manager at Middle Florida Hospital. That means that it is my job to help the hospital and the doctors identify liability risks within the hospital. Those risks might be in the physical plant of the hospital, such as a slippery floor or an uneven stairway, or those risks might involve medical care, such as a doctor whose handwriting is so bad that the pharmacy makes mistakes when they fill his prescriptions."

"What is your education, Ms. DeStefano?"

"I am an RN, a registered nurse. I have a bachelor's degree from the University of Florida, and I went to nursing school there as well. I worked as a nurse for 12 years, then I took additional courses in risk management, and I have been working in that field for 8 years."

"Do you have any particular knowledge of this patient, Mr. Davis?"

"Well, Mr. Johnson, part of my job is to review the chart of any patient who has an unexpected outcome in the hospital. Therefore, I most certainly did review the case. However. I was not involved with Mr. Davis' care at all."

"What was the result of your review of the chart?"

"I felt that Mr. Davis had received adequate care by the doctors and the nurses at Middle Florida Hospital, and that there were no issues of concern regarding patient care."

"Did your chart review specifically address the issue of giving Mr. Davis heparin to prevent the blood clots and pulmonary embolism?"

"Yes, it did. Dr. Boxley had written a note in the chart specifically addressing that issue. He wrote, and I quote directly from the chart, "Extremities are warm, calves are soft, no sign of phlebitis. I have placed TED hose on patient. I'm fearful of bleeding if heparin is used." I think that this note adequately addresses the issue. The outcome is unfortunate, but Dr. Boxley made an informed, intelligent choice in this matter, and the hospital stands behind his decision."

"Dr. Boxley told me that you were involved in a discussion of a similar case at a lecture, is that true?"

"Yes, we were discussing another patient of Dr. Boxley's, a very obese gentleman, and our students and residents gave a lecture on prevention of blood clots and pulmonary embolism. We presented both sides of the issue — bleeding versus clots — and I talked about the risk management issues. It's a sad, but timely commentary on the state of medicine and the law that this medical decision should be brought to the courtroom, rather that taking place in the halls of the hospital where it belongs."

"So, you are telling us that Dr. Boxley discussed his rationale for not using heparin at a lecture before Mr. Davis suffered his pulmonary embolism, and he wrote his logic for this choice in the case in question directly in the chart?"

"Yes, absolutely."

"Thank you, Ms. DeStefano, I have no further questions. Mr. Cuney, your witness."

Cuney went after her immediately. "Ms DeStefano, are you trying to have the court believe that you are an expert in the field of blood clots and pulmonary embolism?"

"Of course not. Why would you say that?"

"You just told us that you reviewed the chart and determined that Dr. Boxley didn't do anything wrong. Wouldn't you call that rendering an expert opinion regarding blood clots and pulmonary embolism?"

"Not at all, counselor. I'm a nurse, and the hospital hired me because of my medical and nursing knowledge. My opinion has to do with the overall treatment of the patient, especially in terms of procedures and the evidence that they were or were not followed."

"How do you know that Dr. Boxley's choice of therapy is correct if you aren't an expert in the field?"

"I do what the doctors do; I read the medical literature. When I reviewed this case, I looked to the journals and found this issue well represented. The medical literature supports Dr. Boxley's actions."

Cuney sneered. "What literature might that be?"

"We reviewed an article in the *Journal of the International Trauma Society*, that article supported using heparin only in selected trauma patients."

Cuney froze, and after a moment Judge Martin coughed to get his attention. Cuney looked up. "I have nothing more, your honor."

Martin looked down at Sandy. "Ms. DeStefano, the court thanks you for your time. You are dismissed."

As Sandy stepped down, Martin said, "We are adjourned for the day. Mr. Johnson and Mr. Cuney, I will see you both in chambers." Martin banged the gavel and the bailiff called, "All rise."

Five minutes later, Judge Martin, Sam Cuney and Matthew Johnson were seated around a small table in the judge's chambers. Martin said, "Gentlemen, if you recall, at the beginning of this trial, I told you that I hate medical malpractice trials and that I expected you to meet each day to discuss an out of court settlement. I will walk out of my office for awhile right now, and I expect the two of you to have that conversation while I am gone." He leaned towards Cuney and added, "Sam, Matthew is kicking your ass. If I were you, I'd get what I could and get out of here." Matthew tried to suppress a smile, but Martin looked at him and said, "Matthew, don't be so smug. I've been a judge for 16 years, and I'm always amazed at the decisions of the juries. They may simply feel sorry for Mrs. Davis and give her some money, even though it seems that your doctor-client did nothing wrong." Then to both of them he added sternly, "Talk to each other." Judge Martin walked out of the office.

Cuney started. "Matthew, I don't agree with the judge. I think we have a great case, and my client is not willing to settle for less than $500,000. Offer anything less and you don't have a deal."

Matthew knew that Sam was bluffing, especially considering that the demand at the start of the trial was $2,000,000. To drop the demand from two million to half a million was significant. "Cut the crap, Sam. Your case is shit. The only risk that I face is a sympathetic jury that isn't listening to the facts of the case. My first witness tomorrow is Dr. Vernon McPeak, the guy that wrote the article that your phony expert choked on. Then, I'll be calling Dr. Boxley himself. After that, your case is worth even less. So, I'll offer you $50,000 to get out of here tonight; otherwise, I'll see you tomorrow."

Cuney excused himself and walked out into the hall. Even though Matthew couldn't hear him, he knew that Cuney was talking to Nadine Davis on his cell phone. Cuney cut the call and walked into the office. "Mrs. Davis says no dice. She won't accept anything less than $100,000."

The two men said goodnight and walked out of the courthouse together.

***

The next morning, the players were all assembled at the courthouse. Cuney knew that Steve Boxley would be testifying that day, so he had an ingenious thought. He stationed David Archer at the door to the courthouse, and as Steve walked in, David served him with a subpoena for the case of The Estate of Susan Parks *vs*. Boxley. He knew that move would shake Steve up, and perhaps even anger him so much that he would not be able to keep his wits about him on the stand.

And in fact, as Steve walked up to the defense table, he was shaking with rage. He slammed his fist on the table and pushed the subpoena at Matthew. Matthew looked at it and stormed up to Cuney. "This is bullshit, Sam. Couldn't this wait?"

"Sure it could, but the effect will work in my favor today." Cuney looked up and said, "I'd like to talk more to you, but the judge is here."

Court was in session and Matthew was asked to call his first witness.

"The defense calls Dr. Vernon McPeak."

McPeak took his seat, and Matthew asked him to introduce himself to the jury.

"I graduated from the Massachusetts School of Medicine in 1980. Next, I did a surgical residency at University of New York, then a trauma fellowship at Harvard. In 1986, I was finished with my training and accepted a position as a trauma surgeon at the Virginia State Trauma Center, where I worked for 8 years. Then I was offered the directorship of the National Trauma Center in Washington, D.C. I have been there ever since."

"Do you publish any articles?"

"Absolutely. I feel that research is critical to the advancement of medicine. I do research and publish on a regular basis, usually monthly. In addition, I am on the editorial board of the *Surgical Treatment of Trauma*. I have published about 100 articles."

"How many of those articles are about pulmonary embolism and blood clots in the legs?"

"Well, sir, that is a particular interest of mine, so I'd guess that about 60 of those 100 articles are about those subjects."

"Have you reviewed the records regarding the treatment of Mr. Davis?"

"Yes, I have."

"Do you have any opinions regarding the care that Mr. Davis was given at Middle Florida Hospital?"

"Yes. I think that the care given to Mr. Davis was exemplary. He had the immediate attention of a third year resident, and Dr. Boxley was in to see him within 45 minutes of his arrival. The appropriate consultations were arranged, and the surgery was done quickly and properly. I could not have done a better job myself."

"Well, sir, as you know, we are here because Dr. Boxley is being sued. Mr. Davis developed a blood clot in his leg, and suffered a pulmonary embolism. The plaintiff's expert has testified that Dr. Boxley should have given Mr. Davis heparin. Do you have an opinion on that matter?"

"I do. But, more importantly, I have done research on that very matter."

"Could you please share that research with the jury?"

"I did a research paper on using heparin on trauma patients. It was published in the journal called the *Surgical Treatment of Trauma*, in the September 2001 issue, pages 23 to 31. To summarize, we found that in patients with pelvic trauma and bleeding, the mortality rate, that's the death rate, actually went up in those patients treated with heparin when compared to those who only had TED stockings placed on their legs."

"Your honor, I direct your attention to defense exhibit 1, as already presented in my cross examination of Dr. Semben. Dr. McPeak, do you feel that this article addresses Mr. Davis' case?"

"Mr. Johnson, it was almost like we wrote the article about Mr. Davis."

"But Dr. McPeak, Dr. Semben has said that Mr. Davis would still be alive if not for Dr. Boxley's choice *not* to give him heparin."

"Dr. Semben is entitled to his opinion. However, I'm led to believe that Dr. Semben is not a trauma surgeon, that in fact, he's not even a general surgeon, and as such, wouldn't be called upon to treat a patient such as Mr. Davis under any circumstance. On the other hand, I am a trauma surgeon, and my field of research is blood clots and pulmonary embolism. So, while Dr. Semben, unfortunately, can render an opinion, you must realize that his opinion in this matter is not consistent with current medical research."

"Based on your research, what might have happened to Mr. Davis if Dr. Boxley had given him heparin?"

"I couldn't honestly predict the outcome, but, based on our research, Mr. Davis would likely have suffered extensive bleeding, and his chances of dying from bleeding would have been higher than his chances of dying of a pulmonary embolism. Now, I know that he did die from a pulmonary embolism, but we are discussing statistics, and Dr. Boxley made the correct choice based on those statistics."

Johnson looked at the jury with an expression that seemed to ask if they had indeed understood the slam-dunk that had just occurred, and said, "Thank you Dr. McPeak. I have no further questions."

Cuney rose and asked, "Dr. McPeak, are you saying that it would have been wrong to treat Mr. Davis with heparin?"

"No, I didn't say that. It would not have been wrong, but, based on the statistics, the chance of complications would be higher if he had been given the heparin than if he were not given the drug. You need to understand. Doctors can make better choices if they allow themselves to be guided by research involving hundreds, or even thousands, of patients, rather than just making choices based on what seems right."

"And don't you agree that if Dr. Boxley had used the heparin, Mr. Davis would not have had the blood clot and the pulmonary embolism?"

"Yes, that is true. But you need to consider..."

Cuney cut him off. "I didn't ask for an explanation. I asked if you agreed that he would not have died if the drug had been administered, and you said that you did. Thank you Doctor, I have nothing else. You are excused."

Judge Martin recessed the court for lunch, and he once again called the attorneys to his chambers. "Gentlemen, I want this case settled. Mr. Cuney, this is a frivolous lawsuit. Your expert is a whore, and you are getting whipped. I'm aware that you had Dr. Boxley served with a subpoena this morning, and I swear that if he does poorly on the stand, I'll declare a mistrial and consider having you arrested for witness tampering. Mr. Johnson, you should win this case if it goes to the jury, but you know that the juries tend to sympathize with sad plaintiffs like the Widow Davis. I'd hate to see a ridiculous Florida award of a million or more dollars for a case like this. So, settle this and settle it now."

Martin stepped out, and the two lawyers eyed each other.

"I'll put $25,000 on the table, that's it. Take it or leave it," said Johnson.

Cuney responded angrily. "Matthew, I told you last night that Mrs. Davis won't settle for anything less than $100,000."

"Right. Make it $50,000 then."

"Deal."

Cuney and Johnson shook hands and called for the judge. They told him about the settlement, and the judge walked into the court and dismissed the case. Mrs. Davis, Dr. Boxley, David Archer, Sam Cuney and Matthew Johnson were herded into the conference room where the necessary papers were signed. Steve Boxley was dumbstruck: just like that this nightmare was over. He felt cheated. Johnson was winning, and he thought that it would be over with a verdict in his favor. Instead, his insurance company was throwing money at a plaintiff just to make the case go away. His mind wandered to Dr. Franks; now he was sure that Franks had killed himself that day, because that was what he wanted to do, too. Steve walked out of the courthouse without saying a word and was grateful for the rain. No one could see the tears streaming down his face.

CHAPTER 19

The plane landed at Hartsfield Airport in Atlanta. Semben and Large said goodbye to each other and went their own ways. Semben headed to the long-term parking area and Large to the Avis rental counter. Semben was going home, but Large had other plans. He got in the rental car and headed towards the coast. From there, he turned south and drove to Savannah. Once in Savannah, he rented a room in a boarding house near the historic downtown area under an assumed name and settled in for a while.

Large walked towards the riverfront and joined up with a walking tour, and from there he paid for a ticket on the tram that circles the historic area. He listened to the drone of the bus driver as he painfully detailed the sights. All of the recognizable attractions from *Forest Gump* were pointed out: "Here is the park bench that Forest sat on to tell his story, and there is the church spire that the feather fell from." The sights from *Midnight in the Garden of Good and Evil* were likewise on display. Finally, he had had enough of the tour and returned to his room.

Most importantly, he tried to blend in. He had a southern drawl in his youth that he had tried hard to lose, and he could turn it on when it was needed. When he used it, he seemed like a local. This affectation allowed him to come and go without being recognized as an outsider, someone worthy of notice and in need of being watched, for southerners are a suspicious lot when it comes to outsiders, and it allowed him to visit some of the seedier places where he definitely needed to fit in. In one of those places, a strip club, Large befriended a bouncer. With this contact, he was able to meet a gun dealer from whom he purchased a Glock 40 caliber handgun with the serial number already filed off. Now he could complete the job.

After a week in Savannah, Large packed up and left the boarding house. He drove all night and entered Semben's hometown at 4:00 a.m. He checked into the only local motel, still using an assumed name, and paid with cash. The next day, he scouted around town: he already knew where Semben worked, and followed him to find his home. The following day, he awoke early and watched Semben's house; once Semben left for work, Large took a shovel and headed to Semben's back yard.

When the workday ended, Semben left the hospital and headed for home. His practice was hardly rewarding, and the bulk of his income was from providing expert testimony for plaintiffs' attorneys. He had a few cases to review, which had come to the office in the mail that morning. He carried the case files into the house and flipped on the light in the living room. As his eyes adjusted to the light, he saw a figure sitting in his easy chair, which made him jump back a step. "Stan, you have to stop doing that to me. You keep scaring the crap out of me."

"Hi, Marcus. We need to talk."

Semben put the files down on the coffee table and sat down across from Large. "Sure, Stan. What's the problem?"

Large pulled out the Glock and waved it towards Semben. "You're the problem, Marcus. You see, we killed that girl. You're what we call a loose end. If the authorities have any suspicion that her death was not from natural causes, they would start investigating. If they did, they'd find you, and you'd talk. We can't take that risk."

Semben had the sudden urge to urinate. He started shaking and whined, "Stan, please. I would never say anything to anybody. C'mon now. If I talked, I'd be admitting that I was involved. I would never do that. I swear."

"Sorry Marcus, but I just don't believe that. You are such a worm that I'm sure you'd talk. In fact, if you ever got a whiff of an investigation, I'm sure you'd run to the authorities and sell Jake and me out to save your own skin."

Large aimed the gun at Semben. "Get up, Marcus. We need to take a walk." Large marched him into the back yard and toward a mound of dirt. Semben could see an empty shallow grave. The urge to urinate was uncontrollable, and as he approached his grave, he wet his pants. Once next to the grave, he felt a slight tap on the back of his head, then nothing, silence and darkness. Large walked around the body and dragged the corpse into the hole. He wiped the gun clean of fingerprints, threw it into the grave and shoveled the dirt back over the body and the gun. Finally, he grabbed the shovel and returned to the rental car.

No more loose ends.

***

Steve Boxley went home and tried to sleep. The thoughts that were forcing themselves into his head wouldn't allow slumber. He got up and walked around the quiet house. He had taken off an entire two weeks in order to help mount a defense in the Davis case, and now, just one and a half days into the trial, his lawyer settled the case. Sure, fifty thousand dollars isn't much in the scheme of things, but it's too much for this case. Steve decided that he wasn't going to call Nan and resume work the next day. Instead he was going to take a few days off. After all, he had told her that he would be gone for two weeks.

In the morning, Steve packed a bag and headed to the beach. He checked in at one of the hotels, changed into his swim trunks, headed out of the hotel and picked out a place to lie down on the sand. There was a beachside bar, and he bought a beer and started drinking. By noon, he was drunk, and finally, by dinnertime, he began to feel better. The next morning, he had a whopper of a hangover, a major sunburn, and a woman in his hotel room he didn't recognize. He made his excuses to the woman, a bleached blonde whose several plastic surgeries were too obvious to make him feel anything but pathetic, packed up and left, heading home.

The short trip cleared his mind and allowed him to start thinking again. He began to fixate on the Susan Parks case. He knew that he was being sued, and he wondered how he could defend himself. He didn't even know what he could have done to make the outcome less disastrous, but there was so much about this case he did not understand, so much no one he spoke to understood either, that all the literature seemed to suggest was utterly impossible. Why had she died?

He began to run through the case in his mind. He remembered the call from the emergency room doctor, filling him in about Susan. She had been fine that day, but had gotten unusually sleepy that evening. She went to bed early, and her boyfriend had been unable to awaken her when he went to bed. She was groggy the next morning and was slurring her speech. Later that day, she was found unconscious.

She was found to have dangerously low blood sugars, but even after her medications were stopped, the sugars continued to dip down, requiring her to be in the intensive care unit. The concern was that she had a tumor that manufactured insulin, but it was never found. She had died of low blood sugar.

Nothing in the rerun of his care struck him as unusual. He thought that it might be a good idea to read through the hospital chart — maybe he had missed something. He called the medical records department at the hospital and asked that the chart be pulled, then got into the convertible and drove to the hospital. He was wearing shorts and sandals, so he entered through the back door and went right to the medical records department.

"Good afternoon, Dr. Boxley," one of the medical records technicians said to him. "The chart on Susan Parks is right here." She handed him a chart that had a bright red label on the front: "THIS CHART IS NOT TO BE REMOVED FROM THE MEDICAL RECORDS DEPARTMENT. THIS CHART IS INVOLVED IN LITIGATION!!"

Steve took the chart to a back room and sat down at a desk in one of the cubicles. He started reading the notes from each of the doctors participating in Susan's care, but nothing jumped out at him. Then he read the report from the doctor in the emergency room. Everything seemed in order. Then he re-read the second paragraph of the history:

> **"Susan felt well earlier in the day, and she made dinner for herself and her significant other (live-in boyfriend). After dinner, she took her Glucophage and sat down in front of the TV. She commented that the pills tasted unusually bitter (?). Shortly, she became very sleepy and went to bed. Boyfriend says she almost fell to floor and was slurring her speech. Next morning, was still tired and slurring speech, didn't feel well, stayed home from work. That evening, unarousable, and boyfriend called 911. Came in with blood sugar from scene of 21. Responded to IV infusion of D-50."**

Steve knew that something was wrong with that paragraph but couldn't put his finger on it. He walked over to the copier and made a copy of the page, folded it into his pocket and went to the main desk in the department. He found the clerk and asked her to make a copy of the entire chart. She told him it would be available later that day. Steve walked to a phone and called his office. He told his secretary to pick the chart copy up for him and asked her to bring it to his house on her way home from work.

***

"Mr. Crandall, this is Jake Morris."

"Good morning, Mr. Morris. What can I do for you?"

"Do you remember our conversation, when you told me that I could respond to the article in your paper about the malpractice situation?"

"Yes, sir, I do. You said that you didn't want to respond at that time, but you would want to soon."

"Right. I want to respond now."

Two hours later, Connie Lombardi, a reporter from the court beat was in Jake's office and sitting across the desk from him. They spoke for quite some time, and Connie assured him that she would be writing an article that would be very sympathetic to the trial lawyers in general and to Jake in particular.

The next morning, Jake read the paper with a look of satisfaction on his face:

Central Florida Times

Orlando, FL

By Connie Lombardi

The physicians in Central Florida will have us believe that there is a malpractice crisis in this area. To hear them speak, the trial lawyers are out of control and the juries are giving away money at the drop of a hat. But, truth be told, the real problem is incompetence in the medical profession.

Susan Parks had everything to live for. She was 25 years old, was in love and had her whole life before her. She had diabetes, a chronic disease that affects millions of Americans. Susan's case was rather mild, and she only needed to take a few pills a day to keep her blood sugar under control. But one day a few weeks ago, Susan's blood sugar dropped suddenly, and her life changed forever. Her boyfriend called an ambulance, and Susan was taken to Middle Florida Hospital. There, she was seen by Dr. Steve Boxley, a general and trauma surgeon. She was told that she had a tumor of the pancreas that was manufacturing too much insulin; Dr. Boxley told her that he wanted to examine the inside of her abdomen to find the tumor. Susan trusted him with her life, a fatal mistake. No tumor was found during the operation, and Susan died the next day of unspecified complications. Throughout her hospital stay, Susan's blood sugar was repeatedly low, and Dr. Boxley did nothing to help her.

Susan died unnecessarily. But, she won't die in vain. Her boyfriend was David Archer, a young attorney who works for Morris, Cuney and Howe, the firm that handles more medical malpractice cases than any other law firm in Central Florida, and Jake Morris himself will be handling this case. Mr. Morris told me, "I take this very seriously, Connie. That doctor is incompetent. In fact, we just wrapped up a malpractice case against him; he was terrified that we'd win, so he settled out of court to protect himself. If someone had chased him out of Central Florida earlier, I firmly believe that Susan would be alive today. I intend to bring a multimillion-dollar suit against him; maybe this time we'll be able to run him out of town."

Morris says that the real crisis in the medical community is the old-boy network that lets bad doctors continue to work on patients rather than disciplining them. He says that if it weren't for the trial attorneys, this kind of thing would happen every day.

This paper will be following the Susan Parks case and will bring you news as it happens.

CHAPTER 20

His secretary dropped off the chart late that afternoon and was on her way. Steve couldn't concentrate on the chart and felt agitated as well as still being slightly hung-over, so he took a sleeping pill and went to bed. The following morning, he woke early, went out for a jog, picked up the newspaper on the way in and made coffee. As he sat at the breakfast table, he opened the paper and saw the article about Susan Parks. He was dumbfounded. He had no idea what to do or say. He jumped up from the chair and almost scalded himself with the coffee. Then he called Matthew Johnson.

When Matthew came to the phone, Steve was screaming. "Did you see the newspaper this morning, Matthew?"

"Yes, I did. I guess you could say that I've been expecting your call."

"What can we do about this?" Steve asked.

"For now, just lay low. It will do no good to get into a pissing contest in the newspapers. This kind of propaganda campaign can get too ugly to undo in court." Matthew asked if Steve could take a few days off, and Steve told him that he was due to be off all week anyway. Matthew told him to expect a lot of phone calls, and he said there would probably be disruption at the office. He also suggested that Steve come to his office with any records that Steve had on Susan.

Shortly thereafter, Steve was sitting in Matthew's office with the copy of Susan's hospital chart. He reviewed the case with Matthew and explained that there was a complete lack of a diagnosis for Susan's troubles. When Matthew asked about an autopsy, Steve told him that it had been normal. No tumor was found, and no abnormalities were ever identified. Matthew suggested that they review the chart together.

After the physician's entries, they went through the laboratory section, and then finally through the nursing notes. Steve needed to take a break and walked out of the office. When he returned, Matthew asked him to review a few of the nurses' notes with him. "I found three notes that don't seem to be worrisome individually, but taken together, I think there may be something here."

Patient returned from x-ray, had a CT scan, results not available. Patient seems confused, is slurring speech and thinks she was injected twice for the CT scan. Blood sugar drawn. I checked with the radiology technician. She was injected only once, by the radiologist. Given D-50 with good results. Blood sugar was 63.

Returned to ICU after MRI scan. Face seems paralyzed, not responding to verbal stimulus. Given D-50 with results. On awakening, she was slurring her speech, but trying to say something about someone playing with her IV. (Checked IV bottles, nothing amiss).

Code note. Patient appeared upset, told her that her most recent blood sugar was 90. She was slurring her speech and said something to the effect of "the maintenance man, my IV," then fell asleep, likely due to morphine

infusion. Boyfriend in to visit and noted her to be unarousable. Code blue called, resuscitation successful, but patient seems brain dead. Blood sugar is 6.

They both were silent, then Steve stood up and took the copy of the emergency doctor's note from his pocket and handed it to Matthew. He watched as Matthew read it.

Steve spoke first. "Matthew, I don't know what to make of this, but you may have found something here. It seems that before each blood sugar crisis, someone may have been doing something with her IV line. Of course, with the dangerously low blood sugar, she could have been hallucinating."

Matthew replied, "Steve, could it be possible that someone was injecting something in her IV?"

"Yes, sure, someone could have done that. But who, and why?"

"I have no idea. Maybe we need to talk with her boyfriend."

Steve jumped up. "Her boyfriend. He works at Morris, Cuney and Howe. He was the guy who was sitting in the second chair at the Davis trial."

"I know that, Steve. But, looking at these notes, it couldn't have been Archer that did it; maybe he might be able to shed some light on this."

Matthew had his secretary put him through to David Archer's phone at Morris, Cuney and Howe. David answered, and Matthew introduced himself as the attorney representing Dr. Boxley. David figured that Matthew was calling to offer a settlement, and asked, "Did the newspaper article rattle your chain, counselor? Do you want to make an offer to keep your client out of the paper again?"

Matthew responded coolly. "Mr. Archer, I'd rather not discuss this on the phone. Could you come to my office?"

David was sure he was about to negotiate a settlement and jumped at the offer to meet with Matthew. He told Matthew that he'd be right there.

An hour later, the three men were seated in Matthew's office. Matthew asked David to listen to Steve and not speak for a minute. He turned to Steve and asked him to begin.

"David, I know that you are devastated about Susan's death. You need to know that I am, as well. However, as you know, the autopsy showed nothing pathologic — there was no tumor to explain her repeated drops in blood sugar. Also, you know that we had her in the intensive care unit to protect her. Despite all of that, she died."

Before he could continue, David spoke. "And that's why we're suing you for millions of dollars, Doctor. If you're trying to make me feel sorry for you, forget it. I want to see you ruined."

Steve continued. "David, please. Mr. Johnson asked you to let me speak, and to just be quiet for a minute. I know that you hate me, and I'm sure that you had a hand in the newspaper article this morning. However, I think that you may be very interested in what I have to say.

"David, I'm giving you pages from Susan's hospital chart. The first page is part of the note from the emergency room doctor. It looks like a typical note, but in it, the doctor comments that Susan said her Glucophage tasted bitter."

David interrupted. "I can vouch for that. She told me that when she took it. I didn't think anything of it at the time."

"Nor should you have. The next note is a nurse's note, written after her CT scan, before her next crisis. She told the nurse that she was injected twice for the CT scan. Shortly thereafter, her blood sugar plummeted. The next note is after her return from the MRI, and she commented that someone was playing with her IV line. The third note is from the code blue. I know that it is painful to read, but please notice that she said something about a maintenance man and her IV. There's a pattern here: each time she had a crisis, it was preceded by someone manipulating her IV line."

David sat silently for a few moments, clearly uncertain as to what to make of what he had just read, and then he spoke. "Mr. Johnson, I can't believe that anyone in the world would want to hurt Susan. But I have to admit that what Dr. Boxley has shown me sure arouses my suspicion." He paused again, as if thinking. "I am not sure if this is a contrivance on your part to throw me off the truth of what happened or not, but it does seem, well, unseemly. Why would anyone want to do something devious to hurt her? I mean, I can't imagine that Susan had an enemy in the world, but this has to be looked into." He scratched his head and then threw the file onto the desktop. "For now, I will have to believe that you are playing this straight up, that you will do your best to uncover what really happened to Susan, so I can drag my feet with the suit to give you two time to investigate, but understand that I have every intention of suing Dr. Boxley to hell and back if you find nothing or if this turns out to be a stalling tactic of some kind. Susan was the love of my life, and I'll never see her again. Someone has to pay for that, and if you can't find anything out that puts the blame elsewhere, it will be you Dr. Boxley."

Matthew said, "David, thank you. Now, I would appreciate it if when you go home, you could think about the last few days before Susan got sick. Was anyone upset with Susan, did she hurt anyone, anger or upset anyone? That type of thing."

David agreed to do that, and left.

***

The phone awakened Steve the next morning. It was David Archer. "Dr. Boxley, I need to talk to you. Could you meet me somewhere?" They agreed to meet at a coffee shop near Steve's office.

When Boxley walked into the diner, he saw David sitting with a man who looked quite familiar. Steve walked over and shook both men's hands; Tyler McNab reintroduced himself to Steve.

David began, "Dr. Boxley, when I left Matthew Johnson's office yesterday, I tried to think about Susan's last week, tried to think about who might want to hurt her. Then, I vaguely remembered that she told me that she had found some problems with the accounting in the firm. She tried to tell me about it, but I really don't understand math very well, and I was working on something, so I pretty much ignored her. But I did know that she went to talk to someone about it. I figured that if she needed to speak to somebody about financial matters, it would be Dr. McNab. He's a full professor at the University, and he and Susan are – I mean were – friends." David looked sad after having to change the tense of his last assertion.

Tyler spoke next. "Steve, I remember that we sat next to each other at the funeral. I mentioned to you that I had seen Susan just a few days before. She had come to me quite troubled. She seemed to have found a large irregularity in the accounting of the firm. She had found that $750,000 of the firm's expenses had been charged to clients. In all honesty Steve, based on the papers that she showed me, I would say that the $750,000 was only the tip of the iceberg. I'm sure that we're talking about millions here."

Steve said, "Could you imagine that someone at Morris, Cuney and Howe could kill for that."

David answered, "Dr. Boxley, Jake Morris is ruthless. I'm sure that he could kill if he felt like he needed to kill to protect himself or his profits." David looked both sheepish and angry now, as if he was still not sure how to feel about the possibility that his employer had a hand in Susan's death.

Steve asked Ty if he could reconstruct the financial information that Susan had showed to him. Ty told him he could do better than that; he had copies that Susan had left with him for safe-keeping. After several moments of silence in which each man seemed lost in his own thoughts, perhaps all pondering the same question, Ty went on, "OK, then, assuming that this discovery of Susan's was enough motive to kill her, if Morris did indeed kill Susan, or had her killed, how could he do it? I take it that the autopsy revealed no sign of foul play."

Steve answered that, based on the way Susan died, if someone was able to inject insulin into her, it could have been what killed her. He excused himself, and told the other two by way of explanation that he needed to do some investigating. He said that he would meet David at his house at 3 p.m. that afternoon. A short while later, he was sitting on a stool in the cafeteria at the county morgue. For the price of a cup of coffee, he had the full attention of one of the coroners. Rob Eckert listened quietly as Steve told him Susan's sad story. Steve then asked him if there would be any way to find out if Susan had been given insulin in her IV.

"Well, yes there is. If a person is producing insulin himself or herself, that insulin can be identified by a protein on it called the C-peptide. Insulin that we give to diabetics comes from pigs or cows and doesn't have a C-peptide. So, if Susan was given insulin into her IV, that would have caused her own pancreas to stop making insulin in response, and the C-peptide level would drop below normal. So, if we had a blood sample from Susan, we could run the C-peptide test. Do we have a sample?"

Steve responded that her body had been autopsied right here, in the county morgue. He asked if they would keep her blood. Rob told him that they might. If they had done blood tests for anything else, they would have kept the tubes frozen. If they had such samples, they kept them frozen for a year. They walked to the laboratory together. Rob checked the computer system for Susan's morgue number, and then looked in a giant freezer with thousands of blood tubes. Rob knew the system well, and he had Susan's blood tube in his hands within minutes.

"Do you want me to call you with the results?" asked Rob.

"Can I wait?"

"If you want, but you'll need to wait a day or two. Now, where can I reach you?"

Steve gave Rob his home and cell phone numbers, thanked him profusely, and was gone.

At three o'clock, Matthew, David and Steve were sitting around the coffee table in David's living room. Matthew spread Susan's chart around the table, and the three of them started looking over the record again. All of a sudden, Steve jumped up. "Wait a minute, I know what bothered me about the emergency room doctor's note," he exclaimed. "Listen to this, 'After dinner, she took her Glucophage and sat down in front of the TV. She commented that the pills tasted unusually bitter. Shortly she became very sleepy, and went to bed.' Now I know what was bothering me. Susan said that the medication tasted bitter. That was unusual. Maybe the Glucophage was tampered with. David, do you still have her medicine?"

"Yes, I do. Since Susan died, I haven't been able to throw her things away. The pills are still in the medicine chest. I'll get them."

David walked into the bathroom and brought the pill bottle back with him. "Holy shit," said Steve. "These pills are not stock medication. They are homemade." He opened one of the capsules and touched the powder to his tongue. Very bitter. It certainly was not Glucophage. Steve gave the pill bottle to Matthew and told him to take it back to his office and lock it in his safe. He kept one of the pills for himself and would later get Rob Eckert to assay the medicine and determine what was really in the pills.

Steve stood up and stretched, and as he did, his arm hit the lamp next to the couch. The lamp fell over and the shade popped off. As Steve was putting it on, he said, "David, what's this?"

He showed David a small wired device in the lamp. David told him that he had no idea, but Matthew immediately recognized it. "I worked in intelligence in the Army. That, my friends, is a bug, a surveillance device." They checked the rest of the house and found a second bug in the lamp in the bedroom.

Matthew suggested that they call the police, but was overruled. Both of the other two had very good reasons to keep this personal.

***

The cellular phone's ringing woke him up. Rob Eckert was on the line, and he said that he needed to see Steve right away. Steve showered, grabbed a cup of coffee and was on his way. He rang David from the car and swung by the house to pick him up. They walked into the county morgue at 10 a.m. Rob was doing an autopsy, so Steve donned a surgical gown and went in. For his part, David cooled his heels in the lounge, not caring to see the interior of some poor dead person. After Rob finished, he and Steve caught up with David in the lounge. Steve introduced David to Rob and explained that David was Susan's boyfriend.

"I have the results of Susan's C-peptide test. I think you're on to something, Steve. The result is so low that we needed to concentrate the blood to get any result at all." He looked at David and asked, "David, are you absolutely sure that Susan did not use injectable insulin. I mean, sometimes people are embarrassed by needing injections and they hide it from their friends and family."

"No, she did not use insulin. In fact, I used to go with her to doctors' appointments with her. Her family doctor told her that if she kept up with her diet and exercise program she might even be able to get off of the pills. And I went with her for a gynecology appointment too. You see, we were talking about getting married and having children, and her gynecologist told her that he doubted if she would have any trouble at all if she got pregnant. In fact, he specifically said that she probably would not even need insulin if she got pregnant."

"Well, then Steve," said Rob, "she definitely got exogenous insulin." He stopped speaking and looked at David. "That means that there is no question in my mind that Susan was given insulin injections, and judging from the miniscule level of C-peptide in her blood, I would say that she was given massive doses of insulin."

Steve told Rob that he had a capsule that he found in Susan's medicine chest, in a bottle labeled 'Glucophage.' He told him that he was quite sure that the medication was altered, and asked if Rob could identify whatever was in the pill. Rob told him that he could use a machine called a spectrophotometer, and if the drug was in the USP, the United States Pharmacopoeia, a listing of all drugs marketed in the United States, he could identify it. He also told Steve that he could identify it in about one hour.

The three walked to Rob's lab. Rob sat down in front of a large machine, and used a computer terminal to turn the machine on. "This is a mass spectrophotometer. It uses light to see the weight of the particles in the medicine. Each drug is unique, think of it as having a fingerprint. If this is a drug for which we already have a fingerprint, we'll identify it."

Rob took the pill that Steve held out and opened the capsule. He poured out the white powder, took a small amount of it, added water and drew the mixture up into a syringe. He then injected the contents of he syringe into a tube and put the tube into the spectrophotometer. Rob told the computer that the drug was supposed to be Glucophage and entered its generic name, metformin. Within a minute, the monitor displayed a graph showing the spectrophotometric fingerprint of the drug in the capsule, with the fingerprint display of metformin overlaid on it. The two graphs could not have been any more different. "Well, Steve, you're right," said Rob. "This is not Glucophage at all. Now, I'll clear the display, and we will see if the computer scan figure out what this really is."

After he pushed a few buttons, the fingerprint display for the mystery drug came up on the screen, and the computer flashed a series of other fingerprints over it, while the processor was trying to identify a match. Finally, after about five hundred compounds had been compared and rejected, the computer beeped and there was a perfect match displayed.

"Diazepam. What's that?" asked David.

"That's Valium," replied Steve. "Rob, can you figure out how much Valium is in this pill that I gave you?"

"Sure I can." Rob took the remainder of the powder and assayed it for purity. It was pure, no contamination, and he then weighed the sample. He determined that the capsule had contained fifteen milligrams of Valium. Steve remembered that the pill bottle label told Susan to take three pills each evening, so she had taken 45 milligrams of Valium.

"How big a dose is that?" asked David.

"It depends on whether or not the patient has even taken that class of sedatives before," said Steve.

"She never used tranquilizers and rarely used pain pills," David replied.

"For someone who never uses sedatives, a starting dose would be two to five milligrams, and if you really wanted to put someone to sleep, maybe 10 milligrams. So, the 45 milligrams that she got is between 4 and 20 times the recommended dose. No wonder you couldn't wake her up that night, or the next morning."

David said, "I can understand that she was sedated and wanted to stay in bed, but I can't understand why her blood sugar was so low when the paramedics got there. Would the Valium do it?"

"No it wouldn't. I have no explanation for that."

They were finished at the morgue, and they shook hands with Rob, thanked him and took their leave. They drove to Matthew Johnson's office and waited for him to finish with a client, then went into his office. They filled Matthew in on the trip to the morgue and the findings. Steve told Matthew that they now knew that Susan had been drugged with Valium, but they couldn't explain why she had such a low blood sugar when the ambulance arrived. Matthew told them he had a simple explanation. "David, I know that you don't want to think about it, but you must understand that at least one, or maybe more, people were in your house, and on more than one occasion. Clearly, they came in to install the bugs, so they knew how to get into your house without letting on to anyone who might see them what they were doing. They were listening in on you, so they knew when you left for work that day. I'm sure that all they needed to do was call your office to be sure that you were there and so could not return home soon, and they knew the coast was clear. Susan was drugged, so she wouldn't be a problem. They got back into the house and injected her with insulin. When you came home and found her, she was already dosed with insulin, and the rest is history. The nurses' notes lead me to believe that the bad guys came into the hospital and injected her a few times there, as well. Now the next question is, why?"

David answered that. "Remember what Tyler McNab said. Susan had stumbled onto maybe millions of dollars of accounting irregularities at Morris, Cuney and Howe; I think that may be motive enough, don't you?"

***

The administrator of Middle Florida Hospital was more than happy to speak with Steve about the possibility that Susan had been murdered. He was quite upset about the threat of yet one more baseless malpractice suit that would nevertheless garner lots of negative attention for the hospital, and if she had been killed that would let the hospital off the hook. Such were the stark considerations for someone in his position.

"Have there been any strange incidents recently?" Steve asked.

"None that I know of, off the top of my head. However, the head of the maintenance department told me that something weird had happened there, why don't we ask him for the specifics."

The two of them walked to the elevator, and took it to the basement. The head of maintenance, a robust man with square shoulders and a substantial belly, was in his office, and he pulled two more chairs into his small glass enclosed cubicle. "What brings you two to the bowels of the hospital?"

"We're investigating something," said Steve. "Have you had any reports of anything strange happening recently?"

"Yes, as a matter of fact, there was," he answered. "One of the day-crew men had his coveralls and ID badge stolen from the set of hooks that we store them on. He had to buy new coveralls, and the security department had to make him up a new badge. Then, when we were cleaning and painting the 11th floor, on the C-wing, we found his clothing and ID badge in a supply closet, along with a white lab coat and a bucket and mop. It was quite strange. We had absolutely no explanation for it. The man in question said he had not been to the 11th floor since it was closed off for remodeling, and I have no reason to doubt his word that these items were stolen. On what little he makes, replacing the overalls was no minor expense, and he complained until I authorized the department to pay for them; and the loss of an ID badge gets an employee written up, you know a report put in his file in the event equipment turns up missing one day and we need a place to begin our investigation."

"Thank you," Steve said, as he and the administrator left. "Clearly, the man or men responsible stole the coveralls and ID badge and used the closed wing for storage of their supplies. That's how they got in and out of the Susan's room so easily."

Steve met up with Matthew and David later and reported his findings to them. The picture was becoming clearer. As near as they could conclude, Susan had found some significant accounting irregularities at Morris, Cuney and Howe, and her boss had found out. This would explain the motive for her murder. Someone had broken into Susan and David's home to plant listening devices, then drugged Susan, and systematically dosed her with insulin to kill her. The killers used a stolen hospital maintenance uniform to be able to move about without getting caught. Morris, Cuney and Howe were using her death to try to show the public that the malpractice crisis was because of incompetent doctors, but in reality, her death was out and out murder.

"I believe that we have enough evidence to show the police that Susan's death was murder, but we need to be able to pin it on Morris, Cuney and Howe. Right now, we have circumstantial evidence suggesting that they would like to see her dead, but nothing to make it stick," said David. "How can we get the evidence we need?"

Steve said, "David, where would Jake Morris get his medical information? I mean, he's not a doctor, and this seems to be a sophisticated plan. How could he come up with this on his own?"

"He couldn't, Steve. But, he has a lap dog, Semben. That guy will do anything Morris tells him to do. I can't believe he'd commit murder, or even that he is smart enough to come up with this plan, given the quality of some of his testimony, but if he could figure it out, he could have indeed given Morris the recipe." David looked almost embarrassed as he said this, because the others certainly had not forgotten that only recently he had taken part in shams that included Semben's malicious testimony, but now it was time to make things right.

CHAPTER 21

Steve and David were on the first morning plane to Atlanta. Before they left, David called his office and got the associates' secretary to give him Semben's office and home phone numbers and addresses. After landing, they rented a car and drove directly to Semben's office. His secretary smiled quite sweetly when they walked in; Steve let David do the talking. David took out his business card and said, "Hi. I'm David Archer. I work for Morris, Cuney and Howe, and as you know, Dr. Semben does a lot of work for us." He pointed at Steve and continued, "Mr. Jones, here, works for the firm, also. We just wanted to speak with him about a case we may need his help with."

"Well, Mr. Archer. I'd like to help you, but we haven't seen Dr. Semben in a few days. He came back from the Davis trial a week or so ago and, shortly after his return, he stopped showing up for work." Her voice dropped to a whisper. "He's done this before. He gets very depressed after he goes to court for you guys. He said once that he didn't go to medical school so he could be somebody's lackey in court. I think he drinks after these trials. He doesn't answer his phone, but I'm sure he's at home." Then she blushed, as if she knew she should not have betrayed these facts to strangers, minions of the law firm who paid her boss for his suspect services.

Steve asked, "How can you run his practice if he's not around?"

"Well, Mr. Jones, it's not like Dr. Semben has a lot of patients. I just reschedule the few that he does have, and cancel the case or two that we had planned, and no one misses him." She looked embarrassed again, but she couldn't seem to help herself and would tell anyone anything.

Larry J. Feinman

David smiled widely and said, "Thank you for your help. I know his address. Could you please give me directions and we'll be on our way."

With the directions in hand, they set off for Semben's house.

About 15 minutes later, they pulled up to the front of the house. It was a split-level and in rather poor repair. They walked up the cracked driveway and knocked on the door. No answer. There were lights on in the house, so they knocked a few more times. Steve tried the door, but it was locked. They walked around the back of the house, and as they did, they nearly tripped over all of the junk stashed on the side of the house. "What a slob," Steve said. As they approached the rear of the house, Steve reached his arm out to stop David. "David, hold it. Something's wrong." Steve slowly walked up to a large red stain on the cement and knelt next to it. He stuck his index finger into the sticky fluid and sniffed at the tip of the finger. "Blood," he said. "We need to call the police."

Soon, there were four Rabun County Sheriff's cars in the front driveway and a Crime Scene Investigation van parked on the front lawn. David and Steve were separated immediately and interrogated; shortly they were released and allowed back to the scene. They watched as the police expertly photographed the area and started an inch by inch search of the property. Other officers opened the front door after checking for fingerprints; later they would find that the only fingerprints on the doorknob were Steve's. Shortly, they found the shallow grave and unearthed Semben's body. The local medical examiner was called, and the body was not disturbed until he got there. After a bit of examination, he pronounced the death to be rather recent, certainly within the past month. The cause of death was quite obvious, a single gunshot wound to the head. A Glock .40 was found in the grave with Semben and the gun placed into an evidence bag.

The officer investigating the inside of the home found very little, but they did find work-boot footprints in the living room carpet that didn't match Semben's. Semben was something of a hermit, and with this exception, all of the other footprints in the carpet were his own. A cast was made of one of the footprints and likewise placed into evidence. The crime scene technician commented that there were no fingerprints in the living room to be found. Not even any of Semben's, not any at all. The room had obviously been wiped clean. Hundreds of prints were found in the rest of the house, all were later found to be Semben's.

The lieutenant leading the investigation asked if David and Steve could stay in town for a few days. Both agreed immediately and checked into the local motel. The clerk eyed them suspiciously and asked what they were doing in town.

"Why do you want to know?" asked David, in as friendly a tone as he could muster.

"Well, this is a small town, and we rarely have guests staying here who are not related to townsfolk or here for hunting season. I know that you're not related to anyone here, because no one called and asked me to have a room ready. And, neither of the two of you look like a hunter and you aren't carrying rifles to your rooms, but then it isn't hunting season anyway. Neither did the other guy, carry a rifle that is. Now, we have the county sheriffs all over town, and you're checking in. Something's going on."

"Wait, wait, what did you say about another guy?"

"There was another stranger checked in about a week ago. He paid cash for the room, and I still can't figure out what he was doing in town. At first, I thought that he was in town for work, but I was wrong. He obviously didn't hunt, he didn't talk much, and when I checked him out, he hadn't made more than two phone calls."

"What was his name," asked Steve.

The clerk checked the register and replied, "John Smith. See, he signed right here."

David asked if he had used a credit card, and the clerk said no. "Like I told you, he paid cash."

"What did he look like?" asked David.

"He was stocky, balding, about 50 years old. He had scary eyes, like he could see right through you if he wanted. I sure as hell wouldn't want to piss that guy off."

Steve asked if the clerk had noticed his shoes.

"Yes, I did. He had work boots on every time I saw him. That's why I first thought that he was in town for work, like a construction job. We have traveling laborers coming to town for work sometimes, and a lot of them stay here, but he never went out like he was going to work."

Steve asked if he had rented the room out that 'Mr. Smith' had stayed in yet. "No, things are slow, and my wife threw her back out," he explained. "She does the housekeeping here, and she's been out of work. We really didn't need the room, so I just left it like it was when he checked out, and she'll clean it when she feels better."

They thanked the clerk and took their bags to the room. From there, they called the police. Within minutes, the Crime Scene Investigation van was parked in the motel parking lot. Yellow tape was placed around the door to Room 103 and the crime scene technicians went to work on the room. Here, they found multiple fingerprints, and most of them were good prints. The work boot prints in the carpet were identical matches for the footprints in the carpet at Semben's house. The cops had no doubt that the man who had stayed in this room was the same man who left the footprints in Semben's carpet.

The police artist tried to make a sketch of the motel guest based on the clerk's description of him, but the picture was unrecognizable to Steve or David. The sheriff put out an all-points-bulletin on the man in the sketch, but they had little hope that he would be caught based on the picture and the APB. The murder seemed to be a professional job, and they were sure that the killer was long gone. The sheriff admitted that it was only the good fortune that Steve and David needed to check into the motel and had struck up a conversation with the clerk, because this had given them their only good lead: fingerprints. The cast of the work boots would be helpful in convicting the killer by proving that his boots had made the prints, but they would need to find him first. Hopefully the fingerprints could lead to him.

The technicians lifted about one hundred high quality fingerprints from the motel room. They fingerprinted the clerk and his wife, so they could eliminate their prints immediately. Steve was impressed with the modern crime lab in the Rabun County Sheriff's office. For example, the fingerprints could be processed by computer rather than by hand. The prints were laboriously developed and placed into the database. The machine hummed to life and began to eliminate the ones belonging to the clerk and his wife. Next, it began to identify those people in the Rabun County database of fingerprints; people with concealed weapons permits, anyone who had been arrested, law enforcement agents. The detectives began to work on the list that remained; once they eliminated people who didn't fit the description of the motel guest, they were left with two men. In addition to the two, there were also two sets of unidentified prints. These were sent electronically to the FBI lab in Washington, D.C. That lab houses the records of anyone who had ever been fingerprinted in any jurisdiction for any reason. FBI searches took some time, usually a day or two, but they were exhaustive.

***

David and Steve decided to stay in Rabun County until the investigation was over. David called Morris, Cuney and

Howe and told them that he had a family emergency and he would be taking some personal leave time, maybe a week or so. Steve called his office and told them to ask Nan Freedman to cover for him; he'd be away for about a week. His secretary told him that, because of the article in the Central Florida Times, his office was not very busy at all, and she was sure he could take a week off without his absence being noticed. That news momentarily depressed Steve, but he knew they were onto the real reason for Susan's death and, with a bit more luck, he would be completely vindicated shortly, at least he hoped this would be the case. He knew, as the source of the only lead suggested, that luck was absolutely necessary to solve most crimes, but especially if the perpetrator was a pro.

The two of them split up, and each accompanied a deputy sheriff to the interviews of the people whose fingerprints had been found at the motel.

David accompanied a young sheriff's deputy who had been on the force for about 6 months. He admitted that he had done little more than give speeding tickets so far. He had never arrested anyone and hadn't ever been involved in a murder investigation. The owner of the prints that they were to investigate was named Herman Werby. Herman met them at the door and invited them in. After the deputy explained the reason for their visit, Herman blushed a bit and told them why he had been at the motel. "I am a widower, and I live with my daughter. She's 23 years old, and she knows that I'm lonely. But she still hasn't gotten over the death of her mother, and I don't dare bring any of my lady-friends back to the house, if you know what I mean. So we go to the motel." At the deputy's request, Herman was able to produce the credit card receipt for the stay at the motel, and the date was a month prior to the murder. The two visitors apologized for Herman's trouble and left.

Steve and his escort were assigned to investigate Samuel Rose. He was quite evasive and would not explain his visit to the motel. The deputy was concerned, and became more so when Rose started stammering and began looking sidelong at the desk. He rose to walk to the desk, and the deputy drew his weapon. "Freeze," he shouted. He looked at Steve and yelled, "Get down, now!" With his gun trained on Rose, he walked over to him and demanded that he lie on the floor with his arms out. He handcuffed Rose, and then patted him down. The deputy and Steve opened the drawer to the desk and found a gun. The office called for backup, and soon, the Crime Scene Investigation team had its third workout in as many days. After a search warrant was obtained, the technicians found about 20 kilos of cocaine hidden in a closet and a methamphetamine lab in the basement. Rose was booked into the county jail, and the motel clerk was asked to come in to view a lineup. He was sure; Rose was not the man they were looking for. He remembered checking Rose into the hotel over three weeks ago and had not seen him since.

Later, the crime scene technicians re-examined the motel room, this time looking for drugs, and found residue of cocaine, ecstasy, marijuana and amphetamines. A few weeks later, Rose pleaded guilty to drug dealing and was sentenced to fifteen years in federal prison.

But, they were no closer to finding Semben's killer.

The next morning, the phone in the sheriff's office rang; the FBI crime lab was on the phone. Of the two fingerprints they found, one belonged to one of the hundred million or more citizens that had never been fingerprinted. But, the other belonged to someone who had been fingerprinted: a licensed private investigator named Stanley M. Large. Steve had a puzzled look on his face. He didn't recognize the name. David, on the other hand, was aghast. "I know him, Steve. He's Jake Morris' personal private eye. I've worked with him a number of times; he's in our office quite a bit."

***

223

The SWAT team surrounded Stan Large's house. The captain took out his cell phone and called Large's home number.

"Hello?"

"Mr. Large?"

"Yes, who is this?"

"This is Captain Jason Miller of the Central Florida Police Department's SWAT team. We are outside your house. We have you surrounded. You have five minutes to come out unarmed and with your hands up."

The police were stationed behind their open car doors and watched Large's house. They saw no activity but assumed that he was simply using the time allotted to him. Suddenly, the garage door flew off of its hinges and a Range Rover came barreling out of the garage, directly at a squad car parked in the driveway. The Range Rover struck the police car in the rear and the police car rolled over onto two policemen, killing them instantly; their car erupted in flames. Large regained control of the Range Rover and shot off down the street. Six police cars took chase, following him at breakneck speeds through the streets of Orlando, joined by an ever-increasing number of new squad cars as they passed. Large reached I-4 and entered the interstate. A police helicopter was dispatched from headquarters and zeroed in on Large. At the same time, two news helicopters picked up the chase and beamed the story in real-time to the networks. Suddenly, the chase was being watched as 'Breaking News' on every television station in the United States.

Back in his office, Jake Morris was glued to the television. He had had the television on in the background and looked up just in time to see a car chase. A Range Rover was speeding down I-4 with countless police cars following it, and three helicopters were in the air, tracking the vehicle. While he watched, he realized that he recognized the Range

Rover, that it belonged to Stan Large. With that, he hit the remote control and turned off the mute; the sound came alive. "For those of you just joining us, the details are sketchy, but from what we've been told, the driver of the Range Rover is named Stan Large. The police were at his house this morning to arrest him for the murder of a doctor in Georgia, and he was able to get into his car and escape. During that escape, he killed two policemen. This chase has been ongoing for about 15 minutes now; we will stay with this story until its conclusion."

Morris started to sweat. If Large was captured and questioned, he would certainly implicate him, and if the authorities were threatening the death penalty, Large could sell Jake out on the murder of the hooker from years ago. Jake knew that there was no statute of limitations on murder. He could be charged anytime. He found himself rooting for the police to kill Large.

One of the news helicopters flew ahead of the entourage and the camera showed the highway about one mile ahead. The police had closed I-4 and placed a nail strip across the highway. When Large drove across it, his tires would be punctured and he'd be forced to stop. Moments later, the video feed showed the Range Rover barreling at high speed towards the nail strip, and then the car was tipping on its left side and rolling. Just that quickly, the chase was over. At least 50 armed policemen approached the crippled car with their weapons drawn, and one of them pulled Large from the broken windshield. Large, who seemed no worse the wear for having rolled a car several times, was handcuffed and hog carried to the waiting armored van.

With a shaky hand, Jake pushed the button to turn the television off. He walked into his private bathroom and splashed cold water in his face. As he dried himself off, he sensed that he was not alone in the room. He looked up, and his secretary was standing just outside the washroom. "Mr. Morris, it's time to head out for Tallahassee."

CHAPTER 22

The news conference on the steps of the state house in Tallahassee, Florida was a trial lawyer's dream. Mike Bloch had arranged it to try to scuttle the malpractice reforms that were working their way through the legislature. What better way to ruin that effort than to have a news conference about the sorry state of medicine in the state. He was hoping that he could turn the tables, and even make more restrictive laws regarding malpractice, maybe double the size and number of the awards given out by the courts.

The Florida Trial Lawyers Association, or FTLA, a lobbying group for the trial lawyers had seen to it that the crowd around the news conference was filled with supporters of Mike Bloch's efforts, mostly the families and employees of the FTLA's members. They erupted in a wild cheer when he took the podium.

"Ladies and gentlemen, thank you for taking time from your busy day to be here with me. As you know, I am the chairman of the House Committee on Medical and Energy Issues and have held hearings on the matter of medical malpractice liability. What we have discovered is that the supposed crisis is one of the doctors' own making. They coddle incompetent doctors in their midst, do not discipline those doctors, and then complain when the trial lawyers expose their incompetence. I must say that my committee is not inclined to offer any legislation to provide relief for this problem, and in fact, I personally intend to introduce legislation to increase the amount of non-economic damages that a plaintiff can be awarded and companion legislation that would allow any plaintiff to recover legal expenses from the defendant-doctor, even if the doctor wins the case. That way, the plaintiff's attorney will not lose any money if the doctor wins." He waited for the cheers to subside, then continued. "Now, I'd like to turn the podium over to a good friend of mine, and an even better friend to the trial lawyers of this great state, Jake Morris."

The crowd erupted again, and Jake received a five minute ovation, as he held his hands up in recognition of the adulation like a politician at a campaign fund-raising event. Finally, he stepped to the podium and began. "The medical profession is pushing the Angel Smith Act, which will seriously limit the ability of our profession to sue doctors in this state. That will mean that our ability to help the residents of Florida will be curtailed. Bad doctors will be protected and everyone will suffer. We need to stop this bill before it goes to the floor of the legislature. Mr. Bloch is right: we need stronger restrictions on the doctors, and we need to make it easier for a plaintiff to recover damages from an incompetent doctor, not harder." He walked off the stage to wild applause.

As Jake walked into the state house building with Mike Bloch, he saw a cluster of policemen in the corner. After he had passed through the metal detectors, the policemen walked over to him. One of them said, "Mr. Jake Morris?"

"Yes, that's me. What can I do for you, Officer?" Morris had hoped that his trip to Tallahassee would forestall this move, that they would at least wait until he got back to his office. The legislator at his side looked mortified, like he wanted to hide his face and run into the building to escape this very public embarrassment.

"Mr. Morris, you are under arrest for the murder of Susan Parks. You have the right to remain silent. Anything you say can and will be used against you in a court of law. You have the right to an attorney, and to have that attorney present with you while you are being questioned. If you want a lawyer and can not afford one, one will be appointed to represent you. Do you understand these rights?"

"Of course I understand my rights. I'm a damn lawyer."

"Come with us, sir, please."

Morris was handcuffed and driven in the back seat of a police cruiser to Central Florida and was taken to an interrogation room. When he got there, Craig Sharp was waiting for him. Craig stood up and said, "Jake, don't say anything. I'm here to represent you. They want to question you about Susan Parks' death." Morris merely winked. He had dodged tough times before and he would dodge this one. It was a minor inconvenience. After all, he was Jake-by-God-Morris, a great lawyer with lots of money to spend on even better lawyers. He would walk away from this. He knew it, and that bastard Large could fry for it, but how to spin this one? He schemed as the prosecutor asked questions that Sharp deflected deftly, like any good lawyer would, thought Jake.

CHAPTER 23

Central Florida Times

Tampa Bay, FL

By Mark Rodriguez

and Connie Lombardi

Police in Orange County made arrests recently in the murder of Susan Parks. This paper covered the story of Susan's death in the course of an article about medical malpractice. One of the authors of this story (C.L.) had taken the position that the current malpractice crisis was due to incompetent doctors, and intimated that Jake Morris was going to use Susan's death due to malpractice as a battering ram to clean up the medical profession in Florida. It turns out that the villains of that story were the managing partner of Morris, Cuney and Howe, Jake Morris himself, and a private investigator, Stan Large, who was the subject of a high speed car chase last week. Not only is it alleged that Morris and Large conspired with a Georgia urologic surgeon, Dr. J. Marcus Semben, to murder Susan Parks and make the murder seem like a case of medical malpractice, but they are also charged with the execution-style murder of Dr. Semben.

It appears that Morris used the murders to cover up a massive embezzlement of millions of dollars from his clients by himself and his two partners, Sam Cuney and Jay Howe.

Jake Morris has been indicted on two counts of conspiracy to commit murder. Private investigator Stan Large has been indicted on two counts of murder in the first degree. Sam Cuney has been indicted for embezzlement, and Jay Howe has been indicted for embezzlement.

The pity of this case is that Morris, Cuney and Howe were trying to use the death of Ms. Parks as a way to show the people of the community the failings of the medical profession. Instead they showed them the seedy underbelly of the legal profession.

This case has sent shock waves through both the medical and legal communities. Representative Bob Hugoll announced this morning that the Angel Smith Act was passed by a 255 to 3 vote and was signed into law. Medical malpractice reform will start today. The changes are sweeping the nation. Doctors' groups are striking while the iron is hot, and reforms have already been passed in 6 states and are on the agenda of legislatures in 15 more states.

Tyler McNab, PhD is an accounting professor at the Business Institute of Florida, and teaches at the University of Central Florida, as well. He was interviewed by the police, and with his help, the forensic accounting department of the sheriff's office identified six million dollars of embezzled funds from the client accounts at Morris, Cuney and Howe. Already, two hundred suits have been filed against the firm by prior clients, and they are being consolidated into a single class action suit. In addition, Susan Parks' parents have filed a multimillion-dollar wrongful death suit against the firm of Morris, Cuney and Howe, as well as individually against Jake Morris.

Steve Boxley, the surgeon at the center of the swirling controversy, said, "I'm just happy to see the end of this insanity." However, he doesn't seem as untouched as he'd like us to believe. He still hasn't returned to the operating room, and the county is still suffering from an acute lack of surgeons. But, with the new laws for malpractice reform, we may soon see a few young surgeons looking to practice medicine in the area.

CHAPTER 24

Steve Boxley and David Archer sat across from each other in the restaurant. They hadn't seen each other in two months, and when they happened to run into each other downtown, they both wanted to see how the other was faring and so decided to eat together at one of Steve's favorite spots, a place he used to take his wife. David asked Steve how he'd been doing, the kind of question meant to segue into small talk, but Steve started talking furiously even before the waiter had walked away to get them a bottle of wine, not fully aware of what he was saying, opening up to his new friend much more that he ever did with anyone else — perhaps because he was lonely, and perhaps because he and David had shared a death and the triumph of catching the killers together.

"I lost my wife because of my commitment to medicine. I even slept at the hospital much of the time, and I missed some of the most important moments of my family's lives. I've been talking to Ellen, that's my wife, recently, and we've agreed to start dating, to see how things go. I called her after I could not stop thinking about her, after...well, after Susan died and I saw that the grief you felt was at least related to my own. I know that Ellen still has feelings for me, and I certainly have strong feelings for her, and maybe we can get back together someday."

Steve looked at David self-consciously, suddenly aware of the private nature of what he was relating, and to someone he did not know that well; but David was listening attentively, a discernible look of sadness on his face. "I didn't mean to bring up tough stuff for you," Steve said." I should not have told you..." But David interrupted him.

"No. Please go on. I am struggling with getting on with life too, and I need the insight you might be able to offer. I at least need to know that it is possible." He smiled in such a way that convinced Steve he meant what he said and so Steve continued.

"I mean, I still love medicine, but Susan's death has put it into perspective for me. None of us knows how long we'll be on this earth, or how long those we love might be around, so I guess we need to make the most of this trip we are all on. Whether I'm in the ER or not, the accidents will still happen, the bullets will still fly, and the knives will still stab. So, I've decided to work on my priorities, and I've come to the conclusion that my family is my first priority."

"So, you are leaving medicine, but for what?"

"No, I'm not leaving medicine, but it won't get in the way of my time with my family. I've decided that I'm going to leave surgery, however. This ordeal has shown me a side of the world that I don't care to ever see again. I keep thinking about Susan, and I know that someone has to speak for the dead. David, if I hadn't become suspicious about Susan's death, think of how this would have ended. You, along with your law firm, and I mean no offense here, would have sued me out of practice, and in the process made a fortune for all the wrong reasons. But, more disturbingly, a murder would have been committed and no one would have been made to pay for the crime, and I know this must have bothered you too, in retrospect. Anyway, I have decided to go into a residency for forensics. I want to be the one to speak for the dead."

Steve looked up from his plate, at which he had been staring intently while he spoke, and asked David what his plans were, now that Morris, Cuney and Howe was closed. David replied that he hadn't quite decided yet, but he knew that trial law wasn't for him. He decided that the whole system sickened him, and he knew that his motives for entering law were not being satisfied by suing people for contrived damages. "After Susan died, I found that the only time I felt alive was when you and I were investigating her murder, and I was on such a high when Jake Morris was arrested. I've decided to go into the district attorney's office as an assistant DA. But, Steve, to be honest with you, my goal is to help clean up my profession. Morris and his partners have left such a stain on the legal field that someone needs to do something. After a few years, I hope to move to the US Attorney's office and work in their Office of Attorney Misconduct, prosecuting wayward lawyers. These bastards have to be gotten rid of so that the real lawyers fighting for real justice can do so without the taint these guys leave in the air of every courtroom in the land."

David smiled at Steve and said, "Who knows? Maybe someday we will work together to catch some other criminal who thinks he can turn both law and medicine against the innocent."

"Yeah, Batman and Robin," said Steve, and they both laughed, "but I get to be Batman. I love that black outfit."

The two of them finished a fine dinner and walked out of the restaurant and into a beautiful Florida evening, warm with just the right amount of humidity for a change. They headed toward the Waterhouse Center to see if they could buy a couple of tickets at this late hour to watch the Orlando Magic take on the Philadelphia 76ers.